Triggers

All The Lies We Told is a dark, psychological thriller that explores dark themes. This includes a list of possible triggers. If you would like to double check these triggers, before delving into this story, these can be found on the last page of the book.

Please be aware that these trigger warnings may be related to twists within this book's story line.

KJ.

All The Lies We Told

K.J. Reed

Lucy

Happy Reading!

To All those who told me I wouldn't.
To all those who believed I would.
For you, Mom. You always knew that I had it in me.

Prologue

It's faster than I thought it would be. Asphyxiation.

I'd been reading up on murder for weeks. The different ways I could kill her. Which techniques were more efficient or more effective. I researched for hours the types of toxins I could buy without any red flags to mix into her tea. Slaved over learning the different knots you can tie in a rope; either to crush and constrict blood vessels or to lever the neck to one side, snapping it. I even practised a few on myself, with fail safes to make sure I didn't kill myself. I'm fed up of the bitch, not suicidal.

That's why it took me so long to finally do this, to finally kill her. Not because of any kind of conscience but because I'm indecisive. I'd been deliberating over it for weeks but then she'd upset me. Spitting her putrid phlegm in my face like I was trash and I snapped.

I lunged at her. Pinned her down. Dug my fingers and nails so deep into her throat that I could feel her heartbeat thumping against my fingertips as I strangled her.

I felt it when her pulse stopped. Now I feel disappointed. I scrutinise the scene for a whole minute. Feeling depleted. I expected it to be better than this. Like the world would be set, somehow, right. That I would be able to breathe again. Except, the air feels the same. Stale and penetrating.

I'd watched her give up, her nails not scratching so hard, her eyes not so petrified. It was almost boring after that. I realise, too late, that it was too quick.

The sound of a piercing scream startles me out of my daze before I realise the sound has come from me. something deep and almost primal taking over.

I want to do it over and over again. Watch her die more than once. See the terror in her eyes for longer than the seconds it took me to strangle the air out of her. I want her to suffer as much as she's made me suffer.

Then, the idea. It blooms beautifully in me, replacing the dread with excitement. I know what I need to do.

I pull her by her fat, swollen ankles onto the floor, my hands pushing so deep down in her chest I can almost feel her ribs straining, ready to snap.

My skin crawls at the thought of having my mouth anywhere near her decaying teeth and tainted saliva but I do it anyway. Breathing the life back in until she gasps, her eyes springing open. Full of confusion at first, then realization, and then pure unadulterated dread.

'Ah, there it is.' The smile feels unnatural on my face. 'You're alive because of me. I brought you back. Maybe next time, I won't'

PART ONE

PRESENT DAY

'Sure, I'll pop round when I've grabbed the kids, mother. Now I really have to go. Bye, love you.' I feel guilty after I've cut the line off that I didn't wait for her to reply. I add "check on my idiotic sister" to the list in my head as I pull out of the driveway.

Chapter 2

No One

'That isn't my name of course. I mean, who would call their child "no one"? *ha*. That's what you can call me for now though. I wouldn't want to give too much away just yet.' I whisper to her as I run the brush through her ash-blonde hair.

Her body shudders as she sobs, and I brush the tears streaming down her cheeks away with my thumb.

'Oh no, no, no. No tears now Freya, you'll ruin your makeup, and we want you looking tip top for your photoshoot don't we.' I bare my teeth in an effort to smile. I've never been able to smile properly. I don't know why but it just feels so unnatural on my face. The way it stretches my lips and plumps up my cheeks, like a chipmunk filling its mouth with chestnuts. It's been twelve hours, twenty-three minutes and eighteen seconds since I watched Freya stumble through her front door, drunk as a skunk as well!

Eleven hours, forty minutes, and three seconds since I crept out of her bedroom wardrobe and felt her hot cheek as she slept. She looked so peaceful, mouth wide and gawking, her eyes moving under her closed eyelids as she dreamt.

Eleven hours, thirty minutes, and ten seconds since I clasped my hand tight over her mouth, watched her eyes open. Slow at first, then fast and wide as she realised what the sensation meant.

My entire body tingles as I remember what she felt like squirming against my grip as I pulled her out of her slumbering bed and tightened my grip around her throat until she went limp and was once again unconscious. It was easy then to carry her down and throw her into the back of my truck. It wasn't difficult to do it without anyone seeing. Especially since Freya didn't come home until 3AM and the roads are quiet at that time of night. No CCTV on Freya's Road either, I checked.

I crept in and crept out with her like an ant scurrying along the road in the middle of the night. Unseen and unheard. It's not going to stay like that though. I won't stay unseen and unheard much longer. I'll make sure of it.

Chapter 3

Ellie

It's 15:17 by the time I pull up outside the kid's school. I'm seventeen minutes late and I can almost hear the water dripping from the shopping as it defrosts in the boot. It hasn't been this hot all year and of course it's the day I choose to wear a long sleeve top and jeans, that the sun decides to make an appearance.

I crank up the AC, pull my wet curls off the sweat on the back of my neck and tie it in a messy *"yes, alright, I'm a mom"* bun as I watch Myah and Matthew run down the school's front steps towards the car. I wave at the teacher at the door who waves back but with a look of utter disgust on her face. *How dare you be such a terrible mother that you're seventeen minutes late to pick up!* Is what that look says to me.

The back door opens and suddenly the car is filled with noise. Myah's holding up a weird looking paper mâché that looks like some kind of deformed alien but what I imagine is actually supposed to be a dog, a massive proud smile beaming across her face as she rambles about the paper, glue and paint she used to make her masterpiece.

'Maybe she's in the bathroom, sweetheart.' I reassure Myah as I walk towards her by the bed and knock on the bathroom door. 'Freya!' I shout through the wood. I'm guessing she's hugging the toilet like a long-lost friend, her hair inches from the water line.

When there's no grunt of a reply, I push the door open an inch and poke my head through. The room's empty. Just a few discarded towels on the floor and some thrown over the edge of the bath.

'You said we were going to play with Aunty Freya!' Myah accuses me angrily.

I feel a surge of panic start to rise in the pit of my stomach. *If she isn't here, then where is she?* I dial her number again and the burst of sound in the corner of the room makes me almost jump out of my own skin, heart thumping in my ears. The phone's sitting on top of the coffee table, in between all of the mess. I pick it up and feel another surge of panic. Normally, she's basically surgically attached to her phone 24/7. I guess that's why she hasn't been picking up.

'Hey, kids! Guess what mommy bought you today?' I increase my voice a few octaves as if this is the most exciting thing to happen all week. Myah and Matthew start smiling automatically, jumping up and down.

'What!? What!? What!?' they squeal excitedly.

'Some really colourful paints!' I actually think the grin I give them is the fakest I've ever done. 'What if we paint Aunty Freya some pretty pictures ready for when she gets home?'

'Yeah!' they both shout, waving their little arms in the air.

I quickly clear off the coffee table, throwing all the rubbish and dirty dishes on top of the already massive pile on the kitchen sides. I clean it down a bit with an antibacterial spray and clean-ish cloth I found under the kitchen sink and fill the last clean cup in the kitchen cabinet with water for the paint brushes. I tell Matt and Myah to sit quietly and be nice with sharing as I plonk them down on the two sofa cushions I've thrown onto the floor.

They're already squabbling by the time I've cleared off the small 2-seater dining table in the middle of the kitchen and sat down with my notebook of errand lists and Freya's phone. Opening her contact list, I think about how she really should put a password on this thing before it falls into the wrong hands. I click on the first name at the top *Adam* and press the phone to my ear. *Please.* I silently beg. *Let one of these people know where she is.*

punish you for that?' I ponder out loud, cocking my head to the side as if I'm really quite unsure what I'm going to do.

'P-please.' She whispers. 'Please, not again.'

I pull her to a standing position by her hair as she squeals. Drag her along the room and down the stairs to the basement. She's pleading with me. Saying she'll do anything. She won't ask to go home again, she'll fix her make up for me, sit nicely for her photos. Too late. I drag her further into the basement and over to the old, rusted sink in the corner. The memory rushes back to me, filling my brain with the smell of soil and freshly cut grass mixed with bleach.

I can picture my mother perfectly as if she's still alive and really standing across the basement at the sink. I hear the water dripping from the tap and splashing off the sides of the sink in an almost song as she scrubs the soil and dirt from the gardening shears and rakes.

She's humming tunes under her breath, but I can't work out which song it's supposed to be. She was gifted with a green thumb but not a decent singing voice after all.

Her blonde hair falls in harsh straight lines down the back of her pink flowery summer dress and brushes over her shoulder when she turns to the sound of my feet coming down the creaky stairs.

Suddenly her smile turns to an angry scowl and the humming is replaced with the sour sound of anger as she screams at me to 'Get out! You know you're not allowed down here!' I see the garden scissors fly across the room and watch as they cut a long slice in my calf.

I see the red beads of blood and feel their heat as they rush down my skin and saturate my sock before the sting of pain works its way up my leg and the tears begin to flow. I run back up the stairs and out of the basement sobbing, leaving a trail of blood in my wake, my mother's still screaming at me as I go.

The scar down the length of my calf throbs and stings with the memory as I pull myself back from the brink and focus on the present.

I shove her body against the edge of the sink, enjoying the sound of metal against flesh, knowing it's going to leave a purple bruise in the small of her back makes me smirk. I fill the sink with icy cold water to the brim, until it's almost overflowing.

She's really sobbing now, big ugly spasms as she snorts and mucous spurts out of her nostrils. I grab a bunch of her hair in my hand and twist it around my fist. Then I shove her head under the water.

She fights against me; her hands are thrashing about violently and I can't help but notice the likeness to how infants squirm when they're new and have no idea what they should be doing with their limbs yet. She's scratching against my arms and kicking her feet, so I push her face deeper so that it's almost touching the base of the sink. I hold her there under the water until her body stops moving and goes limp with death. I pull her out, water dripping from her hair all over my chest. I lay her flat on her back against the stone floor and look her over once from head to toe, taking in the moment. I love this part.

I kneel beside her lifeless body and place one hand over the other one. lining it up to the centre of her chest. I push up on my knees and start to press hard in a rhythm down into her chest. I feel my muscles ripple against my shirt as they work.

Thirty presses and then I lean down and press my mouth over hers. Her lips aren't as soft as they were yesterday, they're a bit drier and I can feel the rough edges of the skin peeling from them. I breathe into her mouth twice, breathing life back into her.

I don't know how long I do it for, longer than the last time for sure but eventually she breathes a gasp of air and opens her eyes wide. She rolls over onto her side, coughing out the water from her lungs all over the basement floor, her body spasming like a fish as it suffocates, desperately trying to take in oxygen from the water that's not there when they're pulled from the depths of the ocean. I pull her up to sit beside me, she's gasping, crying, and shivering.

'Shush now, sweet one.' I whisper, brushing her hair sopping wet back from her face. 'Now. What do we say?' I coo. She looks up at me through her tears, a look of pure despair washes over her face as she whimpers.

'Come on now, where have your manners gone?' I pout dramatically. She takes a few more gasps of air and I almost see the fight leave her eyes as she sags against me, tears brimming the edge of her eyes.

'Thank you. Thank you for bringing me back to life.'

'That's a good girl.' I smirk. 'Maybe next time I won't.'

Chapter 5

Ellie

I push my fingers into my temples and massage in a clockwise motion in an attempt to dull the thumping migraine that's been slowly swelling behind my eyes.

I've made it through to letter J in Freya's phone book and so far, no luck. No one seems to have seen or spoken to her since last night's pub crawl.

I glance quickly over at Matt and Myah, both covered in dried paint, both snoring soundly in the makeshift bed they've made from Freya's sofa cushions and clean washing pile.

How long ago did it go quiet? How long have they been asleep? I glance over my shoulder at the crappy plastic clock over the kitchen window and feel all the blood drain from my face. *9PM!* I knew Freya had a lot of friends but my god, surely, she didn't have enough in her phone book for it to take me until now just to get to the letter J!

'What if something... what if that man... what if he...' Poppy stutters.

'I know.' I sound surer than I feel. 'Keep your phone on you. I'll keep you updated.'

Me and Poppy make our pleasantries, promise to phone each other if Freya turns up or if we hear anything and I dial a new number. A number I've been hoping to avoid.

The dial tone rings three times before it clicks.

'Hello. 911 operator. What is your emergency?'

'It's my sister.' My tongue feels like sandpaper against my mouth, my head swimming with anxiety. 'She's missing.'

Chapter 6

Freya

I'm awake but I can't move. My chest burns, I think he broke one of my ribs. It stings every time I breathe in. My legs feel heavy and tangled, like they're lined with lead and tied in a knot. I try to get my bearings but my eyes sting and blur. I can barely see, just watery, shimmery outlines. My whole body feels damp and cold. The floor smells of filth and the thick layers of mould that seem to cover every inch of this room he keeps me in but there's an undertone of medicinal bleach.

I gag, the pain ripping through me again, the fumes stinging my eyes, nose, and throat. I take a deep breath in, trying to calm myself but my chest bursts with pain and I whine, trying to roll off my stomach and onto my side but it's like my brain no longer communicates with my body.

I taste salt and wonder why before I realise, I've started crying. My body shakes with each sob, shooting the pain through my chest over and over. It's worse this time.

This time my head swims and I feel nauseous and incapable of moving and *cold*. A cold like I've never been before in my life. My fingertips sting like ice and I can't get my vision to focus.

This was the second time he killed me and then brought me back to life. I wonder how long I was out this time, in the sheer blackness that engulfs me each time it happens. I wonder how many times he can bring me back before I'm too far gone. How long can I survive this place? Survive him? My head swims with panic, my field of vision slowly closing in, getting darker and darker as I hear the key turn in the lock.

He's here. He's going to kill me. Please God, let me die.

Chapter 7

Detective Dawson

'So, what we got, boss?' Luke shakes his head roughly as he slides into the passenger seat, droplets of rainwater spraying all over the interior and all over me. He reminds me of a golden retriever as I watch him. Sandy blonde hair flying back and forth as he shakes.

Come to think of it, his whole personality reminds me of a golden retriever we had growing up, an energetic and spritely little thing always so full of energy and so eager to please. He straightens up, eyeing me up and down, the light brown eyes also giving me flashbacks to Sammy the golden retriever. His eyebrow raises, lips smirking. 'What are you staring at?'

I feel my cheeks burn with heat, quickly moving my gaze away, 'Nothing much, just my half an hour late partner who has just drenched my car.' I shrug. Willing the redness to subside.

'I don't think I've ever seen you in a skirt on the job. Good for you, you look... smart.' He shrugs off the compliment, still admiring today's outfit and I feel my cheeks burn again.

He's right of course, I haven't worn a dress into work in almost five years, since making lead Detective in the missing persons division of the station. It's no secret that police work is majorly a male dominated profession and that most of my workforce would have preferred a man to be in my position of power. The other half simply don't care because at least they get to see a bit of ass during their shift.

I've worked hard to try and put to bed the stereotypes of women in power, always dressing down for work. Suit trousers and blazers only. Shades of monochrome and beige, galore. I've even stopped maintaining my hair, letting it grow past the point of comfortable. It ends just above the bum now. It's my natural light mousy brown and curls at the very ends but on days like today, it frizzes with the rain.

Hell, I can't even remember the last time I bothered to put makeup on. In all honesty, I wouldn't have been wearing the dress today if it weren't for the fact that it was the only bit of clean clothing that I had. Working cases upon cases, with no time for laundry, over the last few weeks hadn't exactly left me with much choice, this morning. It was actually the only piece of clothing clean in my entire house. Well, the dress and the black blazer I've added over the top, trying to tone down the feminine even in a dress. Clearly, from Luke's reaction, the attempt was useless.

'Well, when you're done being absolutely mortified that I don't look like a teenage boy today, we have places to be.' I joke, laughing at my own expense, relieved when Luke joins in.

'So, then boss, who's done a runner today then?' he stretches his fingers, letting his knuckles pop in unison. My teeth grind against the sound, a pet peeve I've always had. I feel relieved to finally be pulling out of my spot.

'Name's Freya Dolloway. Twenty-four, divorced, and lives alone. Hasn't been seen or heard from since about midnight Thursday night.

Her twin, Ellie, called it in at around eleven pm last night.' I've read over the report a few times, waiting for Luke to finally drag his ass out of bed so now I can repeat the information we have almost verbatim.

'Midnight Thursday evening?' he raises an eyebrow, flipping through the report. 'And the sister called it in at eleven pm last night? It hadn't even been twenty-four hours at that point. Why are we on this? Why not send a couple of the lower-level Detectives? She's a grown woman, she probably just got busy or needed a couple of days of radio silence.'

'You don't recognize the name? Dolloway. As in, Chief Dolloway? He one of the force's biggest case closers before he died in a house fire at his residence in 0h six?'

'Oh!' A flash of recognition crosses Lukes' face. 'It went down as arson, right? Some kind of home invasion?'

'Exactly. There was a string of home invasions turned arson leading up to it. The perpetrator would break into the homes, tie up and torture the occupants slowly and then burn them alive along with their homes.' I shiver, remembering the absolute mayhem. 'My father worked as part of the task force along with Dolloway to try and find the person responsible but there was never enough to go on. All the leads they had burned to ash along with the houses.'

I remember him working all hours and coming back so downhearted he'd lock himself in his study with his records playing but I could still always hear his sobs over the melodies. I shake the fog of memory away and turn back to Luke.

'Well, all leads until the Dolloway fire. The mad man targeted Dolloway as the lead investigator, he was all over the news so it wouldn't have been hard to identify him. He broke into the Chief's house, tied him and his family up and made him watch whilst he tortured his wife and twin girls, Freya and Ellie. He set the house alight with gas and had planned to watch them all burn along with the house, but the Chief managed to break free. He broke his family free and saved them all. His wife said he went back in for the madman, whether to bring him out or to finish the job we'll never know. The Chief and the suspect never came back out and the home invasions stopped.'

'Jesus Christ.' Luke shakes his head slowly, the look of misery in his face no doubt mirroring my own. 'Did they ever figure out who the guy was? Why he did it?'

'Never.' I grimace. 'The place was burnt to ash, wasn't even enough body left to identify which part of the ash was the Chief, never mind the unknown assailant. The never knowing haunted my own father.'

'Damn.' Luke flips the report shut and throws it onto the back seat. 'I guess we best get cracking then Mols.'

Even after we've been working together for the last eight months, it still feels strange to hear Luke use a nickname. I don't even think the other guys back at the station realise my name is Molly to this day. I think they actually just believe I only have the name Dawson. No first, middle or last. No Molly Sarah Dawson. Just Dawson. No more, no less. I press my foot down harder, wanting this case solved as quickly as possible, for all our sakes.

The house isn't what I expected. Ellie Dolloway and her two children, Matthew and Myah Dolloway live in a very large, very typical family suburban, semi-detached house. The front grass is a little overgrown and scattered with children's bicycles and toys so it's difficult to find the gravel path leading from the driveway to the front patio. The patio swing squeaks on rusty hinges in the breeze. It looks out of place next to the bland, monochrome new builds on the rest of the street with its whitewashed brick and blue panelling.

The door is rather large with a bright shiny chrome knocker, as I lift it and let it fall against the wood, I wonder if Ellie had planned for the house to be as bright as possible. The door opens almost immediately as the knocker hits the wood. I feel the deep intake of breath that fills my lungs at the resemblance as I lay eyes on the old Chief's child.

I didn't work closely myself with Chief Dolloway, he died shortly after I first joined the force, but we had run ins from time to time. The young woman standing in front of me has the same deep dark blue eyes and sharp jawline that he did. Her eyes don't look as calm and wise from years of police work though, they look wide and shining, frantic with worry and fear.

'Miss Ellie Dolloway?' I ask softly, voice full of concern.

'Yes, that's me. Are you here about Freya? I phoned last night, why has it taken so long?' The sheer fear had turned to automatic distaste and disappointment so quickly I just about caught it. It changed Ellie's stance from a defeated and deflated young woman to sheer determination and tension.

'Sorry Ma'am.' Luke and those puppy dog eyes again which seem to be able to woo any woman. Any woman except me that is. 'I'm Detective Lorelle and this here is my partner, Detective Dawson. We work with the missing persons division; we are indeed here about your report. We don't normally get involved in these matters until the person has been missing for at least forty-eight hours which is why it's taken so long to come out, our apologies, but given your family's... position.' He frowns, figuring out the best way to word that we don't want a massive lawsuit on our hands from a prior Chief's family. 'We

ed and strong willed one. I always joke I got all the brains, and she got all the buzz. She got divorced about four months ago and since then, she's only gotten worse. Drinking too much, out at all hours. She's reckless if I'm honest. She gets herself into difficult situations and I'm always the one having to pull her out and pick up the pieces. Not that you'd think that if you spoke to our mother bec…'

'Ellie.' I speak gently, placing my hand over her trembling one across the counter until she meets my eye. 'Slow down. When was the last time you spoke to Freya?'

It's important to keep Ellie on track, missing persons cases are always time sensitive and with the Chief breathing down my neck because of who their father was, I need to make sure we deal with the case as quickly as possible.

'Three days ago. I asked her to pick the kids up from school yesterday and take them for a few hours so I could get errands done.' She takes a sip of her drink, licking her dry lips. 'When I tried calling her all yesterday morning and she never picked up, I assumed she'd spent all night out on the High Street and that I would have to pick the kids up myself. I wasn't happy in all honesty. Don't I feel stupid now.' Tears start streaming silently down Ellie's face. Luke reaches into his pocket and hands her his handkerChief. We both sit patiently as she dabs at her face.

'Do you know if anyone else spoke to Freya within that time frame? Is it possible that she may have… reconnected… with her ex-husband which she may be reluctant to tell you about?'

I don't know how much more gently I could put it. It's usually the case in situations of recent divorce. The missing party isn't missing at all but is just on a weekend rendezvous with their ex and they don't want their family members who didn't approve of the marriage in the first place finding out about it.

'Absolutely not.' She shakes her head vigorously, this idea seeming to be the most ridiculous thing she's heard. 'Freya and Oliver may have been together for years, but it ended horrendously. The whole marriage was horrendous, if I'm being completely honest.

They got together during the summer after graduation. Freya's first love had died in a car accident a few months before and Freya was... heartbroken. If I'm being honest, I think she only tied the knot with Oliver because it was what people expected her to do. She'd known him casually during their school years and they got married young and quick and it only seemed to go downhill from there. They were never happy and when they finally did get divorced, Oliver took everything. Left her with a pittance in his alimony payments. Something Freya and my mother have always been vicious about since finding out he'd been having an affair for two years before they finally called it quits. Freya never fought the settlement, but I think she would have if she knew.' Ellie sips her coffee, visibly trying to control her emotions and if the vice-like grip she has on the cup, which is turning her knuckles white, is anything to go by, she is furious at this whole tale. I make a note to get in contact with Freya's ex.

'I see. You mentioned your mother earlier, that she and Freya are close. Could she have heard from Freya perhaps?' I note down the comments about Freya and her ex's relationship and divorce.

'No, my mother called me and asked me to go check on her. Her flat was empty though.'

'Any signs of a disturbance?' Luke interjects, scribbling in his pocketbook.

'No.' Ellie frowns. 'It was a mess but not trashed or anything. I don't think anything was missing.'

'Blood?' Luke asks it so casually but the alarm that widened Ellie's eyes proved it was not as casual as Luke was making out.

'No.. I don't think so.'

'Could you perhaps lend us a key?' I ask as casually as I can. 'Just so we can follow up. I'm sure there's nothing to worry about.'

Ellie nods, pulling a set of keys out of a dish by the back door and handing them over.

'There's something else.' For the first time during the interview, Ellie actually meets my eye. 'It's not something I think Freya would like to become common knowledge, but I feel the need to divulge everything I know.'

'Understood.' I nod confidently, prompting her to continue.

'When Freya's marriage broke apart, it was a very difficult time for her. She did not cope well with it at all. For all her flaws, Freya has always loved wholly and deeply.' She takes a moment to compose herself, dabbing at the tears emerging in the corners. 'She drank too much, slept for hours a day, she fell into depression quite hard. She lost her job. I was under the impression that since then, she'd been living off of her alimony cheques from her ex-husband. However, I spoke with one of her friends last night who informed me that Freya had taken a job to fill the gap.' She swallows, pulling the tissue in her hands to shreds as she speaks. 'She said Freya's been working at the Kat Club on the High Street for months. That some clients could be threatening and violent. She said she saw Freya leave her shift on Wednesday night and she hasn't heard from her since.' She tears her eyes away from the ripped-up tissue and meets my eye again. Tears streaming freely.

'I see.' I nod. Trying to keep my expression neutral. 'This friend... do you have a name and number?'

'Poppy. I wrote her details down for you.' She pulls a post-it note off of the fridge and hands it over.

'So, to clarify Ellie,' Luke clears his throat, reading from his notes, 'no one has seen or spoken to Freya since her colleague at the Kat Club saw her leave her shift. When you called and asked her to pick the children up yesterday, there was no answer. There's been no evidence of a break in at her place and it isn't unusual for Freya to go missing for a period of time, say, for twenty-four hours since going through a divorce a few months ago which has also led Freya to becoming a dancer at the Kat Club, information which she has withheld from everyone for months?'

I shoot Luke another look. One, I noticed, was very similar to the one Ellie was shooting him herself.

'Listen, *Detective*.' Ellie spits. 'I called you for help. Yes, my sister is hard work. Yes, she has some things to work through, but she is *missing*.' Her voice breaks slightly before she regains control. 'She always texts. Calls. Knocks on my door at stupid o'clock in the morning because she's too drunk to get home. Always. Being gone for this long, with no word to anyone is not normal. If you won't help me then please, just go.'

There's a silent pause of tension. All of us taking a moment to size each other up. I break the silence first. Speaking as softly as possible to not exasperate the situation, Luke and Ellie's stare off still going strong.

'Ellie, no one's saying that. We are just trying to get an idea of the situation to best define where we go from here. Everyone wants your sister home safe. We promise, we will do everything in our power to make that happen.' I rise from my seat, breaking the stare between the two of them. 'Thank you, for these.' I jiggle the keys to Freya's place in the air. 'We will be in touch as soon as we have any information for you. Thank you for your time.' I've never heard a door slam so loud behind us in all my days on the job.

Chapter 8

Detective Dawson

As soon as we've left Ellie Dolloway's house and are on the road, Luke calls Freya's friend whilst I drive. He puts on his best charming phone voice, with that slight edge of flirtation that always seems to work on every female who walks the earth. Well, every female except for me that is.

I listen to his half of the ten-minute conversation, trying to infer what Poppy's side of the conversation is. Frustration stirring that I can't be driving and speaking to her myself at the same time. The control freak in me screaming.

My shoulders relax when he finally ends the call and relays the conversation, more or less, in full.

'She says she doesn't know where Freya may have gone. That they 're only really work friends.'

'But she's as worried as Ellie Dolloway?'

'Seems that way. Although, it could just be that because she and Freya have the same work lifestyle, she's panicking she might be next.'

'Did she say that?'

'No. She didn't say much to be completely honest. She said Freya's been working at the club for about four or five months. That she was quite popular with the clientele but that she mostly kept herself to herself.'

'Did she mention any issues? Work-related or otherwise?' I indicate left when the sat nav tells me to, pulling onto Freya Dolloway's street.

'Nada.' Luke shrugs. 'Said that a couple of blokes could get handsy but that also comes with the territory. To be totally honest, it was basically a repeat of what Ellie Dolloway has already told us.'

'Not much to go off then,' I sigh. 'Let's hope her apartment is more forthcoming.'

When we enter Freya's small apartment, I realize she and her sister, although twins, are truly individuals.

Ellie's house had been all colourful, with home-made furnishings and decorations but very organised and tidy, everything in its place. Children's imagination and love radiated from every picture-covered wall and worn sofa cushion.

Freya's is bleak, devoid of color, and *filthy*. All sharp edges and monochrome colors. Rubbish covers every crevice and surface. It's difficult to know where to start to go through the mess.

The whole place just feels hollow. As if Freya may eat, sleep, and bathe here but she's never really made it home. If I had to guess the type of woman Freya Dolloway is solely based on this place she calls home, it would be... *miserable.*

'You start over there.' I motion towards the kitchen and living room combination to the one side of the small studio. 'I'll look over here.' I make my way to the bedroom half, searching the drawers in the small corner desk. Finding piles of discarded receipts, paperclips, and capless pens.

The bed is unmade and covered in piles of clothes. Whether they're clean or dirty, who knows. I pull some clothes aside, shaking the duvet and pillows out. Searching any places which Freya might use to hide her deepest darkest secrets. Seeking out anything that might give some indication of why she'd up and simply vanish.   Navigating the piles of clothes and crunched-up final notice letters scattering the floors to the bathroom is like navigating the seven seas. There are towels everywhere but nothing that looks too out of place. I rifle through the bathroom cabinet.   The usual culprits; plasters and painkillers, floss and sanitary towels line the shelves. I push a few of them over and find a prescription bottle tucked in the back.   'Hey, Luke?"

'Yeah, Boss?' Luke follows me, showing just how tiny the bathroom is with two of us crammed in here. 'Nothing of much interest in the kitchen or living room. A few last notice rent bills is the only thing worth mentioning.'

'I found a few of those myself actually, in the bedroom. I guess she was having some financial issues. Might explain these.' I hold the pill bottle up. 'Citalopram.' I read from the label.

'Commonly used antidepressant medication, right?' Luke takes the bottle, turning it around in his hand. 'Woah. High dose as well,' he whistles.

'Yeah.' I grimace. 'Ellie did mention past issues with depression. I guess it isn't as much in the past for Freya as she would have her family believe.'

'This can't have helped.' I gesture towards the discarded letters in the waste paper basket under the desk. 'Multiple final notice bills. Electric, gas, rent... doesn't appear she was in a very good financial situation.'

'Seems that way.' Luke agrees, walking back out into the main living space. 'Was there anything on the laptop?'

'Was just about to check.' I walk back across the place to the small desk housing a knocked-over pen pot, a pile of coffee-stained papers, and a laptop that looks way too new and expensive considering the bills. I open the laptop, booting it up.

'We're going to need IT,' I huff when the password-protected screen pops up.

I sit down at the desk and pick the skin down the side of my thumbnail whilst I chew the situation over. Do I know enough about Freya Dolloway yet to guess what words she'd use to protect her files?

In the end, I decide that I probably don't and pull my phone out, dialling the station to request IT support. A few minutes later, I've provided the necessary details from the sticker on the bottom of the machine and the IT guys have remotely hacked the hard drive, providing me with full access.

I open a few files from the desktop, nothing of interest popping up. The email box is mainly full of spam and job adverts.I have almost given up and shut the machine down when I notice a shortcut hyperlink I hadn't noticed saved to the internet browser's favourites. No site name, just a set of numbers with no apparent meaning.

As soon as the web page loads, I know that if Ellie knew about her twins' side job, she would have mentioned it. 'Luke. Come look at this but keep your tongue in your mouth when you do please.' 'XXX Nasties,' Luke reads directly from the website's domain name, nose scrunched in confusion.

'No offence, but I don't think this girl's porn habits are going to help us to find her.'

'No, you idiot.' I'm surprised my eyes don't do a full 360 in my head. I roll them that hard. 'Look at the top video.' The video's thumbnail isn't the clearest but there's no doubting it. 'Shit, she's a cam girl?' Luke raises his eyebrow. 'A stripper and a cam girl. The Chief would have been so proud I'm sure.' Luke sniggers. 'Hey.' I punch his arm, dumbfounded by the fact he would outright say something like that. 'This family has been through a hell of a lot, we can only imagine the toll trauma like that must take. So, keep your opinions on Freya's life choices to yourself.'

'Right.' Luke clears his throat and runs a hand over his face, clearly regretting the decision to mention anything. I click the video thumbnail and within five seconds of the contents loading there's no doubting it, it is definitely Freya Dolloway. 'Shit.' Luke reiterates as we scroll through the other videos on Freya's or "Dirty Dolly's" profile. 'Dolly... as in Dolloway? Kind of clever I have to admit' 'IT are going to have to do a deep dive of this. Looks like she has quite the following on this thing. We need to know who her regulars are. If anyone's got a sheet. Go through all the live chats and private messages, see if anything stands out. She hasn't left it logged in or her password saved, so we can't see anything specific, just the thumbnails and likes.'

I scan the page vaguely, looking out for anything that stands out and it does.

'Check this out, I move over, letting Luke lean down towards the screen, trying to ignore the feel of his breath on my neck.

'Looks like Poppy's got her very own profile on this thing too. Freya's shared some of her videos. Yet, she failed to mention any of it when you spoke to her just now.' 'Maybe she knows who Dirty Dolly's regulars were. Let's ask her to come down to the station, we can drop the laptop off with IT, and see if they can track down the owners of the site and access her private account.'

Chapter 9

No One

The feds leave the apartment with a triumphant stride in their steps. I should be worried. If I left anything in there, this could all be over. What if they looked over across the street and saw me loitering in this alleyway with no honest reason to be hiding here in the shadows?

They could have come right over and questioned me. Noticed the uneasy shift of my eyes or twitch of my fingers. Seen the evil lurking just beneath my surface. They could have dragged me out, cuffed me right there, and read me my rights. Then what would I have done? I'm not done yet... No, no. Not done. I don't know how long I loiter in this spot, long enough for my feet to start aching before I creep out and let myself into Freya's building. She was stupid to leave her spare key behind this loose brick on the building's side. It made it so much easier for me to get in that first time and wait here. Now, her key dangles alongside mine on my keyring. Almost as if it was always supposed to be there. Like I was always supposed to find it. I wonder if she would have realised it was missing by now if she weren't locked up tight back home.

I creep up the stairs, keeping my body crouched and my head low but no one's around to see me anyway. The excitement buzzes through me, making my fingertips tingle. I've always been good at this. Sneaking into places I don't belong.

I check the small flat inch by inch, checking there's no remaining signs of me being here before. If the police were as thorough as they should be, it doesn't show. Nothing is much more of a mess than it was the night before last. My skin prickles. I don't know how anyone could live in such filth, such mess, *such chaos*....1.2.3.4.5..6...7...8...9...10. Breathe. I close my eyes and when I open them, I imagine the room is spotless, that I can smell the mingling sting of bleach, medicinal afternotes of a tidy and clean flat to calm myself. Enough. I compose myself because I'm here for a purpose. I cross the pathetically small flat in two strides, thumb drive twirling between my thumb and forefinger. I stop abruptly, spinning in all directions, scanning the dark room at every inch... but it's gone. The laptop's gone... where is it? Stupid. Stupid. *Stupid, stupid. You fucking stupid idiot. You should have taken it with-*.... 123.45..6...7...8...9...10. Breathe. I should have taken the fucking laptop with me when I snatched her. I don't know how long I stand there trying to decide what to do but it's a few minutes at least.

I kneel down and pull my backpack off, pulling out the physical print outs. This will have to do for now. Now that I have neither her phone nor her laptop. I was too hasty. Too sloppy. I should never have left the devices. I got cocky. Figured I could make it back in time, but she had me... distracted. I had more fun with her then I expected I would and that led to a lapse in judgement on my part. Now I can't use either for my plans. I debate forgetting the photo idea all together. Since I can't use the digital copies, but I've come all this way, made

Rabbit, by the ear. 'Mommy, mommy!' she squeals with delight. *Ouch. It's going to take more than paracetamol.* For half a second I actually glance at the top corner cabinet, debating dusting off the bottle of red at the back. *Absolutely not Ellie, it's 9AM in the morning for god's sake!* I internally reprimand myself.

'Mommy!' Myah's getting inpatient. I rub my eyes, pasting a smile on my face and spin around to face my little princess who doesn't have a worry in the world, except for whether she's getting control of the tv over her brother at some point today. I've told them both that Auntie Freya has been busy at work and that's why she didn't pick them up like she promised on Friday, and no, she's still going to be working tomorrow too so she won't be picking them up then either. I mean, what else was I supposed to tell them? They're just children, they won't understand. The only downside is that now I have to pretend nothing is wrong. That everything's normal. I can see the way Myah tilts her head, resting her eyes on the dark circles under mine for a second too long. She's not convinced. Such intuition for someone so small. 'Yes, sweetheart?' I smile wider, the strain almost too much for my sleep deprived body. 'Nanny's here!' she beams. The blood rushes to my feet. 'Nanny's what?' My palms are suddenly slick with sweat and the mug I'm holding slips through my fingers. It's like I'm watching it shatter in slow motion as the pieces and boiling hot liquid cover the floor and my bare feet.

'*Shit! Shit! Shit!*' I bite my lip against the pain, hopping on my toes. '*Shit! Shit! Shit!*' Matty mimics at the top of his lungs as he saunters into the kitchen, followed closely by my mother. 'Matthew. James. Dolloway. I beg your pardon?' My mother has her hands on her hips, glaring down at my child the way she used to glare down at me and Freya when she caught us smoking behind the trees at the end of the back garden. 'Sorry Nana.' Matty pouts out his bottom lip, looking at his feet and swinging his arms in that sulky childlike manner which always manages to melt my mother's ice-cold heart.'That's ok, darling. Mommy shouldn't be swearing in front of you anyway.' she nods. 'Myah pudding, help your brother get some towels from the upstairs cupboard to help mommy clean up the mess she's made.' I scoff at the way she still manages to wind up reprimanding me, even now I'm older with children of my own.Once she's sure the children are firmly out of earshot she turns her stern face towards me and I feel all my resolve and fight vanish in an instance. I'm sixteen again, standing in front of my strict mother, holding my breath to prepare for the inevitable verbal abuse. Again, much like my sixteen year old self, when it comes I'm still not emotionally prepared for it.'What kind of a mother are you, Ellie?' She spits and, just like that, I'm seventeen again...

Seven *years ago*

It's almost midnight and I focus on the frost that's slowly climbing along the window, stretching out from the corners to meet each other in the middle. Separating us from the outside world, almost as if it's trying desperately to hide my shame. I look up and meet my father's eye in the window's reflection. He looks old now, the job wearing him down and stripping his youth. His brow is furrowed in that line he always gets sweeping across his forehead when he's in deep thought. It's always amazed me, how deeply brown they are, almost black. They peer back at me through the reflection and I can't quite tell what they're trying to say to me. He's rubbing that line in his brow and shaking his head but he hasn't said a word since I told them. Just his head moving back and forth in confusion and frustration, the only sign he's heard me. The sudden wave of betrayal surprises me and I feel myself wiping tears from my cheeks again. I really thought he'd support me, take me into his arms and hold me tight like he used to do when I was little. Kiss my nose over and over in the same way, tell me that it's all going to be ok. Not this time. This time he just stands there, rubbing that crease in his forehead and shaking his head in disbelief. I tear my eyes away from his reflection, not bearing to look at the expression on his face for another second, and look past him instead. In the reflection, to the far end of the living room wall. Where my mother's pacing back and forth, back and forth, back and forth along the length of the living room. Her shins just nearly miss the coffee table each time.

She's crying… not the gut wrenching wailing I expected but instead silent but fast tears. dampening her face, she keeps dabbing her nose with a crumpled tissue but it doesn't do much, instead it's just smearing the snot across her cheeks. Her mouth is moving fast but I can't seem to hear what she's saying properly. Her voice sounds muffled, as if I'm under water. You know in movies where the main character daydreams and the voices of people around them are all muffled and unclear. That's what it feels like. I'm wondering whether this will all be just a movie, a dream I'll wake up abruptly from, panting and sweating. If the unclear voices will suddenly drown into shouting beep beep! Beep, beep! Until my alarm clock pulls me out and I realise none of it was real. My mother turns abruptly, locking eyes with me in the window's reflection. 'I'm going to call Dr Francis first thing tomorrow.' She declares. 'We're going to get this all straightened out.' 'What does that mean?' I turn to face her properly from my spot on the sofa, still hugging my legs and rocking back and forth gently - trying to rock myself out of this nightmare. I kick myself at how feeble my voice sounds. I know better than to show her weakness. My father stops rubbing his head and turns to my mother too. 'Kathrine, this is Ellie's decision. You must let her make it for herself.' He's insistent but his voice sounds as feeble as mine did. He gives me a look as if to say, I'm sorry I didn't say something sooner; before the screaming and the following agonising silence, before my mother started rambling and pacing across the living room. 'Don't start with me, James!' My mother shrieks. 'She can't possibly want this to end any other way. What will people say!? What will people think!? The Chief's daughter... pregnant at age seventeen. Not even an adult yet, herself. Never mind when they find out...' she trails off, catching the astonishment in my eyes that she would mention it. 'We can't let this happen.' 'It isn't your life, you can't just decide this for me.' My voice is barely a whisper, barely an argument but I feel it deep within me. This resilience I didn't know I had, this resolve. That this is my child, a part of me, living and growing alongside me for the past few months without me even knowing it. 'No, Ellie. I won't have it. A baby can't be born of your childish mistakes. How could you bring this child into this world when you are still a child yourself. No job, no money, no father...' again, that look. 'If you bring a baby into all of this mess then just what kind of a mother are you even?'

Chapter 12

Detective Dawson

We're both quiet on the drive back to the station from Freya Dolloway's flat. Both deep in our own thoughts, turning things over, trying to look at them from different angles and perspectives to evaluate the information we have so far before we move forward with next steps. I let Luke drive so that I can take notes. I sit, chewing the rubber on the end of my pencil, staring at the notes I've already made in my pocketbook. I'm debating over how to approach such a significant case, an old, respected Chief's daughter, a part of the deep, wide, dark web.

I read through my scribbles for the tenth time since we set off; Freya Dolloway, daughter of renowned Chief Dolloway who died in a B&E arson gone bad, is there a connection? Nothing points to it at this stage. No sign of break-in or forced entry at the property but multiple final notice bills suggest debt. Possible connection to half-empty anti-depressant pill bottle, suggestions of financial difficulty and depression. Need for escape from problems? Could she have run away from her problems? Possible suicide? But no note or body has been found so far.

Bad divorce angle; possibility of ex-husband being involved or connected to sudden disappearance. Family and friends have mentioned Freya going off the rails recently since divorce was finalised. Is the ex-husband involved?

Risky lifestyle angle; Freya is on at least one cam girl site on the dark web. It's possible that it could be a regular customer gone wrong. Also, possible Freya ran away from risk? I underline "Runaway?" four times. I spit bits of pencil eraser from in between my teeth, realising I've been chewing too hard.

Luke glances over when we hit a red light, quickly skimming my haphazard notes. The years of experience working with me and deciphering my notes are coming in handy for him to make any kind of sense of them before the light turns green again. 'Runaway scenario looks like most likely,' he nods slowly. 'Unless you think that possible suicide could be a legitimate concern?' 'I don't know. Out of the two I would be more inclined to think that the pressures and changes in her life recently were too much for her. The divorce might have been the tipping point in making her feel like she needed to just get away from it all so she upped and left.' I flip my notebook shut and stuff it back into my blazer pocket 'I think we'd have something if it was a suicide. A note or something.' 'Could be a suicide note on the laptop.' He suggests it but he doesn't look convinced either.

'I guess we'll let IT figure that one out.' I nod. 'Although, there's normally signs beforehand with suicide. It's almost like the victim accepts their fate before they do it. They take steps and precautions to get their affairs in order beforehand. Tie up loose ends. That kind of thing. We haven't seen anything like that from Freya.'

I'm certain that if that were Freya's plan, she would have shut down and deleted her online profiles. Otherwise, why make sure your family had no idea, only to then leave it all for them to find after the fact. I don't think she would have agreed to pick up her niece and nephew either. I take my pocketbook back out of my pocket and cross off "suicide" as an explanation. 'I agree,' Luke nods. 'but I do think we need to wait for Jasper and the lads to confirm there's no note on the laptop before we completely rule it out.' By Jasper and "the lads" he means the head of IT and his fellow experts who run the stations' forensic IT department. 'You know partner, the usual culprit is normally the most obvious, the one closest to the missing person.' Luke shrugs, indicating to turn down the high street where the station is located. 'Usually it's the spouse, or in this case, the ex-spouse.' I nod slowly. 'Although, that's normally in cases of crimes of passion and when one of them winds up dead. Or if it's the abduction of a child. None of those seem relevant in this case.' 'Not yet anyway.' Luke raises an eyebrow at me as he pulls into the station's small parking lot. 'But I do think we need to speak with this Oliver bloke all the same.' 'I'll ask him to come in whilst we wait for the lads to give us anything back from Freya's laptop or phone.'

We leave the laptop with the IT guys downstairs and head back up to our office on the fifth floor. The balls of my feet are aching, and my head is thumping from lack of caffeine, but something tells me this case is far from over.

I'd called Poppy as soon as we left Freya's apartment, walking down the front path back to the car to ask her to come down to the station to give an official statement. I'd also left a message for Oliver White, Freya's ex-husband, during the drive. He'd sent me straight to voice-mail the three times I tried.

I'm about to finally sit down and drink a cup of coffee when Juniper from the reception calls up to say Poppy has arrived to see me. I ask her to bring her up to one of the interrogation rooms instead of the more comfortable family waiting rooms. We give it twenty minutes before we head over to join her. Whilst I understand her inclination to protect herself from federal scrutiny given that these sites aren't always exactly legal, her friend is missing. Given that, I would have expected her to disclose this piece of crucial information which could help us find her sooner. Without hesitation even. Instead, she conveniently chose to keep this information to herself, costing us time on the investigation which could prove crucial. The whole sordid situation has me grinding my teeth with aggravation. So, I've put her in this bare, uninviting room to sweat instead and as Luke and I join her, I realise that's exactly what she's been doing for the last half hour. I take a seat directly opposite her whilst Luke walks to the far wall and leans against it, leg up against it supporting his weight with his arms crossed in front of him. I guess we're taking the good cop, bad cop routine, of which he's stepped into the role of the latter and I willingly step into my role and smile at her.

'Ms Ryan. Thank you for meeting with us here.' I begin with a much chirpier incline to my voice than usual.

I watch the beads of sweat form on her forehead, the shuffle of her feet, the way she's wringing her hands so hard that they're turning blotchy with redness. She sees me looking and squirms in her seat, pulling her hands from the table top and hiding them from view

a man in the room, even one as gentle and handsome as Luke, will only remind her of the type of men that watch her from afar. It will make her uneasy. She'll hold back. I know Luke isn't going to get water, in a few moments he'll be behind the glass mirror spanning half of the wall behind me. Watching and listening. For a brief moment, I wonder if Poppy knows this too deep down. Hell, there's enough cop shows on the TV nowadays telling the nation the habits of our police force on a daily basis for her to figure it out, and yet, these tactics still usually have their desired effect. 'Can you tell me about the site? What does the content usually involve?' I uncross my arms and place my hands flat on the table in front of me. Another tactic, this will make me look more open, less threatening, even subconsciously, that I'm open to her disclosures. 'It's mainly sexual content.' She confesses, her cheeks reddening. 'There's another, softer side to the site though. People looking for friendship and just honest to god relationships, whether romantic or platonic, but those chat rooms and pages seem to be few and far between nowadays.' She sniffs. 'That's how I started on the site. Working late shifts at a dance club can be lonely. It's unsociable hours, there aren't many others awake the same hours I am. I didn't have many friends.' 'So, you didn't start off on the site... performing?' I chose my words carefully. 'Not for months, no.' She shakes her head. 'It was just a place to meet like-minded women in a similar profession to me who would understand the toll it takes, you know?' 'I do.' I nod, trying to build rapport. Even though the truth is, I can only guess and imagine what life is like for these women. I imagine it's similar to my own in certain respects. Unsociable hours, people either love or hate what you do, either understand or feel threatened by you. Stressful shifts, men feeling they have the right to comment on a woman making her own choices and choosing her own path. Whether that be on the streets with a badge or on a stage in her underwear. 'So

I started off in a few chat rooms, mainly women with similar hours and interests, we'd vent about clients, about long hours, the aches and pains, the constant demand and being used for the entertainment factor your body could provide and not the depth of your person. That kind of stuff...cheesy I know.' She scoffs, picking the skin around her fingernails absentmindedly. I can see from the flecks and scabs it's a nervous habit she has.

'So when did you begin taking part in the content side of things?' 'Only a couple of months ago. The club is under new management, they cut our hours in half, hired new agency dancers who would do longer hours for less money. I had to decide between paying my rent or paying my electric and gas.' I pass a tissue along the table when she starts crying. We sit in silence for a few moments before she takes another deep breath and continues. 'It was when I was shivering in the middle of the night. I had four jumpers on and three blankets on the bed. It still wasn't enough but I couldn't afford to put the heating on. My teeth were chattering and I knew then I had to find some other way of making money. Then my phone chimed, it was one of the women from the site replying to one of my messages. It sounds silly, but it was almost as if it was a sign.' 'That's when you decided to film your first video?' 'No. it's where the most money is so I did start streaming a few weeks later but in the beginning I did calls.' 'Calls?' 'Yes. Men mostly, a couple of women. They would pay five dollars every five minutes for a phone call. No cameras. I never saw any of them and they never saw me. It was just...voices. Sounds sometimes.' She blushes again and I nod, not feeling the need for her to explain further. 'Freya found out about the site from you?' I can feel my pocketbook burning a hole in my blazer and I hope Luke is taking notes because I don't want to take it out and put Poppy off.

'Yes,' she sobs. Covering her mouth. I wait until she's ready to carry on. 'We went for a coffee one morning after a long shift. It was a bachelor party, one where they had deep pockets and very little inhibition. She had a breakdown. Told me about her husband, the nasty divorce, that he left her with nothing. She was struggling; she didn't know if she could make her rent.' 'So, you suggested the site as a way to supplement her income, to help her during a rough time?' 'That's right. I actually helped her to set up her account.' She sniffs. 'She did the calls to begin with aswell. She only started streaming in the last few weeks.' 'Did she ever tell you about any clients, whether at the club or on this site, that made her uncomfortable or that she may have been afraid of?' 'A couple. They were real creeps, said some vile things to her but she never said she was afraid, only disturbed, they made her uncomfortable.' 'Did she disclose their names?' I sit a little straighter, trying to not look too desperate for the information. 'The site doesn't use real names but I think she said one of them was "Slitter" or something,' she makes air quotes with her fingers as she says it, 'I remember it because it just sounded... creepy.' She visibly shivers. 'He started commenting on her videos, saying how he wanted to feel what her body would feel like with no skin on it. The moderators blocked him from her streams but then he started to DM her.' 'DM meaning direct messaging through the chat function?' 'Yes. He would send her messages daily, they got more and more disturbing, she reported him a few times but he kept creating new accounts, it would always be *Slitter* but he'd put different numbers at the end. That kind of thing.' 'Did you ever have any contact with him through your own page?'

'None. I asked around too, none of the women had ever heard of him. It seemed he was completely focused on Freya.' 'Did she ever report this? To the police? To the site administrators?' 'No. It's like

I said, very few of us chose this career path because we like it. Most of us do it out of need and desperation, the police aren't exactly fans of our line of work.' She rubs her eyes, taking a deep breath and she starts picking her fingers again. She's stopped crying but I can see she's still shivering. I decide she needs a break. 'I just have one last question and then you're free to go home.' Now I take out my pocketbook. 'You said you helped Freya set up her account. Does that mean that you know her username and password?'

Chapter 13

Ellie

I hate Freya. That's harsh but it's how I feel. I think, as I sit in front of my mother at her kitchen table, that I've always hated her. Maybe not as deeply as I have over the last few years, but I think it's always been there. Bubbling below the surface, threatening to boil over the top of me. It's strange, to finally accept that all I feel for the woman who shared almost every second of my life with me, even when we were nothing but mere cells in our mother's womb, is pure strong hate.

I dropped the kids off at school this morning, their uniforms crumpled and un-ironed, their lunch boxes full of cheese strings and crisps because that's all that was left in the kitchen. As I watched them run up the steps, clearly both uneasy because of their mother's mood, I found myself hating Freya with every inch of my being. That she would just up and disappear like this, to the point my children are suffering. I see it in Matty's face when he sees my unbrushed hair and dark circles, the fear and concern. He should be worried about whether he wants chicken nuggets or cheese sticks for dinner, not whether today is the day that his mother finally cracks.

I drove to my mother's straight from drop off, my body sizzling with apprehension because I knew how this conversation was going to go before I even rang the bell. As I sit here, at her table, nursing a now lukewarm cup of tea, watching my mother endlessly sob into crumpled sopping wet tissue, I find myself thinking about how much I truly do hate my twin. I wish I'd been an only child. Maybe then, there would have been enough love to go around, instead of Freya sucking up every last drop and hoarding it to herself like a dehydrated vampire. Although, I guess I can't blame Freya entirely for that, there were other factors at play for my mother to decide I wasn't worth even the dregs of her love. Although, regardless of my mother's beliefs, the things that happened weren't exactly my fault either. As much as they weren't mine, they also weren't Freya's.

My mother sobs loudly, her breath coming in and out more like heaves. I sit silently, staring into my too strong tea. My mother never did learn that her two daughters prefer their tea differently. She only bothered to learn Freya's. Strong as a builder's, barely even a dash of milk but three heaped sugars, enough to rot your teeth by the time you're forty. She doesn't seem to know, or care if she does, that I prefer my tea milky with only a dash of sugar. *God, get a hold of yourself. Freya's missing. Surely that is more important than your lack of milk in your goddamn tea.* I chastise myself.

'What are the police doing to find my daughter?' My mother sniffles, pushing her untouched coffee away like it spat at her. 'I need her home! I don't know what I'll do if she doesn't come back to me.' I stifle the urge to roll my eyes, reaching across the table to take my mother's hand. She visibly flinches, moving her hand away suddenly and tucking it into her lap.

She looks out of the window, trying to pretend she didn't just recoil from me like I was a viper. I feel the pang of resentment and hurt flow through my chest but I sigh and sit back, folding my arms as if they alone can protect me from my mother's scorn. 'They are doing everything they can mother,' I sigh. 'They've taken her keys; they're going see if they can find anything to indicate where she's gone. Once they know anything, they will be in touch. You know how this works. They don't even normally start looking this early when an adult goes missing so I'm grateful they're looking into this at all. It's only because of dad th-' I stop short and swallow my words as I meet my mother's eye.

She's stopped looking out of the window now and is instead fixing me with a stoney glare. Her bottom lip quivering and if I didn't know her so well, I would think it was sadness and grief. Except I do know her, and the look she's giving me isn't that it's pure unadulterated anger and resentment.

'You dare speak of your father to me again.' She whispers it but the emotion behind the words may as well be screaming across the table at me. I wonder if it was always there: the venom.

She spits it at me so regularly now I've become almost numb to it. Since my father died, she doesn't even bother to hide it anymore and I wonder when I started noticing the spitefulness within my mother. It always shocks me when she shows it, even now. Maybe it's because I've never seen her act that way towards anyone else. It's like a version of herself she reserves solely for her eldest daughter, the worst version of herself. I'd understand if I was a problem child and I guess when I got pregnant - I kind of was for her. But she had started to dislike me before then; I was always the bad one. The tainted one. The unwanted one. Freya got showered with love and I got drenched with spite and I wonder if that's just who my mother is.

My eyes sting but I refuse to let her win. I haven't cried in front of my mother in years. Not even at my own father's funeral. She made it very clear that I wasn't allowed to grieve in the same way her and Freya were. The silence fills the space between us like a tensioned whip, ready to snap for what feels like forever until my phone ringing breaks the silence. My boss' number lights the screen and although I've already told her that I need to take a few personal days and she really shouldn't be calling me when I'm taking said personal days, I jump at the opportunity to apologise to my mother and say a quick, emotionless goodbye.

Chapter 14

Detective Dawson

The interview with Poppy Ryan leaves me feeling uneasy. I can't count the times a missing woman has turned up dead or as part of a sex trafficking ring where they were targeted from being part of a site like XXX Nasties. They promote the safety of their users, confidentiality, and the end-to-end encryptions but the truth is, none of them can assure absolute safety.

As soon as Poppy had left the station, red eyed and puffy, I brought the log in details she'd given me down to Jasper. I feel for the girl. I can imagine the fear she feels right now. Both for her friend and for herself, if Freya's sudden disappearance really does have anything to do with this site. It would make anyone else on there a potential target too. The IT office is stifling hot in the summer, all of the servers and technology whirring away, filling the room with a thick electric heat. Jasper has his desk fan on full and rotating so that it hits my face every few seconds as I sit next to him, waiting for him to pull up Freya's account. All the fan really does is throw a blast of stifling heat straight into my face. I tie my hair up tightly in a bun and revel in the small reprieve I get on the back of my neck.

As we wait for the account to buffer and log in, I find myself needing to fill the silence.

'Have you found anything else useful yet in the files?'

'Not yet, no.' Jasper yawns.

'Any suicide note?'

'Nothing at all. No recent searches or forum visits which suggests any sort of suicidal ideation either.'

I cross suicide as a possible explanation off of the list in my pocket-book – relieved to see it go. I'd checked my messages on the way down here. I was hoping that Freya's ex-husband would have called me back during the couple of hours we had been with Poppy but after checking my voicemail and emails twice, it would appear that either Oliver is extremely busy and has not heard my voicemail yet, or he's avoiding me. My money's on the latter.

'Looks like this woman posted every other day. Mainly live streams, doing... sexual acts for specified amounts of money, all of which were paid via bank transfers through the secure services, so I can't access their encryptions of which accounts were paying.' Jasper clears his throat, moving over slightly so that I can pull my chair in and take a closer look.

'Can we get transcripts of the live streams? Who commented what? If there were any threats or unconventional requests which Freya may have discarded or ignored?' I skim the comments on the latest video, cringing at the uninventive usernames. Nothing really catches my eye at first glance but that doesn't mean it isn't there.

'Sure. That will take time though.' Jasper nods, snapping his fingers at one of the lads on the desks opposite who comes over obediently.

Jasper relays my request and gives the tech guy the login details I had passed to him.

'Can you check her private messages? Looks like there's an inbox icon.' I point at the small envelope icon in the top right.

Jasper pulls it up and reveals several private chat conversations. Going through them quickly, it looks like Freya ignored most of the direct messages she received. From the amounts at the tops of the chat, it looks like users had to pay to direct message content creators but in Freya's case, this didn't seem to guarantee they would get a response. Most of the messages she's received are filthy and crude, so I'm not surprised she decided not to reply. There seems to be a few chat conversations which Freya had indulged, some involving regular payments and private photos and videos but Freya never seemed to cross professional boundaries with clients, even when she did reply.

There's one thread between Freya and what looks like a handful of other content creators too, warning their fellow performers away from certain users as well as general tips for content and what makes the most money.

'I'll do a search on the guys they mention avoiding.' Jasper starts making notes, already anticipating what my next request was going to be. 'But you'll have to speak with the website domain owners to try and get these guys' real names and personal information. I'll only be able to search their handles through the site.'

I nod, knowing that it will be a long road with a lot of red tape. 'I need you to look for any constant messages from one particular person. It's possible that Freya blocked them and reported them but they kept making new accounts under different email addresses. See if you can find multiple threads with similar usernames. One of the girls on the site said his username always involved the word "Slitter" in some way or another.' I wait for Jasper to finish cringing and add the task to his list. 'Can you pull that thread up there, with OJ6969?' I point to one of the chats which jumps out at me, stifling a scoff at the user's unimaginative handle name. 'Can you scroll to the top?' I frown, trying to figure out why this name in particular has my instinct stirring. After reading the first few lines of conversation, it's almost a cliche how quickly my brain goes *Ping!*

The conversation is full of insults and harsh words on both parts between OJ6969 and Freya. Degrading language and expletives fly back and forth until Freya eventually blocks them.

Reading the last couple of lines solidifies my suspicion. Freya's last message to OJ6969 is telling them that they no longer have any right to pass judgment on her exploits because he was no longer her husband. OJ6969 is Freya Dolloway's ex-husband Oliver James and from their conversation, it looked like Oliver was infuriated by Freya's choice of supplementary employment. Ironic really, considering *he's* on the site too. A fact clearly lost on him, considering his last message to her had been; ***Fuck you Freya. You're going to regret this. I'll make you pay. Watch your back.*** Which is a threat if I ever did see one. I need to get in touch with Mr James sooner rather than later.

Chapter 15

No One

I need to do something. The police are still sniffing around, and I know it's only a matter of time before their trail leads my way. I can't let that happen. It's going to ruin it. Ruin the game. Ruin my fun. I won't let them do that. I won't be rushed. I want to take my time, indulge. So? Sue me!

She passed out about an hour ago and I've been sitting here watching her ever since.

She stinks. I need to clean her soon. How am I supposed to enjoy it if she stinks like a whore? Like used sex and urine mixed with three-day old sweat. That's not going to be fun. No. I'll wash her. For now, I look her over, running my finger up and down her side, admiring the bruises and cuts that trademark her body as mine. I brush her greasy hair from her face and admire her sleeping face. When she's out of it like this, I can almost pretend she is who I wish she were. I can pretend that we're frozen in time, that she was never ripped away from me. The warm feeling is fleeting, like it always is. The excitement gives way to a numbness that has become so familiar that I cannot tell it and myself apart. My skin crawls and my teeth grind, the hollowness drowning out all of my senses and I need to find something to distract me. To take the edge off. I find myself wishing she was awake so that I could see the terror in her eyes. Her fear always seems to relieve these feelings. When I first brought her back here, she didn't sleep at all, barely even stopped weeping to breathe. Now look at her. Sleeping soundly like she has no care in the world. Like she has nothing to worry about. As if I'm not a threat. How dare she!?   I feel my lips curl back over my teeth, feeling the rage start to bubble up. It seeps into the numb hollow and ignites the senses. She must sense it because her eyes flutter open, filling with fear when she realizes how close to her I am. She starts pushing away from me and screaming so loud it makes my ears ring.

I guess she knows what's coming.

Chapter 16

Detective Dawson

I push open the door to the family waiting room. Mr James isn't what I expected. He's a tall, lanky man. Dark salt and pepper hair, the silver glistening in the sunlight from the window. It's in desperate need of a cut, flopping across his forehead and he keeps blowing it out of his eyes. He's quite handsome with deep coffee eyes and aside from his unkempt hair, looks very well-to-do and put together. His suit is expensive and the watch on his wrist and the shoes on his feet look designer. I have no doubt that they each cost what I make in a month.

He's pacing the room when I walk in, his hands on his hips and his brow furrowed. He sets me with a hard look and just from the angry quiver of his mouth and the irritation colouring his face, I can tell he's a hard assed, sour, middle-aged man. From his activity on XXX Nasties, he's also a very angry, short fused and entitled man with a superiority complex. All reasons why he's been put here, in this cushiony and welcoming room. Because his money and entitlement make the Chief nervous. My blood boils but I paste on my sweetest smile and motion towards the worn brown sofa under the window. Arse licking is the only language men like this understand.

'Mr James. Thank you for coming in to see us.' Luke and I take the sofa opposite and as I cross my legs, I notice Mr James' eyeline travelling down. I cringe.

'What the fuck is this about?' he snaps. 'I don't have time for this; I'm a very busy man. Why on earth you needed me to travel all this way is beyond me. I've already called my attorney.'

'Why would you do that, Mr James?' Luke fakes confusion and I see the itch of a smirk at the corner of his mouth, 'Do you feel you've done something that requires an attorney?'

'Of course not,' he scowls. 'Don't twist my words like that.'

'Ok, Mr James.' I hold my hands up in mock surrender, 'Please excuse my partner. I for one, am extremely grateful you were willing to come down. Shall we get this over and done with? I know you must have much better things to be getting on with, a busy man like you.' I dive straight into the good cop, bad cop routine. I'm sure Oliver James regards all females as weak, submissive creatures and I'm willing to play my part. 'We are not trying to twist your words. We just need your help.'

He sits back, stretching his arms out wide on either side of him on the back of the sofa, consciously trying to make himself look bigger, puffing his chest like some idiot. Luke coughs and I know he's trying to stifle a laugh. I pinch my wrist to distract myself from the laugh tickling the back of my throat, trying not to show my amusement.

'Right. Well, this isn't the way to go about getting my help now is it lady?' he rolls his eyes.

'Detective Dawson.' Luke corrects him but I can tell Mr James isn't paying him the slightest bit of attention. His eyes leer across my body as we talk and I want to rip my skin off just so he can't look at it anymore.

'It's regarding your ex-wife.' I smile sweetly and watch his face fall into one of disgust and reproach. 'Freya Dolloway?'

'That bitch.' He spits, rolling his eyes. 'What's she gone and done now?'

'She's missing, Mr James.' He scoffs, rolling his eyes yet again.

'Is that all?' His dismissive tone shocks me, and I realise that I doubt this man has ever truly loved anyone or anything and I feel sorry for Freya Dolloway.

'You said you didn't want us to twist your words, Mr James.' Luke cocks his head to the side, regarding him with almost the same level of reproach he's shown towards his ex-wife. 'So how about we use your exact words. Like, for instance, when you told Freya, and I quote,' Luke pulls a printout of the conversations between Freya and Oliver from the file in the middle of the table. He flips it and pushes it towards him, pointing deliberately to the line of text from the printed conversation as he reads it verbatim, 'Fuck you, Freya. You're going to regret this. I'll make you pay. Watch your back.'

We let the sentence hang there. Watch Mr James shuffle uneasily, looking down at his sleeves and fidgeting with his cufflinks. I'm convinced he's going to fold, grovel at our feet and beg us not to arrest him. That he'll tell us where Freya is, tell us whatever we want but that's wishful thinking.   Instead, he works a kink out of his neck, popping it loudly and straightens his back. I catch a glimpse of a tremble in his hands before he balls them into fits, squeezing them tight and looks me dead in the eye. His stare is filled with spite and it sends an uneasy shiver down my spine. He speaks through clenched words, his words spitting out from between them.

'Freya is a bitch.' He laughs without humour, 'Even now, even after she managed to convince that judge to give her *my* money because she's a little fucking sponge, she's still managing to fuck with my life. She posts those vulgar videos and photos all over that site, speaks to those strangers like that and she thinks that's ok?' he laughs hysterically, and I feel the gooseflesh prickling along my arms. A moment ago he seemed like any other self righteous man. Now he's making me uneasy, and I can see why Freya felt like she needed to get away from him. 'She's not your property, Mr James.' Luke shrugs, clearly unphased by his sudden anger.

'She's no longer your wife either. So, what? She starts working on this site and you believe it's your right to, what? Stop her? What did you do, Mr James? Where exactly is your ex-wife?' Mr James laughs louder and holds his stomach as if this is the funniest thing he's ever heard.

'You can't seriously think I'd waste my time on that pathetic whore?' He shoots a look between me and Luke, 'as soon as she put some other bloke's cock in her mouth she was used goods. Dirty little cow, her screen name was fitting alright.'

I watch him closely. The rage he showed only moments ago is not the kind of rage that can be fed, satiated purely by preventing Freya from taking any more of his alimony. No. That was control, ownership. Something only a true narcissist can feel to that level of fury. Those types of men are not satisfied by merely making sure a woman doesn't have access to their money. He's greedy for sure but he would have wanted to put Freya firmly back in her place. I know there's more to it, there's things he's not divulging, and we need to rile him more if he's going to really lay it all out on the table. I'm suddenly wishing we had asked to meet him in an interrogation room where the light isn't as soft and seating not as comfortable but when you ask a man like Oliver James - with as much sway in the district attorney's office as he has - to come down to the station, you put him in the family room until you're sure they've committed a crime.

He finally stops laughing, sniffing and wiping away the tears of laughter and I'm about to wind him up as much as I possibly can. I clear my throat, signalling to Luke that I'm taking the reins. Oliver James clearly hates women. Hates feeling inadequate, especially when it's a woman making him feel that way and only I can feed into that.

'I wonder Mr James,' I smirk at him and see his mouth fall into a straight line and his eyes flash. I guess he doesn't like it when I'm not playing malleable. 'Does your distaste for Ms Dolloway's... excursions... stem from jealousy? Perhaps you wanted to get back at her for making you feel belittled? Perhaps when you couldn't satisfy her sexually?'

His face burns hot red, a bead of sweat forming on his hairline and there's a vein in his neck throbbing because he's clenching his teeth so hard.

'Is that why you were also using this site, to try and find something that would do the trick?' Luke chimes in.

Oliver narrows his eyes which sparkle with hate and pure, unimpeded rage. I hold my breath, ready for the blow up, when the door to the room bangs open. 'My client will not be answering any more questions.' A large African American man enters the room. His shoulders broad and his heir of authority much stronger than that of Mr James. He crosses the room and beckons Mr James to stand.

'Unless you are going to arrest my client with probable cause, we will be leaving now. I trust you will strike anything he has said without me present from the record. Given that this isn't an official interview and all.' He raises an eyebrow at me and searches the room for cameras and recording devices. He's right of course, I hadn't set this up to be a questioning of a suspect. Although, given everything that has unfolded in the last half hour, I wish I had.

Chapter 17

Ellie

The kids know something's wrong. I can tell. I've sat them in front of the tv to watch some kind of Disney film, I didn't even pay attention to which one I shoved in the player. I pour out marshmallows and popcorn out into two bowls, getting more on the floor than in the actual bowls and draw the curtains in a pathetic attempt to make it look more like a movie theatre. Myah is hesitant at first.

'But we never get to eat snacks in the middle of the day!?' she questions, cocking her head at me.

'Well, you do today!' Even I can hear the fake strain of cheer in my voice.

She glares at me another few moments before shrugging and shoving a fistful of marshmallows into her mouth. She clearly decided not to question the situation too greatly and would rather just reap the rewards of sugar filled snacks in peace. Matty takes a little bit more convincing. His eyes are full of concern, my little prince. He's always been more emotionally intelligent than his sister. He can tell all still isn't well, he's guessed I'm just trying to distract them so I can go spend another day on the edge of my nerves in private, out of their view. I've been trying to shelter them from what's going on. A task which is markedly more challenging with Matty than with Myah.

'What's wrong, Mommy?' Matty whispers, the genuine concern in his voice and in the small frown line that creases between his eyebrows every time he's worried just about breaks my heart.

'Nothing sweetheart.' I lie, kissing his head. 'Mommy's just tired today, that's all. You enjoy your snacks. Ok?' I smile, kissing him on each cheek.

'Ok.' He frowns, clearly still not convinced but willing to let the subject go, at least for now. He sits down on the floor next to his sister who has cheeks full of marshmallows and starts asking her about which princess she would rather be. I guess I've put on Cinderella.

I watch them for a few minutes, my little angels. It's always struck me how close the two of them are. The connection they share is almost unfathomable to me, given how strained my relationship is with my own twin. After that scan, the one where the nurse had turned the screen and shown me the two heart beats, I was filled with anxiety so raw it choked me and filled almost every thought for the rest of my pregnancy. Me and Freya had built a bond out of necessity and duty as siblings rather than true love and I prayed that my twins would do anything but that. Their whole childhood has been such a relief, seeing how they interact and connect, it's like they move in sync, and I couldn't ask for anything better. The lights from the telly are reflecting on their faces as they giggle and prod each other, throwing bits of popcorn in each other's faces. The smell of the fresh popcorn fills the space, and I'm suddenly pulled back to before everything that happened, when life was normal, or at least when I thought it was.

Seven years ago

The bottom of my shoes stick to the floor as I walk between the seats. I have to actively pull them free as I walk along, sweeping the popcorn and abandoned sweet wrappers into a pile at the end of the row. With each step, I'm convinced that at some point, the sole of my shoe isn't going to be prised away as I lift my feet. The bottom of my shoe left behind, fused to the sticky floor. My hair is frizzy and I can smell my sweat as I sweep. The movie theatre has air conditioning so its not exactly hot in the screening room but it's a sunny Saturday afternoon in the peak of summer where everyone is pulled by the prospect of a few hours watching a movie in a cool room with cold drinks and sweet snacks so I've been rushing around, perspiring even in the cool conditioned building, since the start of my shift at midday. I feel tired and hungry but I push all of my mental complaints away because I'm just grateful to be here, working my first real job and making some extra cash.

Mr Fuller had interviewed me at the start of summer for the job at the local movie theatre. At least, he'd grunted about giving me a trial for the next two weeks and then we'll see. So, I was working harder than any of my work colleagues to prove myself.

There are four of us who work the weekends: Bobby, Phoebe and Reggie. I go to the same school as Bobby and Reggie and I'd been dating Bobby for a few months already when I started at the theatre.

Phoebe's older than us and had dropped out of school a few years ago, working at the movie theatre ever since.

She's bold and blunt but has taken me under her wing when I started and we've become fast friends.

Reggie's quiet and withdrawn. He has a shy and complicated air about him but has been nice to me ever since I started. He's helped me learn how to use the ancient and complicated cash register, but he also stares at me when he doesn't think I can see him.

He seems sweet and innocent though and he knows I'm with Bobby and uninterested, I've made that very clear. I find it flattering in a way that he clearly has a crush on me. Freya normally hogs the spotlight, overshadowing me.

Bobby's my first serious boyfriend, unlike Freya who is on her fourth. Although, I do think this time is different and her and Scott are end game. I hope it's the same for us.

This weekend all four of us are on shift. I'm trying and failing to get as much of the rubbish into the black bag in one go when I feel the back of my neck prickle. I look over my shoulder and lock eyes with Reggie, he's standing at the bottom of the stairs by the door, watching me. I smile and wave and he quickly looks away at his feet and shuffles out of the door as fast as he can. 'Creep.' Bobby laughs. He's carrying a full, heavy black bag from his half of the room, the grimiest seats towards the back. 'He's just shy.' I playfully swat him with the back of my dust pan and he grips his bicep dramatically, fake whining about being basically stabbed with a blunt dustpan base.

'I think he wants to be friends with us but he doesn't know how.' I say seriously when the laughing has subsided. 'He's a freak with no friends. Which is no wonder when he stares at people like that. It's so intense.' 'You, Bobby Williams, are lucky you're hot.' I roll my eyes. 'But seriously, you're starting to sound like a bully. Reggie doesn't do us any harm. He's just quiet and lonely and doesn't know how to interact with others. He's not a creep.' I can't stand bullies and Bobby knows it. I think that's why

he lets the subject slide and shrugs, crouching down to help me clean up the last of the mess.

I do love Bobby, with everything I have. I know people say teenage love is just that... teenage. Childish. Not real, never lasts. But that's not how I feel. I feel we're two halves to one whole. That we bring out the best parts of each other and it's not an immature love, but a true one. Except when he acts like this, says such spiteful things, it makes me second guess whether I really know him. Freya's a bully. In school, to everyone else who isn't in her clique, and at home to me, her personal punching bag for verbal insults and psychological torment. I know Bobby isn't a bully. I wouldn't be with him if he was but situations like this make me really second guess whether the nice guy persona is just that, a persona. Whether the real Bobby lurks beneath the surface and every now and then, the mask slips and he lets out the venom brewing there.

A shriek cuts through my memory fog and forces me back to the here and now. A shot of adrenaline stings my fingertips until I realise it was just Myah, shrieking needlessly at the cat which has sprung up against the living room window.

They've asked me about Freya a few times this morning, they're so used to her calling them every day, using inappropriate language and making them giggle whilst I seethe and tell Freya to pack it in. That's what had triggered this sudden need for them to be distracted, to stop asking me where Aunty Freya was, when she was coming back.

It's always shocked me; how close the kids are to their Auntie. It's so much closer than Freya and I have ever been with one another.

Our relationship was more that of tormentor and tormented, me unfortunately drawing the short straw. It had always been that way, since I can remember but it was only heightened when I got pregnant so young. I'd become the outcast of my family. Suddenly, it wasn't just my sister who loathed me but all of them. I was always the one who brought them shame and disappointment. Freya had always been the favourite, even before that, but the pregnancy had well and truly pivoted her up there in the family pecking order. I was just the spare part; the child who was born to be a visually spitting image of her better version but who, ultimately, wasn't wanted and whose failures were only highlighted by her better twin's success.

Even in adulthood, I'm still that same girl. Nothing like her family, still struggling to find her place in an otherwise perfect family bond between all other parties. Freya has never understood. So similar to our mother, she has never empathised with my situation. In all honesty, I don't think she's felt anything but indifference towards me. A spare part who serves to make her look better, to ensure that no mistakes she herself ever makes is deemed of any real concern or issue because at least Freya isn't like Ellie. The divide between us only worsened once my father was gone. The chasm between us became an all-out canyon.

They didn't see my hurt, how my heart ached just as much as theirs did. That my father was the only one who treated me like I was worthy, even after I got pregnant. He never made me feel like a lesser person. He always made sure I knew I was loved, even if only by him and that was enough. Once he was gone, taken from us, there was no love left for me. At one point when the twins were still infants, I considered packing up and whisking them away from here. Away from my mother and sister's meddling and constant need for control. They would constantly try to parent *my* children. They didn't feel any sort of way about letting me know that they believed I was doing wrong and how I should be caring for them differently. I wanted to scream in their faces, tell them that the twins weren't their children - they were mine. That I'd parent them exactly how I wanted. How, if it were up to my mother, they would never have even existed. If I'd done what she wanted all those years ago, she wouldn't even have two grandchildren to soil with her poison, like she did to me and Freya. That I would never let her ruin them like she ruined us.

I thought about it so often that one day I did actually pack our things. Just the essentials, into a small suitcase in the middle of the night. I wrapped them in warm clothes because it was the middle of the winter, sung softly under my breath to keep them calm and quiet as I strapped them into their pram.

That's how she'd found us, the twins sleeping soundly in their pushchairs, the suitcase shoved on the bottom rack when I was halfway out the front door. I guess the sound of the door unlocking and the rattle of the old hinges as I'd pulled it open, had woken her. It was the look in her eyes, the way her body deflated against the banister, and she shrunk down on to the step and looked so heart broken, that had stopped me. I realised at that moment that she needed them.

She needed me. She needed what was left of her family to pull her through the grief my father had left her with now he was gone. That even though she viewed me as nothing but a shameful burden, she needed the twins. She needed them to give her own broken life purpose. So, I'd said I was just going to the lake for a couple of nights to clear my head, some bonding time with the twins. That I'd be back Sunday afternoon ready for tea. Since then, I've resigned myself to the fact that I can never leave. Even if I physically left this town, cut them off, I'd never cut off the guilt I feel.

Now I pace the kitchen back and forth, begin to fill the kitchen sink with soapy water and then abandon it midway through. I can't bring myself to wash the dishes. I walk over to the kettle, fill it to the top and click the electric on, I pull out a mug and stick a tea bag in it and a dash of sugar. Leaning against the countertop whilst I wait for it to come to the boil.

By the time the water bubbles and the light flicks off I've already left the cup on the side and have started shoving clothes into the washing machine from the basket of dirty laundry that has been sitting by its side for days. I fill it a quarter of the way before I spot the pile of junk on the dining table.

Old leaflets and empty crisp packets and dirty plates. I start emptying the rubbish from its surface into the bin until I realise it's too full to fit anything else. So instead, I begin emptying the bin. I pull it out with a heave and tie the top as tight as I can. As I lift it from the floor with great effort, I hear a snap and the contents plummet from the gaping hole that's opened up in the bottom.

I drop the bag and drop to my knees, my body heaves, tears soaking my cheeks in streams. I hold my breath and cry silently there on the floor. Every day has been like this. I can't keep my mind occupied; I can't bring myself to do the mundane things I should be doing because I keep thinking about the past and how we wound up here.

When I begin to feel normal again, I feel like I'm betraying Freya because how can I be here, making cups of tea and washing the dishes when she's out there somewhere. God knows where. Going through God knows what. If she's even alive, that is.

I know if my mother was around she'd be screaming at me, telling me that it's not fair that sweet, perfect Freya has gone whilst I, the broken and useless one, am left.

She'd be screaming at me to do more. That this is all my fault because everything bad that happens to this sorry excuse for a family is always my fault. I'm in a constant battle with myself. I flick back and forth between feeling guilty because I should be doing more and shouldn't be bothering with making dinner or watering the plants, and then instead, feeling guilty because the house is a mess, the kids haven't had a home-cooked meal in days and I should be acting normal for them because they have no idea that their Aunt has disappeared, seemingly forever. Maybe she's right. Perhaps I should be doing more, should care more. Instead, I feel like I'm going through the motions, pretending to care like a sister should. In reality, it's a facade. Whilst I am anxious and worried, I feel like that's my innate instinct and a way for me to prove I'm worthy. That my family shouldn't hate me.

It's when I'm sitting on the floor in the middle of the rotting food, dirty paper plates and used plastic cutlery that we've been using because none of the kitchenware is clean, that my phone buzzes loudly on the kitchen counter.

The sound of it cuts through my feelings of self loathing and pity, a jolt of adrenaline stabbing my chest and burning through my limbs.

I force myself to my feet. *You have to keep going, for the kids.* I repeat this mantra that I've been using the last few days over and over as I cross the room to where my phone is charging. It's a text message from an unknown number and if it had been any other day I wouldn't have given it a second thought. I would have deleted the message without even opening the damned thing but something in the pit of my stomach surges and I swipe it open.

Back off Ellie. I don't need you looking for me. I don't need any of you. I'm not coming home. I hate you. I hate mom. I hate my life. I've decided to put myself first for a change.

I throw my phone across the room and watch it bounce across the floor. I'm panting with fury. Of course she would do this. Make my life a living hell. Make it all about her. Have our mother sobbing to me and blaming me whilst she saunters off and lives her life.

I didn't even realise I was screaming until I heard a shout from behind me, begging me to stop. I spin round. I hadn't even noticed Matty come into the room. He's standing, shivering, with tears streaming down his cheeks. He creeps forward and whispers, 'Mommy, what's going on?'

Chapter 18

No One

I'm so glad her kitchen faces the street at the front of the house. I've figured out all the best angles to watch them from the street and from the back garden but it's more exposed round the back. I much prefer it when she stays at the front of the house like this.

There's an alley way directly across the street, separating the two houses which sit parallel to hers. It makes the perfect spot for watching them.

The Living room, kitchen, and the master bedroom sit at the front of the house, facing out onto the street. The dining and utility rooms sit at the back, under the children's rooms. From this position, I can see clearly into all of the former.

Even though it's almost too easy for someone to see directly into her bedroom at night when it's illuminated against the outside darkness, she rarely closes her curtains before half past ten. Or at least, that was the case before I took the other one. Now she goes up to her room, but the light stays on well past midnight into the early hours.

Sometimes she tiptoes down to the kitchen and, under the delusion that no one is watching, pours herself a large glass of wine. She always nurses the first glass, drinking it sparingly. Almost as though, if she drinks it slower, she won't end up pouring herself the other two she needs to sleep. She always does in the end. Most nights she sits like this; drinking, staring blankly out of the kitchen window into the black night.

Last night I was sure she saw me, lurking in the shadows. But, she only caught my eye for a few seconds before her drunken hazy stare moved away.

I'm surprised at her reaction to her sister being gone.

She's usually the seemingly strong one who holds it together but she's crumbled under the pressure. I didn't even think they were close enough for her to be so stricken by the other one's disappearance. In all the weeks I followed her before I took her, I never once spotted even an inch of affection between them. It fascinates me that even though they appear to despise one another, they are still connected because they share blood. The actions of one, still affecting another. I feel hollow and lonely in the fact that I've never experienced this myself. It makes my headache.

The children seem oblivious to the tragedy happening to their family. To the suffering I've caused. I've been wondering if she's been keeping it from them. As I watch her now, in the kitchen comforting the boy in the middle of the mess I've helped to create, I know she has.

Mothers, they always think they can keep things from their children. I knew as soon as I saw the Detectives leaving the other one's flat with her laptop in tow that I needed to do something. I needed to adapt. I can't have the police sniffing around, it would ruin my plans. My hands trembled with anger that they were involved at all. It's far too early for any police presence. No matter. I adapted to the situation forced upon me like I always do. I purchased a prepaid cell from a low rent gas station with no sort of surveillance on my way over here to watch my pets

It would have been better if I'd had her phone, but I'd been foolish and rushed. In the ordeal of removing her from her home and putting her in the back of the truck, I'd failed to grab her phone from her coffee table. That had been my first and only mistake. It won't happen again.

I realise now though that leaving the phone may have worked out in my favour. If I hadn't, then I wouldn't have been able to enjoy this moment. The text was just to throw the police off of the scent. A necessity really but watching her reaction to opening it sent a rush straight up my spine. A sort of kick you could say. I think I'm going to enjoy this.Yet, as much as I enjoyed watching the disruption, watching her lie to her son makes my skin crawl. The way she holds him to her and strokes his hair, plastering on that overbearing and fake smile, I know she's lying to him again. Telling him it's all going to be alright. It's not. I'm going to make sure of that.

Her dishonesty brings about my rage. It feels like a living thing, moving through me inch by inch. A slight tingle in my extremities at first. Then it moves, like a villainous creature, along my veins and fills every cell until it's burning hot.

Why do mothers lie to their sons? As if it will help? As if it will make a difference? Do they seriously believe that we don't already know what's going on? That we're dumb or too slow to understand?

As I let the rage overtake me, the memory also creeps close behind. I try to suppress it, willing it to go away but the black spot at the corner of my vision grows, covering my whole line of sight until I succumb to it.

Seven Years Ago.

My mother's baking. The smell of dough and sugar wafts through the house and I breathe it in deeply, but I feel the pang of panic in my chest. If she's baking, that means she's upset. When she's upset things don't work out well for me.

The last time she'd baked was almost seven years ago, when I was eight and she wanted to apologise for cutting my leg open with her garden shears when I'd disturbed her. I ate the syrup-covered pancakes so fast, it gave me a stomach ache. She rarely ever bakes so I'd been so excited when the smell had wafted through the house back then.

The excitement had been extinguished quickly though. As soon as I'd finished the pancakes, my stomach gurgling and aching, she'd taken my empty plate and her own barely touched, to wash them in the sink, and declared as she scrubbed them that she had something to tell me.

I remember her sleeve riding up slightly as she'd washed the plates and the garish purple bruises that dotted her arms stared at me as she spoke. She told me that her friend Victor, who I knew was the reason for the bruising, was going to live with us.

She'd made such a huge false show of pretending that this was a good thing and that him and his own son, who was also apparently going to be moving in too, were going to be one of the best things to happen to us since dad left.

Little did I know at the time that the pancakes were just to soften the blow before they moved in and made my life even more unbearable than it had already been living with her.

Victor, I'd find out a year later, was to become my stepfather and his son my stepbrother.   Two bullies moved into my home that year and never moved out. Victor was an angry drunk who stumbled around the house, hitting everything and everyone in sight. His son would then take out his frustration of being beaten out on me. Meaning, I got pummelled twice on the worst days.

I've learnt to count the small round raised scars on my arms from the cigarette butts which have been extinguished on them when Victor or his son come for me. It helps to distract me from the torment. I stroke my finger over each one and count them silently in my head as fists punch my stomach; 1...2...3...4...5...6...7...8...9...10. Over the years, it's become a comfort, more than a distraction and I find myself counting them even when I'm not being beaten.

That's how I know the sweet baking smell means nothing good. I'm older now and so close to legal adulthood I can almost taste it. I've come to realise that my mother isn't one of those mother's who will do anything and everything for their child. Instead, she's the type of mother who marries bottom feeder men who beat her and beat her son. Bottom feeding men who also come with bottom feeder sons who also beat and bruise those around them. She's the type of mother who ignores her only child's cries for help when said bottom feeders are beating him black and blue because at least it isn't her going under the fist today.

I stretch, climbing from my bed and locking myself in the bathroom across the hall. I wash my face and frown at my reflection in the mirror. There's spots all over my chin, bright red and sore. No matter how many times I pop them I just get more. The other kids at school keep talking shit about them, cornering me in corridors and bathrooms stalls to lay in to me. Or at least, they did. Until I fought back, punching their ring leader so hard that I broke his nose in two places and knocked out one of his front teeth. The rest of them are too pussy shit to touch me now. Still though, I hate this place. I can't wait to get out of here. Two more years and then I'm gone.

It's as I'm drying my face that I hear it. Something smashes, my mother screams, then something thuds heavily. I stand there for a few moments, motionless and soundless. I try to listen past the sound of my heavy breathing and the blood rushing through my ears but the house is silent. I try to ease the bathroom door open quietly but it squeaks loudly on its hinges and I cringe.

Goddamn Victor, he never fixes anything in this shit pile of a house. I'm used to the crashing sounds of Victor on a rampage and the cries of pain from my mother as she's beaten and her bones break. My usual reaction is to lock my bedroom door and put my earbuds in with the music turned up loud, pretending my life isn't really my life.

This feels different though. The usual signals didn't happen. There were no loud, raised voices, no cabinet doors slamming, my mother wasn't crying. I creep down the stairs on my tip toes and move slowly through the house like a member of a FBI SWAT team. I find my mother in the kitchen. She's standing motionless, her back against the counters. She isn't crying but her bottom lip trembles, her eyes wide and full of terror as she stares at the floor. There's small splatters of blood drying on the front of her pale yellow summer dress which hangs loosely over her, making the years of weariness and weight loss from alcoholism even more apparent. Her hands are at her sides and are trembling along with her lip, the sharp half broken vodka bottle swaying in her right hand at her side. She's holding the neck so tight her knuckles are white with effort and the sharp corners of the broken end are shining with crimson. I follow her line of sight to the floor at her feet.

That's when I see Victor. He's lying dead still on the floor between my mother and the dining table. He's face down, a puddle of blood pooling around his head, expanding by the second. He's cheek down, facing sideways so I can see his eyes are open. If he were alive, he'd be staring directly at me. Except, his eyes are glazed over and his pupils are dilated, one bigger than the other. I silently thank God as I stare at his lifeless body on the floor that his son isn't here this weekend. He's on some stupid sports trip down south and won't be back until Monday

'I had to,' my mother whispers, pulling her eyes from Victor's to meet mine. 'He was going to kill us. Maybe not today, but he would have eventually. You know that don't you?'

I nod once. I reach for the landline on the wall but my mother steps over Victor and grabs my wrist, her nails digging into the flesh. I flinch, dropping the phone. She grabs it from where it hangs loosely on its cord and throws it back down hard into the console. Her eyes pierce me.'

No police.' She demands. 'They won't believe me that I had to do it. They'll take one look at the bottles in the bins and under the sink and then they won't believe a single thing that comes out of my mouth.'

'We can't just leave him lying in the middle of the kitchen, Mother!'

'I know that.' She snaps, licking her lips which are peeling from the dehydration that happens when all you fill your body with is cheap vodka and nicotine. 'We'll say he came at you... that you had no choice but to defend yourself. That he was a monster, always hitting you, hitting me.' She's nodding at me, a small smile playing on her lips, dread completely washed from her face.

'No, Mother.' I shake my head violently. 'They'll lock me up.' I feel frantic. What exactly is it that she's suggesting? She can't possibly want me to take the fall for this. Does she really want me to admit to killing a man for her?

'You're sixteen. You'd only go to juvenile detention, out when you're eighteen. Even sooner with good behaviour.' She grabs both my hands and holds them to her clammy chest.

Her eyes are rapidly moving back and forth between mine and I can smell the strong stench of vodka on her breath, 'but if they lock me up, I'd be gone for good. I'd rot in jail and I wouldn't be able to live like that. In some dirty women's prison full of psychos, murderers and baby killers.' I don't mention the irony of her talking about murderers in a derogatory manner when she just ended a man's life with a three quarters empty off brand vodka bottle. I peel my hands out of her clammy hold. I breathe in deep. I try to think. My mother continues to rant about all of the obscenities she'll be subjected to if she goes down for this. That she'll hang herself in her cell. I run my fingertip over the scars on my arm to focus and block her out. 1...2...3...4...5...6...7...8...9...10. Breathe.

I push past her into the middle of the kitchen and peer down at Victor. I was going to feel for a pulse but from this close I can tell I don't need to; the man's dead. I look around the kitchen, trying to think of some way to explain this away because she's right, as dramatic as she's being, my mother isn't built for prison. Even if she didn't hang herself in her cell like she's threatening to do, she'd die from the sudden alcohol withdrawal or a spiked, bacteria filled hooch made in a skanky prison bathroom.

It's standing there, looking down at the congealing blood that I realise the only way to stop either of us going to prison for this pathetic excuse for a man, is to get rid of the evidence. What is it they say; no body, no crime? I need to get rid of him now, before his devil spawn comes home. I can feel an idea pulsing in a corner of my brain but as I try to pull it to the forefront, my mother's sobbing screeches make my ears sting.

'SHUT UP!' I whirl around and snap in my mother's face. 'Just shut up and let me fix this.'

Chapter 19

Detective Dawson

I stretch my neck out, rubbing my knuckles into the groove between my neck and shoulder to try and ease the tension. I sip my coffee which is almost stone cold now. We've been trying to research Freya Dolloway's history and routines all day whilst we wait for IT to hopefully get us more information from her laptop.

The office has been slowly emptying out. Now there's only a handful of us left, burning the midnight oil. Everyone else has gone home, to their wives, their children and their hot showers and comfortable beds. I wish I could go home and curl up in front of the television, bundled up in a comfortable blanket, watching cheesy late-night soaps but my brain won't let that happen. It never does once I get given a case. Once I know there's someone out there, missing and whose loved ones are in agony, unable to simply sit still and relax in front of their own televisions and their own shows. It's an unhealthy habit. An obsession really. I can't stop until I find them. With a case like this, I don't think the powers that be would let me rest anyway. 'So then boss, what have we got so far?' Luke drops a fresh cup of iced coffee on my desk and I could kiss him. I'm so grateful for the extra caffeine. He takes his own seat at his desk opposite mine and slurps his own coffee far too loudly for my level of tiredness. 'How many times have I told you to stop calling me that?' I roll my eyes, thankful for the coolness of the coffee against my fingers.

Summer is coming to an end and soon the heat will break and the leaves will turn warm and start to fall. I can't wait. I hate the summer, always have. All of my friends used to go on extravagant trips over the summer break but my dad was always in the middle of a case or five. So I used to spend my summers in the hot house, drawing the curtains and sweating in darkness, trying to block the heat out because my mom used to hate having the air conditioning on too high. I wonder if Freya is somewhere cool or whether she's burning in a stifling hot room, her sunburn peeling and itching, no relief from the heatwave. 'Right, right. Sorry. What we got Mols?' He quirks an eyebrow and I feel myself rolling my eyes again. I hate being called that too and he knows it. I decide not to give him the satisfaction of a reaction, choosing to pretend I didn't notice the nickname at all.

'Oliver James' credit card transactions proves he wasn't even in the country the night Freya went missing.' I massage my shoulder, a dull ache from the tension blooming.

'Fantastic.' Luke spits sarcastically. 'So, we're back at none for suspects.'

'Yep.' I sigh, frustration scratching at my head. Before long, the ache behind my eyes will match the ache in my shoulder. 'Anything else?'

'Well, after scouring Freya's social media accounts, it looks like she's very much what Ellie described her to be. She enjoys parties, posts all of her dalliances all over her social media accounts. Has a large following but doesn't interact with them a lot. She's very much a showboat kind of girl.'

I pull my hair from the tight elastic band it's been held in since lunch when I decided I needed a clear field of vision to concentrate. I rub my fingers through my hair, massaging my scalp, wishing I could be doing this with shampoo in an ice cold shower.

'I called a few of the other women at the club, they didn't give me much, unsurprisingly.' Luke taps the side of his coffee cup, nodding as if he's assuring himself of the facts. It's a sweet mannerism I've noticed he does when he's thinking. I smile inwardly, watching the action with affection. *God Molly, pull yourself together. He's your work colleague, stop thinking with body parts that aren't in your head.* I clear my throat, shuffling slightly in my chair, almost as if I can shuffle the affectionate feeling away.

'I'm surprised none of her friends tried to contact her or even report her missing. The general public don't often realise the whole twenty four hour general rule.' I skim the list of posts Luke had pulled from Freya's respective social media accounts over the last few weeks. 'Considering how much she appears to socialise, every night from the looks of things, you'd think someone would have noticed her radio silence.'

'Right, that's what I thought.' He sits up a little straighter, flicking through his notes. 'So, I did some digging, called a few of the friends who appear more frequently in her posts and have their numbers attached to their profiles. According to those who answered my call, Freya was slowly distancing herself from all of her friends over the last couple of months.'

I flip through some of the more recent pages of posts. Looking for signs that Freya was becoming distant. I can't find any. She posted every other day at least, photos filled with friends, cocktails, fancy meals at fancy restaurants, parties and shows. There were a few solo images here and there of a more relaxed atmosphere, Freya in comfy baggy knitted jumpers with a mug of coffee in a quaint coffee shop, the type you only know about if you're a local. A few images of books with corresponding book reviews but otherwise, it was full on, full time. I guess Luke reads the confusion on my face because he wheels his chair round to my side of the desk. I'm sure the goosebumps that pop up on my arm are noticeable so I pull the sleeves down on my dress, ignoring the proximity.

'I asked a few of these women who have appeared in the more recent pictures.' He pulls a couple up simultaneously, circling the women with the cursor. 'The response was pretty similar. They said that these pictures were taken months ago, during the spring. That they had met up, had a girls day and took some pictures but that it was ages ago. They were pretty pissed that Freya had been uploading them like this, claiming it to be more recent. Tagging them too like they wouldn't notice. Janine... here...' he pulls up another picture. Freya and a small petite woman with deep copper hair and warm brown eyes, smiling up at the camera from over the pitcher she was drinking from with a singular straw. 'She said Freya uploaded this picture on a day she was off sick from work. Home with a flu so bad, she slept for two days straight, through and through. Someone at work saw her tagged in the photo and reported her to the manager. They didn't believe her when she tried to convince them it was old. She rang Freya, texted, and emailed but Freya never replied and never took the image down. Janine's been given a disciplinary at work.'

I try to put myself in Freya's state of mind. Why actively take a step back from the people in your life whilst also simultaneously wanting to portray a world full of friendship and life? Why not just actually meet with your friends? Why not just invite Janine out for lunch. Why post old photos as if that's what you're doing but then distance yourself so completely that no one hears from you in months except for work. To tag the people in these deceiving photos is just the very confusing cherry on top of the even more complex lie.

'I can see the cogs turning,' Luke smirks. 'You're frowning so hard, your ears are going red.' He chuckles. I blush and take a sip of coffee. Luke yawns loudly and stretches exaggeratedly. 'Maybe we call it a night here aye? Go home, get some food, get a shower and a full night's sleep. Pick back up first thing?' I nod agreeably even though I have no intention of going home anytime soon.

'You go ahead, I'm going to check in with IT on the way out, see if there's anything yet, before I go.' Luke stands and starts pulling on his jacket.

He eyes me knowingly. He knows I'll be going to the IT department, but he also knows I won't be going home after that. I'll be right back here, at my desk, working until my eyes blur. Besides, Jasper wont have found anything so quickly. They may be brilliant but they're not miracle workers and they're covering the whole department with just the three of them. It's as he's pulling his bag onto his back that my phone rings. A sudden loud shriek which makes us both jump. I see Luke roll his eyes and start taking his coat off. I clear my throat and answer the phone

'Detective Dawson.' I try to disguise the excitement in my voice. Praying it's IT. Praying they're going to say that Freya conveniently left a whole address of where she's gone and full contact details for who she's gone there with.

'It's Ellie,' Ellie answers, a clear edge to her voice. "It's Freya. She texted me. I've been so stupid, I'm so sorry.'

'Miss Dolloway?' I glance at Luke over my monitor who is now sitting back down as if he never planned to leave at all. 'What exactly was the text message Freya sent you?' I hit the speaker button so that Luke can hear both sides of the conversation.

'She says she's not coming home, that she... hates us all. That she needed to get away and that she won't be coming back. I'm so sorry, I've wasted your time, your resources. All for my stupid, immature and inconsiderate goddamn sister who decided to leave without a word.' I realise then that the edge in her voice is inhibited irritation. I noticeably relax, sitting back in my chair and rubbing my eyes. 'I'm just so sorry,' she huffs and at that moment, she sounds as tired as I feel.

'It's ok.' I blow out the breath. 'The most important thing is that Freya's ok. That she's safe. Get some sleep. I'll be over in the morning to get an official statement, to take a look at this text.' It takes a further ten minutes to calm Ellie down. To assure her she doesn't need to keep apologising before she finally hangs up.

By the time I end the call and look up again, Luke is back on his feet. Coat and bag both already on. 'In the morning Mols.' He nods. I ignore the nickname yet again. 'Oh and don't worry, I won't bother saying I told you so or anything.' He winks at me.

I stand too, feeling how stiff my limbs are, getting ready myself to go home to my bed. 'Don't worry, I won't mention it either.'

I stumble through my front door around 1AM. I did make a stop at the IT department after all but to tell them to stop the search, that it wasn't needed anymore. Vada greets me as soon as I step in, rubbing up against my shins, circling back and forth. She purrs loudly and mews simultaneously, letting me know that I have about two point five seconds to fill her bowl before she starts knocking things off my living room shelves.

'Come on then, girly.' I coo, dropping my bag by the door and kicking my shoes off. I nestle my toes into the high pile shag hallway rug, enjoying the softness on my sore feet, before I venture to the end of the hall to the kitchen.

I pick Vada's bowl up off the floor and start filling it on the small island counter. She sits patiently at the other end, still purring. Her pure black fur stands in contrast to the white clinical feel of the kitchen. I put the dish back on the floor and watch her jump down and eat as if she's never been fed. I remember the day I found her. A tiny kitten, abandoned in an alley bin when I'd gone to take the trash out. I knew then, when she looked up at me with her bright blue eyes that I'd love her. I named her Vada for her colour, stereotypical I know. Black cat called Vada, after Darth Vader, very original of me but I think It fits her well. I debate throwing one of the microwave meals from the freezer in but I know I won't be awake by the time the microwave dings. Instead, I drag myself back down the hall into the bedroom. Collapsing onto the bed fully clothed, not bothering to switch a light on and get undressed first.

Chapter 20

Ellie

Matty has been giving me the silent treatment since last night. He ate his cereal in stone cold silence this morning, his face glum and it only fuelled my rage towards Freya. He stayed completely silent all the way until school drop off. My usually vibrant and chatty boy is suddenly silent and moody.   Myah was glum too, but she at least was still speaking to me, giving me the usual 'bye mommy, love you!' shout as she ran up the school steps.

I drop to the sofa as soon as I get home, knowing that I should be getting up and getting back to the office. My manager has been harassing me all week asking when I would be back. I guess the rich, well-to-do parents of the snobby upper-class children I tutor are getting inpatient with their no-show, overly priced private tutor. I need to call Elaine back. I know I do but I feel so deflated that I decide to give myself one more day. One more day of feeling sorry for myself that my twin, the person I'm supposed to - according to all the laws of nature - be thick as thieves with, has let me down once again.   All of this is her fault and yet, my mother still blames me for her perfect twin getting up and going off of her own accord. As if I somehow made her do it. As if I'm to blame for the fact that her favourite child has now acted in defiance.

I felt almost ready to go back to work this morning when I woke up until my mother had called first thing. Screaming and sobbing down the phone that I've driven Freya away. That I didn't support her during her divorce and piled on the pressure by asking for her help with the kids. She's convinced herself that if it weren't for me then Freya wouldn't have upped and left. I guess even this isn't enough for her to realise Freya's a flake. Now I feel exhausted inside and out. Just one more day. Then I'll drag myself, kicking and screaming, out of this slump and get back to normality. My phone buzzes loudly and I realise my last day of peace is non-existent as Elaine's name flashes up in front of me. This is her fourth call this morning. I just want to curl up in my bed and sleep away my life until it resembles something normal, but mothers don't get the luxury of that. So, instead, I sigh loudly, trying to shake the lethargy that comes with summer every year and tell myself I should call Elaine back today and take whatever punishment she sees fit to inflict.

I'm so glad the summer season will soon be drawing to a close. The recent heatwave has been scorching the streets and windowpanes for the last fortnight, and I feel clammy. My hair smells like week-old sweat and the house smells just as bad. I sit staring at the dust that has started to cover the mantel for at least ten minutes, trying to prompt myself to get up and wipe it down, when I hear the front door slam.

My heart rate picks up instantly and my limbs tingle with adrenaline as I scan the living room for something to use as a weapon. Someone knocks on the living room door and I'm about to lunge, nails first, off the sofa at whoever comes through the door when Tilly's fiery red hair pops into the gap.

'Jesus Christ Elle, you look like *pure* shit, girl.' She grimaces, bounding into the living room and throws herself down beside me.

The relief rushes through me and I suddenly feel completely at ease. Like the last week or so never even happened. 'Thanks, Tills. That's the look I was going for.' I smile.

Tilly's been my best friend through thick and thin for almost the entirety of our lives. The only real family, even though not by blood, I've ever had. I see the look on people's faces when I tell them that. Half of them look like they want to vomit all over my shoes at the cringe worthy cliche but it's true. Her turning up at my door this morning is just what I need.

'You pull it off better than I do. Right, what's going on then?' she raises an eyebrow, picking strands of my limp, greasy hair up and examining it with a look of pure disgust as if she can physically see the grime lacing it. 'You haven't responded to any of my texts or calls the last four days and we both know that, besides the two little toerags, I'm the most important person in your life.' She says it as a factual statement rather than a question. Which if I'm honest, it is. The relief that filled me three seconds ago is suddenly dissolved into guilt. She's right of course, I've been screening her calls since I found Freya's flat abandoned. I just couldn't bring myself to tell her. I knew what she was going to say; she's always hated my family and how they treat me, Freya especially. She would have told me to let her rot, wherever she is.

She believes that sisters should stick together no matter what and she never really understood the dynamic between me and Freya. Her own relationship with her older sister, Ginny is the complete opposite to ours so she's always resented Freya for how she treats me.

'Sorry, Tills.' Suddenly, I'm crying. Ugly sobs rake through my body. I feel so fed up. So exhausted and resentful. Why has my life always revolved around Freya and our mother? Why couldn't I let the guilt I felt go and break free from their toxic grip years ago.

Tilly rocks me gently back and forth, shushing me and reassuring me in soft whispers until I can finally catch my breath and sit upright by myself. We sit like that, me sniffling and calming my breathing with Tilly stroking my arm softly and searching my face for answers, for what feels like forever.

'Tell me.' Tilly urges, 'what's happened?'

By the time I've relayed the whole horrid tale, Tilly has turned a noticeably paler shade.

'That goddamn...' she struggles for the words in her anger, 'damn... inconsiderate, toxic *bitch.*' She scoffs. 'Let me see the text.' She holds out her hand expectedly. 'Jesus. She's such an attention seeker.' She tuts, frowning as she reads over the message a couple of times before handing me the phone back.

'Isn't she always?' I sigh, resting my head back on the sofa.

'Yet, she'll still be the golden girl.' Tilly huffs, throwing her head back onto the sofa too.

'You know what my mom said when I called and told her?' I laugh without humour. 'She said that "at least she's having some fun. It's just what she needs after that awful divorce".' I mimic my mother's voice perfectly, 'and then she proceeded to tell me that she definitely needs a break after having to always help me with the twins. That she isn't surprised she needs to get away for a while having to help me all the time with children that aren't hers.' My heads started throbbing again.

'It's settled.' Tilly throws her hands up, almost as if in surrender, 'your family is officially dysfunctional.' We both laugh at that. Real, deep belly laughs, for a good five minutes until the doorbell chimes.

'I'll get it,' Tilly reassures me. 'No one deserves to lay eyes on the mess that you are in today.' She teases, pulling herself up from the sofa and heading for the front door. As she leaves the living room she looks back over her shoulder and says, 'you should shower, girl. You stink.' I drag myself off the sofa, preparing to do just that when she comes back into the room.

'Elle... the police are here.' I look behind her and see Detective Dawson and her partner... Luke something? standing in the hallway.

Chapter 21

Ellie

'Don't worry.' Tilly turns back to them. 'I've already told her she stinks. I'll pop the kettle on,' she decides, heading for the kitchen. My cheeks burn and I'm suddenly hyper aware of my hair greased to my scalp and the coffee stains down my shirt. I pull my cardigan tighter around myself.

'Please.' I motion to my grubby looking sofa with its squished cushions and kid's dried food stains. 'Take a seat.' I start to apologise again for wasting their time as they sit down. My cheeks flame an even darker shade of crimson. 'I'm sorry for the state of me and the house. It's been a long few days.'

'Miss Dolloway, please. No need to apologise.' Detective Dawson reassures me once again, smiling at me kindly. 'We're just here to tidy things up. Dot the I's and cross the T's, if you'll excuse the cliché.' I take a seat on the other sofa, ignoring the stab of some sort of toy in my backside.

'Of course, I understand.' I vividly remember my fathers same logical and methodical way of solving cases. Even when a case was over, he'd still spend hours tidying things up, doing last interviews. He would also complain over many a family dinner about the time wasters and false reports, how much of a strain they would put on the force. That it took away from the real crimes, the real police work. I hated Freya for making me one of them.

'So, you say you've received a text message from Freya?' Detective Dolloway looks at me expectantly and I pass my phone over to her, the message already on the screen from mine and Tilly's conversation mere minutes ago. The Detective takes a couple of seconds reading the message, passing it over to her partner to also have a look.

'Have you and your sister always spoken to each other in such a... blunt manner?' her Partner asks.

'Unfortunately,' I sigh. 'I guess everyone's perception of twins is that we would be thick as thieves. Two halves to a whole.' I have to stop myself from scoffing. 'But Freya and I, we've never been like that. Sometimes I think the only reason we ever speak is because we're supposed to.' 'That's a shame.' Detective Dolloway grimaces a little.

'Freya's a bitch.' Tilly states matter of fact from the doorway. I hadn't even noticed her appear. I notice she's not holding any cups, just standing against the doorframe with her arms folded. I guess she never went to put the kettle on after all. She's just giving the illusion of privacy whilst standing outside listening. I should've known really, it's never been Tilly's nature to mind her own business.

'That's quite a statement Miss...' The other Detective raises his eyebrow.

'Parker. Tilly Parker.' Tilly smiles at him, holding out a manicured, ring covered hand. 'Nice to meet you Detective...'

'Luke Lorelle.' He smirks, holding out his. Lorell! I knew he'd told me his name last time we met.

It could be the lack of sleep or the stress but I'm almost certain I see Tilly start to sweat as she clutches his hand and Detective Lorelle seems to be noticing it too, his smirk deepening. 'Miss Parker, you sound as if you have something you'd like to say in regards to Freya Dolloway?' Detective Dawson asks her, a clear note of annoyance in her voice.

Although, I'm not sure if her annoyance is the result of Tilly's interruption or the fact that Tilly and her partner seem to be in the midst of a weird flirtation. How she glances at their clasped hands, which linger, and clears her throat loudly makes me think it's the latter.

'Where to begin Detective,' Tilly blows out a breath of exasperation and - a little reluctantly - lets go of Detective Lorelle's hand. 'Freya is... how shall I put this...' she taps her bottom lip dramatically as if in deep thought. 'An inconsiderate and self-absorbed embarrassment to herself, her sister and her mother. To put it lightly.'

'That's... descriptive.' Detective Dawson raises her eyebrow and glances over at me. She clearly expects me to jump in and defend my sister. Instead, I nod curtly, and she looks surprised but doesn't comment.

'You'll have to excuse Tilly,' I shrug, 'she's never had much of a filter. She can be a little blunt.'

'I take it you've known the Dolloways for quite a while?' Detective Lorelle asks.

'Since we were in the same daycare.' Tilly nods. 'I've known both Freya and Ellie nearly our entire lives and can safely say that this is exactly the type of crap Freya would pull and Ellie will, no doubt, get the brunt of it. So whatever you've come to say about her wasting precious resources or police time, I suggest you keep it short.' It sounds like a threat and the way that Detective Dawson stares and Detective Lorelle smirks, I can tell they think so too.

'Actually Miss Parker, that isn't why we're here at all.' Detective Dawson visibly turns her body towards me, completely cutting Tilly out of her sight. She's clearly making a statement that Tilly's input in the conversation is now over. 'Miss Dolloway, over the last few days we've been looking through Freya's laptop and speaking with her friends and colleagues, trying to get a picture of the type of person your sister is and where she may have gone. I'm happy to report that everything we have found so far, the text message you received from her included, points to Freya leaving of her own accord. At this moment in time, we don't suspect any foul play and following this conversation, plan to close your sister's missing persons case.'

'Everything?' I repeat, noticing that Tilly shoots me a look to say that I shouldn't be questioning anything. I should just agree with the Detectives and let them end this whole embarrassing charade.

'Yes.' Detective Dawson shuffles uneasily and I imagine the conversation she's having with herself in her head. What to say, what not to say. 'Our IT technicians found some posts on a...' she glances over at her partner, clearly looking for guidance on what should be said. From her next sentence, it looks like she's chosen not to divulge much at all. '...forum.' She holds out her hand as if offering the word to me like a suggestion. 'It seems Freya was unhappy in her day to day life which has gradually gotten more and more apparent over the weeks. She has been distancing herself from her usual routines and friendship groups as of late.'

'I'm sorry, what? As I've told you before Detective, Freya has experienced depression before. If she were struggling again we would have noticed.' If I frown any deeper I'm sure I'm going to give myself frown lines.

'To be frank, Detective,' Tilly interrupts. I watch as she folds her arms across her chest, and I'm suddenly thrown back a decade to when we were teenagers. When she used to take this stance at least twice a day. 'Freya's a complete attention seeker. I don't think she's ever even been *really* depressed in her life. She just likes to garner sympathy.'

'Well,' the Detective falters and I can see a muscle twitching in her jaw. She looks like she wants to hurl Tilly out of the room by her hair.

I can tell she's wavering on the line between telling me too much and not telling me enough and she's struggling to decide which side of that line to fall on. Her partner decides to fall on the side of the former.

'What my partner is trying to say,' Detective Lowell leans forward, resting his elbows on his knees and I'm surprised at how casual he looks when he tells me, 'is that your sister was in a lot of debt and from some personal posts which were found on a number of different sites, she seemed to be very unhappy with the current state of her life. She mentioned getting away from it numerous times and from statements made from her closest friends, she had been becoming increasingly withdrawn over the last month or two. These findings paired with the antidepressant prescription your sister appeared to be taking and the text message you have received, points to your sister deciding to up and leave. We have no suspicions of foul play in this matter, we are ruling your sister's disappearance closed.'

'So, the prim and proper, self absorbed bitch basically just ghosted her family? That's Freya right down to a T.' Tilly scoffs. 'And anti-depressants? What the hell did she have to be depressed about anyway? goddamn woman's so self-righteous.'

'Tilly, stop!' It comes out more of a snap than I'd meant it to and I see the flicker of hurt cross Tilly's face but I'm still trying to process what they've just said to me, so I don't apologise.

'You seem to have a real hatred for your friend's sibling?' Detective Dolloway directs the question to Tilly but looks directly at me as she asks.

I can feel the judgement in her look. She's wondering how someone can just sit back like that and listen to someone so openly insult their family but she doesn't know Freya. She doesn't know me. Tilly may be blunt but she's more of a sister to me then Freya has ever been and I'm grateful for her. Tilly shuffles slightly from foot to foot and I know she's getting agitated. If I don't diffuse the situation, she'll declare all out war on these Detectives who are just doing their jobs. She's blunt but she can also be short tempered.

'Thank you for coming all this way to let me know, Detectives.' I smile and stand, a cue to them that this conversation is over.

'Of course.' Detective Dolloway rises and taps her partner on the shoulder to encourage him to do the same. 'Thank you for your time Miss Dolloway. We wish you and your children all the best.'

Tilly sees the Detectives out for me whilst I head upstairs to the shower. By the time I come out and crawl into bed, my hair sopping wet and soaking the pillow, Tilly has made me a cup of tea and brought it up to me.

'Here,' she says gently, 'for your sorrows.' 'What would I do without you, Till?' I smile, my voice already full of sleep. 'I've already told you before,' she smiles, stroking my wet hair out of my face, 'you'd be positively screwed without me, darling.'

Seven years ago

He stares at me across the counter, mouth hanging slightly open, eyes glazed with confusion. I regret telling him instantly. I knew I would. I'd been second guessing telling him all week; Tell him. No, don't. He deserves to know. He won't understand.

I'd decided, only two minutes ago, to confide the truth. Well, it feels more like it just fell out of my mouth, rather than an actual decision. This is the first shift we've worked together in months, so it had to be tonight. I might not have gotten another chance. But now, watching him react with deafening silence, I wish I'd kept my mouth shut.

We both used to work the Friday and Saturday late night shifts. Mr Fuller, the owner, preferred to keep "the kids" as he called us, on the same shifts. I guess because none of the older employees were willing to work weekends, whereas the high school kids were so desperate for their mere pittance he paid per hour, some individuality and sense of adulthood, that we didn't complain about working the weekends.

Mr Fuller has always been a creature of habit and tended to stick to the monthly rota without much allowance for movement. If you wanted to change shifts or patterns, you had to find someone who was willing to swap with you.

I guess he'd picked up the thick cloud of tension between Bobby and I which had gradually gotten worse over the last few weeks, because we hadn't been on the same shift all month. He'd swapped so I was now working predominantly with Reggie in the evenings and Bobby worked the mornings with Bea.

Today though, I'd finally managed to get Bea to swap her Sunday morning shift with me. She hadn't been happy about it. She hated working the late night shifts but many a negotiation later, she had finally huffed in resignation, rolling her eyes and agreeing to the swap.

I guess that's why I had felt the need to confide the truth right this second because I'm not sure if I can convince Bea to swap with me next week.

Bobby had been avoiding me all shift and there was only an hour left. So when he was filling the popcorn mixer, avoiding my eyeline whilst the only customers in the lobby were busy at the pic 'n' mix, I had let the words fall out of my mouth. He'd stopped, physically tensing every muscle and letting popcorn kernels spill to the floor. He'd turned and searched my face. He's still standing stock still, just staring at me. I want to pull the words back in but of course, I can't. 'You...you're...what?' He stammers, almost falling into one of the counter seats across from me. My tongue feels too heavy in my mouth for words but I've come this far.

'I said, I'm pregnant.' I hold my breath.

He just stares at me, silent. I go to speak again but the group of kids across the lobby come over with their bags full of sweets, laughing and debating whether Antman or Ironman stand a better chance against Superman in a one on one battle. It gives me the few minutes I need to collect my thoughts as I weigh their respective bags and ring them up. Bobby doesn't waste a second. As soon as they've gone through to screen one, he picks up right where we left it. 'How can that be Elle?' he asks, still searching my face as if he could find answers there. 'We were always careful.' I feel sick. I don't know what to say or how to explain, how could I? I barely understand what has happened as it is. How am I supposed to look him in the eye and tell him everything? I just can't bring myself to do it. Not now. Maybe not ever. 'I don't know,' I lie, looking away from his face and hoping he doesn't see the sweat beading at my hairline. I've never lied to him before. I don't know whether he'll be able to see it in my eyes. I can't risk that. 'How far along?' He collapses on to the stool behind the counter, almost as if they can't keep him upright anymore and holds his face in his hands. It's as if he can't stand to look at me and I can't blame him for that. I can barely look at my own reflection these days. I have, after all, broken his heart without any explanation. I'd refused to look him in the eye when I'd ended things. He'd searched my face then in the same way that he just did. Saying we could work it all out, whatever it was, we could fix it. I'd snatched my hand away from him and told him there was no fixing it, how could we fix the fact I didn't love him anymore.

I'd felt as sick lying like that then as I feel now, having to tell him that after all of that, I'm going to make him a teenage dad. That from here on out, nothing will be the same again. 'About five weeks, I think.' I mumble, grabbing a handful of cheap, two-ply napkins from the counter and dabbing my face.

'Ok.' He swallows, nodding his head as if he has it all figured out. 'So, there's still time to fix this.' He stands up and comes round the counter, gently taking my hand twisting me so that I have no choice but to look at him.

'What does that mean, "Fix it"?'

You know...' he glances down at my still flat stomach and nods meaningfully at it. 'It's not as if we're going to keep it.'

I snatch my hand away so fast that I only just catch the pained look on his face. I recognise the same look in his eyes to the one I'd seen the last time I'd snatched my hand away. Telling him it was over between us. I expected my mother to push the subject, but I really thought Bobby would be more supportive. His reaction makes me feel utterly alone. '

No.' The venom in my voice shocks even me. 'No. No. No. No.' My breath catches. Panic and anxiety mingle and vibrate through my head. The room spins and I feel lightheaded. I try to blow out the breath that's caught in my throat, but it feels like a knot at the back of my throat and that just makes me panic more.

'Elle... come on. You can't be serious!? We're seventeen. We can't be parents. We're not even adults. How are we supposed to do that? We're

not even together anymore!' He's started shouting and I feel grateful that the foyer's empty. 'You made it perfectly clear that you don't want me! Why would you want to keep my baby!?' His voice sounds like it's booming inside my head, bouncing off the inside of my skull.

The baby's mine too,' I rasp, willing the panic to calm. 'Oh come on, Ellie! Grow the fuck up!' he spits. I'm taken aback by how vicious he sounds. I've never seen him like this before. 'You can't be serious. It's not even a person yet. Just a bunch of cells.'

He steps towards me. Clearly oblivious to the fact that I can hear the blood rushing in my ears, my heart thumping so fast I feel like It's going to crack a rib. I'd been worried about how he would react but never in a million years did I think it would be like this. Not Bobby. He's gentle, so sweet and understanding. How could he turn around and say something like this so flippantly. As if the decision has already been made. The edges of my vision have started blurring and I don't know how to calm down.

Maybe I shouldn't have done this. Maybe it was a mistake to even tell him at all. 'Hey, Ellie. Are you alright?' I hadn't even heard Tilly come in. I'd completely forgotten we'd planned for her to pick me up at the end of my shift. 'Jesus Christ Elle, what's happened!?' She rushes around the counter, crouching on the floor next to me. I hadn't even realised that I'd slid down the side of the counter to the floor '

Get some water you goddamn idiot. What's wrong with you!?' she shouts at Bobby who has stopped dead in his tracks. He's looking at me like I've grown two heads, and I want the ground to swallow me whole.

'I'm ok.' I whisper, taking big gulps of air as Tilly holds my hand. I suddenly feel physically exhausted in the aftermath of the panic attack. 'I'm ok now. Take me home Till, please.'

Tilly drives me home in silence, the radio playing quietly in the background. I've never heard her this quiet before. She normally can't go two minutes without finding something to talk about. I'm relieved for the peace and quiet, my head aching from the aftermath of the adrenaline. It's only when we pull up outside my parent's house and she kills the engine, audibly taking in oxygen to fuel the upcoming interrogation, that I know she isn't going to let me go without an explanation.

'So, do I have to squeeze it out of you?' she asks me calmly, but I can see her jaw twitching with anticipation. She rolls down the window and lights up a cigarette. I screw my face up like I've just stepped in something disgusting, and she rolls her eyes at me. 'I'm going to quit. Just not yet. Anyway, we're not talking about my bad habits. We're here to talk about yours. So, you going to tell me what the fuck that was back there?' I slump down in my seat, almost as if I can make myself so small, she won't be able to see me. '

It was my fault,' I mumble. 'I shouldn't have told him. I knew it was a mistake. I guess some part of me just hoped I was wrong.' I pick at the skin around my fingernails, trying to fight back the tears prickling at the corners of my eyes.

'Woah.' Tilly shakes her hand back and forth in disagreement, blowing out a billow of rank smelling smoke through the open window. 'Bobby's a dick. We knew that as soon as he broke it off with you because you wouldn't fuck him.'

There's that guilty feeling again. I only have myself to blame though and I know it. I never should have lied and told her that Bobby had ended things with me and not the other way around. I just couldn't cope with the interrogation when the break up was so raw and it's not as if I could tell her the real reason for me ending things with the guy I'd been smitten with for years. I'd told her he'd broken up with me to protect myself, knowing that if I made out that he'd broken my heart and not the other way around, she would spare me the interrogation. She's good like that. She'd let the subject go with a simple "Well, he's clearly just a dick then. Good riddance," and we left it like that. Now I'm reaping what I've sown. '

I did.' I sigh, pulling myself back into the present. Tilly stops puffing on her cigarette and stares at me, blinking. 'A couple of months ago, we slept together a few times.' I blush.

'Well, shit.' Tilly laughs, pushing my arm playfully before her face shadows over again 'In that case, he's even more of a dick than I thought. Getting what he was after and then fobbing you off.'

'He didn't break up with me, Tilly. I broke up with him.' I whisper, picking the skin on my thumb harder, ignoring the sting and bead of blood.

'You what?' Tilly frowns, shaking her head and I know I have to put her out of her misery, but I just don't know how to form the words. 'Then what? Him kicking off back there was because he wants you back?'

'No,' I sigh, taking a deep breath.

I just need to say it. She's going to find out eventually anyway. It's not as if I need to tell her the whole thing. Just the essential part. I pause, my panic growing with every second whilst I try to muster the courage, until I panic and just blurt out the words. 'We argued because... because... well... I'm pregnant.' The silence stretches. Tilly opens and closes her mouth a few times as if she keeps forgetting her words. She looks like a fish. I can't bear the silence anymore. 'I'm keeping it.' I say it with such conviction; Tilly just nods firmly.

'And Bobby he...' Tilly motions towards my stomach, 'it's his, right?'

My chest bubbles with anxiety; creeping up my throat, threatening to spill all over Tilly's car interior. I swallow it down and take a breath. 'He doesn't want it.' My voice comes out a pathetic squeak and I start crying. Loud and ugly sobs wracking my body. Tilly throws her cigarette out of the window and drags me closer across the car, hugging me tight and shushing me gently. A cloud of strong nicotine encircles us but I barley notice the stench. Not like I normally would.

* 'It's going to be ok,' she soothes, 'that peanut doesn't need a daddy anyway. Not when he's got a mommy like you and an Auntie like me.' I laugh at that. Tilly always finds a way of bringing me back from the edge and I'm grateful for it. 'What would I do without you, Till?' I smile, wiping the snot with my sleeve.She leans back and smiles at me mischievously. 'You'd be positively screwed, Darling.'*

Chapter 22

Freya

My eyes sting and there's a constant ache behind them that won't subside. There're fresh bruises up my thighs and on my hips where he pinned me down again.

I knew the moment I opened my eyes, and he was lying next to me, what was about to happen. His proximity was enough for me to smell his breath, see the sweat on his neck. The tears sting the cuts on my cheeks as they fall down my face. I peel myself from the rough floor, my skin burning as it separates from the boiling surface, the ache in between my legs as strong as the ache behind my eyes.

I don't know how much longer I can take this. It takes all of my effort to peel the sequined dress from where it's stuck to my skin. He's left it on me since he took those horrid photographs the first night. I don't know how long it's been, but the dress is saturated with sweat and grime.

It's so stiflingly hot in here I can barely breathe. The hot air circles my nostrils and clogs my throat. I drag myself on my knees across the room and push myself up as close to the far wall as possible. It's cooler here. The small window of the room has been bricked up, so the only bit of sunlight that gets in is from the fan near the ceiling but it's red hot and lets all of the heat into the confined space. At least in this bit of shade, it's breathable.

I can hear how raspy my breath sounds in my own head, and I can tell my ribs are still broken from the sheer pain ripping through my chest every time I breathe.

I feel more alert today. As if he hasn't given me as many sedatives as he normally does and I don't know whether that should make me feel relieved or petrified. Is his resolve weakening? Has he forgotten? Or does he just want me alert to everything that's happening for this next part? I wonder how he can stand to wear that wretched mask he always has on. It's one of those cheap latex Halloween masks you can buy at the mall. The face is garish. A rabbit with massive teeth and fake splatters of blood. Although I wonder if the blood's real.

He never takes it off and I wonder how stifling hot it must be under all that latex in this heatwave.

I've always loved the summer. The cocktails and beach parties, skimpy clothes and expensive day trips. To me, it always feels like summer is full of possibilities. Not this year. Now it feels more like a threat, a death sentence.

A week ago, I was foolishly concerned with the direction my life was headed. I'd never wanted to get into the working girl industry and I've been feeling sorry for myself ever since.

I stopped going out with friends, stopped speaking to people all together really. I felt trapped in the mess that had become my life. Reminiscing about when times were simpler back in the good old days. Pathetic.

I'd give anything to go back to my mundane boring life which I was convinced was a waste of time and pulling me under. The bills, the depression, the pills. All a vicious circle I was desperate to escape. Now I wish all I had to worry about was money and an addiction to prescription meds to keep me functioning.

I sweat in the blaring heat and find myself daydreaming about the last summer where I truly felt happy.

Eight years ago.

It's the last day of summer before our final term of classes start and teenage anticipation hangs in the air. This summer has been the best yet and I feel disappointed that it's almost at an end. The gin and tonics I was knocking back at lunch time are still giving me a buzz and I feel elated. The last month has been filled with boys, booze, sex and parties and I don't want it to end. We've all decided to spend the last day getting pissed in the movie theatre, paying more attention to each other's mouths and bodies in the back row than to the actual movie. I guess that's the advantage to being a friendship group full of couples. We can spend time together and with our significant others and not be teased for it or left out because we were too busy getting laid in the backs of cars to be present.

Courtney and Sebastian are the newest and sweetest couple of us all. Still new and fresh and a little bit shy around the rest of us. Courtney's also the newest addition to our clan and Seb has been wooing her ever since he laid eyes on her at the start of the year. She's quiet and reserved but Seb is loud and a bit of a wild cat and she seems to be coming out of her shell this summer.

Harriet and Austin, on the other hand, are the high-strung couple. They've been together the longest. I guess that's why they argue the most. Harriet's independent and strong willed and hates how much of a cling on Austin can be. He knows Harriet is way out of his league and he's convinced someone is going to swoop in and whisk her away. Little does he know they already have. Multiple times. Usually in some skanky club toilet.

Scott and I fall somewhere nicely in the middle. We've been friends for years and together for a few. He's sweet and loving but is also witty and well-liked. I know people normally laugh at teenage love, claim it won't last once the euphoria passes and we grow up. I disagree. I think we're definitely end game material.

As we walk into the movie theatre's sweet, air-conditioned release from the outside heat, I subconsciously reach up and stroke the small silver locket clasped around my neck. Running my fingernail over where the small S is engraved. A small trinket of the massive amount of love he has for me. That's what he said when he gave it to me on our first valentines, clasping it in place with a gentle kiss. I rub the small dent in the one side, marvelling at how something can be so perfect, even with its imperfection, just like Scott and I.

We all huddle into the foyer, audibly relieved by the air-conditioned chill of the main lobby. We stumble half drunk, arms interlocked and laughing up to the main counter. I huff and roll my eyes when I see Ellie working the register. I know she's going to ruin my mood and I'd rather not have her spoil the last day of my summer.

'You're drunk.' She scowls. There it goes... the high. She just has to ruin everything fun, doesn't she? I lean across the counter shaking her shoulder.

Ells. Lighten the fuck up, would ya?' I laugh. 'We don't all have to be boring bitches like you.' I scoff.

Harriet and Courtney giggle and I feel accomplished when I see the red-hot blush move up her neck and into her cheeks. 'Four tickets for Camp Massacre, three popcorns and six Colas please, honey.' Austin winks at Ellie as he hands her a twenty-dollar bill, clearly amused when she blushes bright red.

I notice Harriet's neck flushing red too, but I guess it's for a whole other reason when she sneers at Austin. Clearly as unimpressed as me by Austin's flirtation with my sister. Ellie tuts, trying to pretend she isn't bright red, moving away to the other side of the counter to get us our popcorn and as my eyes follow her I notice one of the lads she works with glaring at me.

His eyes bore into me like a drill. His face is set in stone and there's something there I can't quite read but a shiver crawls up my spine. I wrap my arms around myself, the air conditioning suddenly feeling too cold. We stay, eyes locked, until Ellie pushes three large bags of popcorn across the counter.

'Hey, Freya! You coming or what?' Harriet calls from the screen entrance, her red hair looking garish under the door light.

I hadn't even noticed them take their drinks and head for their seats. I clear my throat and break the piercing stare with the creep. I grab one of the bags of popcorn and sneak a quick look back at the lad, he's stopped staring at me and is looking at Ellie like a lost puppy. Ha, I guess Ellie's found herself a little admirer. I follow Harriet inside. Ellie all but forgotten, as she normally is. As the lights dim and the movie starts, Scott's hand moves up the inside of my thigh and I know this has been one of the best summers of my life.

I pull myself out of the haze of the memory and silently pray to a God that I'm not even sure I really even believe in that I make it out of here alive.

I vow that if I just make it out of here in one piece, I'll never complain about my life again. That I'll make sure that next summer is the best yet. Pushing that last high school summer off of the winning podium.

Except, I think God and I, if he really is out there watching this, knows that it's just a little bit too little, too late. If the heat and dehydration doesn't kill me first, he will.

Chapter 23

Detective Dawson

I finally finish my paperwork on the Freya Dolloway case and sit back in my chair debating what to do for lunch. It's a bit deflating once a case is solved. Don't get me wrong, it's always a relief when a disappearance turns out to be a simple mid-life crisis or someone who left of their own volition. It's what happens most of the time to be completely honest but it's the time between closing a case and getting assigned a new one that seems to make me wish I chose an easier line of work.

I'm just filing away my own personal notes in to my electronic files when the lieutenant walks out from his office and calls my name. All eyes fall on me and I feel like a kid on their way to the principal's office. It's rare that Lieutenant Forester calls any of us into his office specifically. We don't normally see him at all unless there's a problem. I guess that's why my stomach suddenly feels like it's going to fly out of my mouth as I pass through the desks towards what I'm sure is nothing good.

'That one too.' Forester motions towards Luke back at our desks.

I turn slightly and motion for Luke to follow me. He looks as uneasy as I feel, if not slightly offended that the lieu doesn't seem to know him by name, following me across the room. Once we are all in the office with the door closed, Forester closes the blinds on the windows facing the rest of the office. Another bad sign.

'Sit.' He orders, walking back to take his own seat behind his desk. Forester is a big, bald, middle-aged man who's seen a lot of bad shit in his three decades on the force. Over the years, his features have hardened as much as his resolve and his emotions. His stomach has also gradually grown into a significantly obvious beer belly. I imagine that alcohol helps him to cope with the stress of the job.

I'd feel sorry for him if he wasn't such an arsehole. All about the figures and the costs rather than the people and their families. Managing the department with a hard fist and no empathy.Luke and I both take our seats opposite his excessively large desk, which takes up the majority of the small office. A design choice, I'm sure, which was made to make Forester look as important as he believes himself to be. He struggles to squeeze himself into the seat which was once much too big for him and sets me with a firm and unblinking stare. I refuse to blink or look away. Instead, clearing my throat to break the tension.

'How can we help, Lieutenant?' I ask.

'I heard that you closed Freya Dolloway's case as no reason for concern?' Forester fiddles with the waistband of his trousers which are digging into his sides, giving him a distinctive muffin-top shape.

'That's correct.' I nod. 'Ms Dolloway's financial situation, witness testimonies from her friends as well as a text message her sister received, all point towards Freya having chosen to leave of her own accord.'

'But, you haven't spoken to Ms Dolloway *specifically*?' he puts emphasis on the last word, like I'm too thick to understand what he's asking. Annoyance twitches in my eyebrow.

'No, sir. We have been unable to contact her directly. It appears she does not wish to make contact with anyone.' Luke nods slowly.

'Right. But you are sure?' Forester directs the question to me, his eyes boring into my face. 'Because if that shit blows up in our faces, it won't be me going under the knife, Detective Dawson. I can assure you of that.'

'We understand this case has significance.' I lick my lips, trying to keep the anger out of my face and voice. 'Given the relationship to the prior station Chief, we know that this case needs to be airtight. I had assumed, Lieutenant, that that was the precise reason you specifically put myself and Detective Lorell on this case. Given our experience, skill sets and case resolution rate.' Forester's gaze is unrelenting. His mouth is set in a hard line, clearly unimpressed at my response.

'I hope Detective, for all of our sakes, you are correct in your opinions of yourself.' Forester clears his throat and straightens up, the buttons on his un-ironed shirt threatening to pop open. He throws an open case file down on the desk between us and motions for us to look. We both lean forward and take a look at the front page. 'That...' he motions towards the photograph of a young, blue eyed, brunette woman, who is pushing her smiling face into the side of a happy looking German shepherd. I recognised her immediately.

'It's Amelia Taylor,' I finish the sentence for him. My mouth suddenly dry. 'You don't need to tell me. It's the only case I've had in the last five years that's still open and unsolved. Do we have a new lead?' My heart is pounding so loud in my ears I'm surprised I even hear his reply.

'There was a body pulled out of the Vicory Canal this morning. The prints match Amelia Taylor.' Forester says it without feeling. 'The body is now in the morgue downstairs. It's unconfirmed but the cause of death appears to be homicide.' The room spins and it takes all of my effort not to scream.

Amelia Taylor. Missing for six months and four days. She was last seen on her way home from her job at the Rolling Bowling Alley on Ainsley Lane at eleven fifty seven, buying a pint of milk from her local corner shop on her way. Somewhere between the shop and the three streets back to her house, she disappeared. Her parents had alerted authorities when they found her bed empty the following morning. Amelia had never wavered from her weekly routines in the four years that she'd been working in the bowling alley, her parents had said. They also said she hadn't spent a single night away from her toddler, Callie, since she was born. In fact, the only time she ever spent away from her was to work. She'd been trying to save enough for them to finally move out of her parents house. Single parents didn't get the luxury of working sociable hours when they were desperately fighting for a better life for their child.

It didn't reach my desk until she had already been missing for seven days. The former Detective on the case hit a dead end and asked me to take a look. My expertise in the department had outweighed their own eighteen short months of experience. Luke and I had spent weeks working on the case. Trying to find any more leads or evidence we possibly could but we didn't find much. The pint of milk and pack of digestive biscuits in a ripped plastic carrier bag with the corner shop's logo printed on the front had been found midway through the badly lit local park. Amelia's parents confirmed that the park was the route Amelia took every day, to and from work. There were skid marks found on the road which ran parallel to the park but the tire treads didn't match anything in the system. All we could ascertain was that they belonged to a large four by four, probably something resembling a pick up truck. The scuffed and broken foliage found between the roadside and the footpath could have suggested a struggle, that Amelia may have been dragged through and loaded into a vehicle but the light rainfall in the early hours of the following morning made it difficult to tell.

We couldn't ascertain anything further than what had already been surmised from the evidence and the investigation and the case went cold. A copy of the case file has been burning a hole in my bottom desk drawer and I still check every news radio station each morning, expecting to hear something. For a body to be found matching Amelia's description but until now, nothing had surfaced.

I knew deep down that Amelia was probably dead. That her body was buried somewhere out there, which would eventually be found. In how many years, I had no idea, but I had convinced myself I would never find her.

I leave the lieutenant's office without saying a word, ignoring Forester's shouts at my sudden departure and demands of coming back, heading straight for the stairs down to the basement morgue. As I run down, I hear Luke hot on my heels.

I guess Charlie, the coroner, was expecting me because at the sight of me, she abandons her current cadaver and circles round to one of the back examination tables, beckoning me to follow.

'I knew you would want to know, Molly. So I made sure Amelia Taylor's initial external examination was top of my priority list this morning.' Charlie squeezes my arm, giving me a sympathetic look.

For someone who sees so much death on a daily basis, Charlie always manages to remain a glass half full kind of woman. What I like most about her is that her fifteen years working as the station's medical examiner hasn't hardened her. She still empathises with the victims she examines, treating them with respect and compassion. Ensuring she speaks of them as the person they were, not just the slab of flesh and bone that holds clues of the crimes viciously committed against them. We have worked more cases together than I can count at this point, when missing person's cases result in the worst possible outcome, and I'm proud to say that Charlie is my friend as well as my colleague now.

'Tell us what you know.' I nod, trying to push down the anguish that's filling me. I know I've failed this poor woman and now I'm doomed to have to hear and relive what happened to her when I couldn't find her. I refuse to look down at Amelia. Not wanting to see the horrors which her body lays bare. Instead I keep my eyeline firmly on Charlie's face as she explains her findings.

She circles the table as she speaks, pointing out significant things on Amelia's body but I refuse to let my eyeline sway from her pinched concentrated face. 'She was found floating in Vicory Canal. It's quite deep for a canal bed and the cold temperature of the water has preserved her body quite well, slowing down decomposition.'

I find myself getting distracted as she talks. Realising that the Canal sounds so familiar because it was read out to me a few days ago. By my car's navigation system when we went to search Freya Dolloway's residence. Coincidences happen all the time but I still find it surprising that Amelia was found in a Canal so close to another apparently missing person's apartment. Charlie pulls on her gloves, moving to the end of the table near Amelia's feet and I can see the blue tinge of her toes in my periphery. I know I have to look so I do. Trying to ignore the parlour of her skin as Charlie turns her foot gently.

'You see these ligature marks?' she points to the dark purplish rings around Amelia's ankles. Her feet are covered in bite marks and I feel a gag moving up my throat at the degraded flesh, half her foot missing.

'She was weighed down by something, her ankles are fractured. Looks like some kind of thick rope. I imagine it was tied to a heavy stone to keep her body below water level but the aquatic life bit through the soft tissue, loosening it and letting her body rise to the surface.'

'Was she dead before she went in the water?' Luke's voice is levelled and calm but I know he's feeling the same stab of guilt that I am. We both failed her. We should have looked harder, never stopped. Maybe then we'd be speaking to her about what happened instead of learning it from her corpse.

'Yes.' Charlie sighs, rounding back up to the top of the table. 'I found no traces of water in her lungs, she didn't breathe it in. Given the cause of death as well, I believe she was deceased when she entered the water.'

'Cause of death?' I ask, needing to know the type of monster we're dealing with. If it weren't for the ankle marks and broken bones, It would still be possible that her death was an accident but the tension in the air lets me know that's not the case.

'Strangulation.' Charlie says the word quickly and it feels like a kick in the face. 'Whoever this psycho is, he's strong. He strangled her with his hands, so hard that he broke her neck. I'm assuming her assailant was male, given the strength needed for some of her injuries, but they could of course be a woman.' The violence is unfathomable, but I'm not surprised. Amelia has markings all over her body as I look, burns and bruises, cuts and blisters. He took his time and he was vicious, anyone can see that.

'Do we know how long she had to endure this?' I motion towards the marks littering her body and Charlie looks at me remorsefully.

'It looks like he started as soon as he took her. Given the oldest markings and their stages of healing, it looks like he kept the torture up regularly over six months. As I've said, the water slows down decomposition but it also makes the time of death much harder to determine. Given everything I've found, I'd say she died between six and seven days ago.'

The timeline sends another shock wave through me. I realise he probably moved her body, submerging her in the canal around the same time we started working on Freya Dolloway's case. I feel relieved to know I won't have to find out Freya Dolloway's last moments were this. Charlie pulls her gloves off and we follow her back across the examination room and out into the hall towards the lifts, the conversation clearly over and I'm glad to be leaving.

'Thank you for this, Charlie.' Luke nods to her. 'We know you didn't need to share all of this with us and that you're very busy. Have the homicide Detectives assigned to the case been by yet?'

'Not yet, no. I asked the receptionist to let Detectives Jennings and Harding know the preliminary external examination report was ready once you had both left.' Charlie takes Luke's outstretched hand and shakes it firmly. I'm relieved to hear that Jennings and Harding have been assigned to the case. We've worked with them a few times over the years where our cases resulted in unhappy endings where their services were required. Charlie hugs me tight and promises to let me know about any other developments once she's completed the full autopsy before she heads back to her office.

As we head back upstairs in the lift, I suddenly feel fatigued and I check my watch, silently counting the hours to when I can go home and cry in peace.

Chapter 24

No one

The boy looks bored. Sitting with his classmates on the large outdoor table the teacher set up early this morning. The other children are beaming, shouting, and laughing, full of pent-up childish energy as they make colorful banners and hats.

I saw a sign for the school's summer fate haphazardly sellotaped to one of the trees lining the street outside the school's main entrance as I passed. I'm guessing whatever the children are making is in preparation for that. Their excitement buzzes in the air, tickling my nostrils and throat, making me want to gag. Not the boy though. He looks stoic. Clearly too mature for his years and his peers to join in their childish antics. He sits towards the end of the table, cutting and gluing quietly. He looks up every so often, his eyeline travelling along the chain-linked fence which corners off the large school grounds from the rest of the street.

Earlier, I thought he'd noticed me, crouched behind this tree, but his eyes only remained for a moment before they carried on. I wonder what he's looking for. I wonder If he's hoping that something more interesting than the nauseating playfulness of his peers will suddenly pop out from behind the trees. I'm the only one out here, though. The girl is a little more adventurous, although still more subdued than her peers. She doesn't run around and screech, misbehave and throw things like her classmates but she does seem to enjoy the lesson.

She takes meticulous care in her work. Her tongue sticks out slightly as she focuses on cutting out shapes, eyes unblinking and focused. She laughs with her peers at their jokes and turns her face to the sun, absorbing the happiness in the air. I find myself obsessing over what that feeling of joy must feel like. How other people feel when the warm sun hits their face. To me, it's claustrophobic but she seems to find it pleasant. I wonder if, in some other life, I might have found the sun charming too. In a life where my mother wasn't my mother and my sordid life wasn't really my sordid life. I push the curiosity aside. That isn't what I came here to do. I draw my attention back to the children. They seem to move in sync. Their mannerisms are similar, their movements happen almost simultaneously even though they are at opposite ends of the table and their resemblance is obvious. An invisible connection, bonding the two of them seamlessly.

The jealousy of their companionship claws at my chest. I breathe in through my nose and out through my mouth, counting slowly to ten in my head to calm the mounting anguish at something I'll never have.

1...2...3...4...5...6...7...8...9...10.

I used to have a connection almost as strong as theirs before it was ripped from me, betrayal so sour I could never enjoy the heat of the sun again. The teacher stands abruptly and puts her hand in the air, her other hand covering her lips with a quieting finger. The children start to mimic her like mimes, raising their hands and pushing their sticky fingers against their mouths. The sound of laughter and chatter slowly dies down. She barks instructions to the students who all stand and follow her quietly, all in a neat line, back into the main school building. None of them take any of their bags or crafts inside so I know this is probably a short reprieve that won't last long. I need to act now, before they come back. I cross the distance between the trees and the chain link fence, crouching down behind the large oak tree at the perimeter where the children have left their bags. I crouch low to the ground, pull my cap tighter onto my head and move low and fast.

Given that the school promotes a high security of students on their site, the chain link fence is easy to snip through with my cutters, and I reach through, grabbing the girl's bright backpack from the top of the pile. I open the small, zipped pouch at the back and slip the present inside.

I hear the large school doors bang open and the teacher shouting to tell the children to slow down. The bolt of adrenaline which shoots through my arms makes my fingers tremble and it takes me three attempts to zip the pocket back up. I don't even manage to get it done up all the way, but it will have to do. I throw the bag back on top of the others and quickly straighten up.

As the children round the corner of the building back towards the table, I'm already halfway down the adjoining road. I know she's going to be missing me by now; I should get back.

Chapter 25

Ellie

I pull the kids closer to me as we weave through the graves. The sun is setting so there's finally a bit of a breeze to the day and I know the kids are glad it's the weekend. Their school clothes are dishevelled, and Myah's pig tails have started coming undone, loose strands of hair poking out all over the place and there's at least one strip of her hair caked in sticky glue which I'm going to have a nightmare to get out. Sometimes I think the teachers do these crafts with them just to ruin the parents' nights with hyperactive, glitter smothered children. I let the irritation wash over me and decide to take the win, because at least they seem content.

The moodiness from this morning seems forgotten and I suppose it's because they've had a craft day which has ended in me agreeing to take them to the park after school. I even caved and bought them both ice creams. Even though they haven't eaten dinner yet. My loose-fitting summer trousers and vest feel suddenly cold as the sun sets but I'm glad for the reprieve from the sticky, sweaty feeling of the heat wave.

The kids are playing hopscotch on invisible tiles between the headstones, their ice creams dripping down their hands and onto patches of grass as they go.

I read the names engraved on the headstones as we pass by, a ritual I've gotten into the habit of doing every time we come here. I try to work out how old these people were when they died from their engraved birth and death dates. It still shocks me, even though I do this every time, just how young so many people are when they die.

The kids don't seem to notice the significance of the place. They laugh and joke, playing some secretly devised game between the two of them as they jump from invisible tile to invisible tile. I watch them with swelling feelings of love and jealousy in equal measure. Myah and Matthew have always been so close, so inseparable. Their relationship has always felt to me the way that twins should be. They love each other unconditionally and are the best of friends. They laugh and play and share without me having to encourage them to. They squabble and fight too but it's short-lived and they always make up before they go to sleep, their disagreements never running too deep or lasting too long. I do wonder whether Freya and I may have been the same in different circumstances. We would always have been incredibly different, because even though we are twins, we are our own person.

She would have always been the firecracker, the one to take risks and have mountains of friends. I would have always been the quiet and reserved one, preferring the fictional characters in books to the real people around me. The studious one living in her brilliant twin's shadow. But, I wonder, if all that had happened had not happened, would we be close now? Now that we are older and more mature. Would we have accepted our differences for our individuality and became closer as adults? I guess I'll never know and I guess, just as Freya believes, that's my fault. The twins carry on through the graveyard to the open playing field on the other side of the fencing. My voice seems to be lost on the air when I shout to them to stay close. I listen to their laughter and smile, deciding that as long as I can still hear them, they haven't gone too far.

I stop next to my father's grave and kneel down in the dry warm earth. I empty the dead flowers from the small flowerpot, replacing them with the bright sunflowers I brought. I sat in silence for a few moments, wishing that I could talk to my father.

I imagine his face and his voice when he used to help me with my maths homework. The slight tilt of his glasses on his head. But as it always does when I think of my father, his face turns into something dark. His mouth twists into one of agony as he shouts through the flames. Telling us to run.

I can smell the smoke and hear the flames licking up the walls and I have to hold my breath against the panic attack threatening to overtake me. I hear him screaming out in pain as he burns along with the person who decided to burn our house to the ground.

I blow out my breath, reminding myself that I'm not in a burning building anymore. I'm out and I'm safe. I look across to where I last saw the children playing and my stomach drops into a bottomless pit when I don't see them. I listen closely for their laughs but all I can hear is the slight breeze rustling through the trees and the birds singing. I scramble up. I run.

My legs screaming against the effort in my muscles as I run through the field, screaming their names. There's that bottomless feeling of parental panic you always hear people talk about. I feel it now. I am frenzied, spinning around, calling to them in shrill tempos. Praying to God that I find them. Promising that if I do, I'll never lose sight of them again.

Then I see them.

At the corner of the field, just in the tree line of the woods. They're standing there speaking to someone. The person's only a shadowy figure from here and I curse the fact that the sun's setting, so I don't have a clear enough view of them. The only thing I can tell is that their build is tall and I think that they're male.

He leans down and passes Matthew something and I start screaming at them to come to me. To get away from the stranger. They both look up, startled and hurtle towards me. I watch the man turn around and disappear back into the depths of the forest, not bothering to apologise or explain why he was talking to two seemingly unaccompanied minors.

I put my hands to my hip and look at the twins expectedly when they finally reach me.

'Who was that?' I ask them both urgently, looking between their faces. 'Who was that man? Why were you speaking to him? Haven't I told you we don't speak to strangers!' Myah's bottom lip trembles and I realise I'm shouting.

'He lost his dog,' Matthew mumbles. 'He wanted to know if we'd seen him. He said his name was Biscuits.'

'We told him we hadn't seen him.' Myah moans, kicking the ground with her toe.

'Right.' I sigh, lowering my voice. 'Well, you never, ever do that again. We do not speak to strangers, and we do not run off. You scared me half to death; I couldn't see you!'

I pull them both in close and squeeze them tight to my legs. 'Sorry Mommy.' Matty mumbles into my legs.

'Sorry Mommy.' Myah echoes. 'We did ignore him at first because he looked a bit funny but then he said he was looking for a dog.'

'Here.' Matty encourages. 'He gave me this to say thank you for trying to help. You can have it, we're sorry.' He stretches up and hands me the flower and I feel my blood pressure spike.

I silently try to reason with myself. These flowers are found everywhere. It's just a coincidence that it's the same as the one he sent to our house the day he set the place alight. I tell the kids we're going to race back to the car and as they bolt off back through the graveyard, I search the treeline for any trace of the stranger. Of course, there's no one there. I drop the purple Dahlia on to the ground and crush it with the heel of my sandal. Wishing I could crush all memories of that day with it.

Seven Years Ago.

I'm going to be sick. My stomach retches and I run for the nearest bush. There's nothing even left to come up. Just tangy sharp bile and I'm not surprised. I haven't been able to eat a full meal without throwing it back up in weeks. It's as if my unborn children want me to be punished for choosing to bring them into this world, into this situation.

I've been thinking about what my mother had said for days. Maybe I'm really not ready to be a mother. Maybe I should do the best thing for both me and my babies and terminate.

I'd gone to the doctors with the idea of requesting termination at the forefront of my mind. That was until she'd pressed the probe hard against my stomach and found two heartbeats.

Twins. I can't decide if it's a twisted game of fate. Especially given my relationship with my own twin. Do I really want to bring children into that dynamic? Do I really want them to feel responsible for another person? To compare themselves to one another and for one of them to find themselves never truly measuring up? It gave me reason to pause and now I'm walking home from the clinic, the ultrasound picture burning in my back pocket. I wish I'd taken Tilly with me. I went alone and now my head is swimming and I don't know how I can make it home alone, but I do. I stumble up to the porch, the decision firmly in my mind. I'm going to be a mother. It's only as I'm turning the key in the lock that I notice them. I don't know how I didn't see them as I was walking up the steps. I guess I was just too deeply in my own head because they're definitely there.

Wrapped tightly in light white paper. I spin around, my eyes scanning the street, trying to see who left them. I pick them up, the smell of dahlias filling my nose and making me gag again. Everything makes me vomit these days.

I search through the stems and pull out the small white card pushed deep between the flowers. I'm assuming they're going to be from Scott to Freya. Although, why he wouldn't just give them to her himself instead of having them delivered strikes me as bizarre. I guess he was just trying to be romantic.

Except, when I read the card, my legs suddenly feel weak. I chastise myself, it's clearly just a stupid prank. I storm back down the steps and shove the flowers into the bin and look around the street one more time. Hoping that whoever pulled this vicious prank sees that it was foolish and ineffective. I throw the card in after them and it lands face up, the words staring at me.

None of you are safe. I'll be there soon.

Chapter 26

No One

I watch her from the treeline. It seems somehow *right* that this moment would be in the graveyard where their father's buried. The first sign that something isn't quite right. That her sister isn't quite as safe as she thought. She takes the flower, her face dropping in dread, and I know she understands.

I laugh quietly under my breath, thankful for the heavy treeline for hiding me from her view.

This is going to be fun.

Chapter 27

Ellie

I'm bone tired. I thought this last day of relaxation would be all I needed to get back to normality and back to work. Turns out, Freya's sudden realization that she's too good for us has taken it out of me more than I thought. I'm teetering on the edge of a caffeine high from my last coffee of the day and I've been counting down to the kids' bedtime for three hours.

The kids seem more relaxed tonight, and I feel relieved. Any remaining unease around me seems to have passed and they both chat happily as they do their last pieces of homework at the table.

I glance at the clock and feel a wash of relief as I realize it's finally time for them to go to bed. I guess I'll be going to bed at eight tonight as well. 'Right, that's enough for tonight kids.' I smile at them from the kitchen sink where I'm washing up from dinner. 'Go and brush your teeth.'

They both groan loudly like they always do but I'm grateful that neither seems about to put up too much of a fuss tonight. I listen to their little feet on the stairs as I finish up. When I follow them both up, they're already in their beds and ready for their good night kisses and tuck ins. I smile, thanking my lucky stars that I was blessed with the two of them. They drive me up the wall sometimes but generally speaking, bringing them up hasn't been as difficult as it could have been if they were harder to handle.

I go to Matty first, like I always do. My little prince. I tuck his covers in around him and tell him not to let the bedbugs bite, kissing his head gently. He's asleep before I even turn his lamp off.

I walk along the landing to Myah's room next door and realize bedtime isn't going to be as smooth as I had hoped. She's sitting up in her bed, wide awake with a book in her lap, and looks at me eagerly when I walk in. I sigh and climb in next to her.

'Just one.' I laugh, kissing the top of her head too as she gives an excited squeal and snuggles down.

I'm not even through the first chapter when she starts snoring. I maneuver out from under the covers, trying my hardest not to make any noise or sudden movements that will wake her up.

I trip and stumble loudly across the room, just about catching myself on her chest of drawers before I completely topple to the floor. I curse under my breath and turn slowly, flinching, expecting to see her wide eyed and sitting up. I breathe out the breath I didn't know I was holding when she stirs for a second, rolling lazily to her other side before starting to snore like a freight train. I suppress a laugh. How such a tiny little girl could make such a racket every night is beyond me. I pray for the man she winds up marrying one day.

I tip-toe back across her room and pick up the culprit of my near topple. Her school backpack sprawled across her floor. I roll my eyes so hard I'm surprised they come back around the right way. I've told them so many times to put their coats and bags away properly when they come in. If I had a penny for every time, we'd most definitely be in a much nicer house than this one by now.

I pick the bag up and am about to turn around to go and put it away myself when the glint of something which has fallen from the half open compartment catches my eye. A silver slither now sprawled across the pastel pink carpet. I crouch down, my brow aching with the force of the frown filling my features. I pinch the chain between my thumb and forefinger and hold it up in the dull lamp light, watching it twirl in the air.

The locket is old and a little tarnished, but I can still make it out. The small S engraved into the heart of the locket. I'm so confused my head swims. Why would Myah have Freya's locket in her bag? A locket she hasn't taken off for half a decade since Scott died all those years ago. Determined that even in adulthood, she would still carry him with her.

I always thought the two of them were near to a breakup in the days leading up to his fatal car crash. They were arguing in her adjoining room, their shouts obvious and loud through our shared wall.

Our parents had gone out and Scott had come over ten minutes after their car had left the driveway. I'd plugged my earphones in as soon as I heard them giggling as they climbed the stairs. I was used to Scott's visits and I wasn't about to listen to any teenage lust unfolding in there if I could help it.

It was a while later when I could make out muffled raised voices. Voices which were clearly not the type of raised voices I had been expecting to hear. I had listened closely, trying to make out what they were shouting about but couldn't work out much. Scott had stormed out, slamming the front door behind him and I pretended not to hear Freya crying once he'd left. Freya had eventually cried herself to sleep but at breakfast the following day it was as if nothing had happened. She was her usual spiteful self over breakfast. Having digs at me subtly whilst she spoke to our parents. They cooed over her like a child. Full of compliments like they always were.

Then my mother's eyes drifted to my swollen stomach like they always did and she'd suddenly lost her appetite and excused herself.

It was when we were getting ready to leave for school that Freya got the call from Scott's brother. When he had left the night before, he'd gotten drunk well above the legal limit, but had attempted to drive home. Except, he never did make it back and instead had wrapped his car around a tree, dying on impact. Freya was traumatized, and she's not taken the locket off since. The only exception had been her wedding day and even then, it was only because it was what she was expected to do.

I don't think Oliver expected her to put it back on afterwards, but she did. Right there on the first day of their honeymoon. He thought it was morbid and I'm sure it was a big instigator in things finally ending between them. My mother used to tell Freya that it was completely natural and she had done nothing wrong, it was Oliver who needed to get over himself. Figures. Freya can never do anything wrong in my mother's rose-tinted eyes.

Staring at the locket now, in the low night light of Myah's room, I don't know how it could have possibly gotten into her backpack.

Did Freya give it to her at some point? Surely not. She never took it off, why would she suddenly decide to part ways with it now. Plus, if she had purposefully given it to Myah before she upped and left, surely I would have already found it by now. I empty the kids bags out at the end of each day. I would have seen it. Myah would have told me if Auntie Freya gave her a gift. Wouldn't she?

I look over at my sleeping daughter and debate waking her to ask her why she has Auntie Freya's locket in her bag. How it got there. But I know better than to wake a snoring six-year-old late at night and it will only serve me a night of fitful sleep and tired tantrums from her and I'm too tired for that.

I push myself up from my crouch on the floor and feel the ripple of old age creeping in through my knees and shins. I resolved to ask Myah tomorrow during breakfast. It's not important, it can wait until then. I slip the locket into my dish on my side table before I shower and climb into bed. I check the clock, seeing that it's after ten and I wonder if I'm going to actually manage to sleep tonight now that I know Freya isn't in mortal danger. That it's not my responsibility to find her and comfort my mother because of my guilt of what happened before.

My eyes feel heavy as soon as I pull the cover up to my chin. Yet, sleep eludes me. Questions racing through my mind; If the locket wasn't there yesterday when I emptied the kids bags and Freya's been off gallivanting God knows where for the past week, then who could have put the locket in Myah's school bag?

Chapter 28

No One

I'm on my way back from leaving my present in the girl's backpack when I hear it over the radio. I tune into the station mid-monologue. The presenter's voice is nasally and is teetering on the edge of being grating. She speaks almost in a monotone, in that way that radio presenters often do. Like she doesn't actually care about what she's reporting to the masses.

I break. The horn of the car behind me blares and the balding man driving it gives me the finger as he overtakes me. On any other day, I would have made note of his license plate to find him later and teach him a lesson in manners that he'd never forget. Not today though. I'm too distracted by the news report. I pull the truck over, off of the road, and turn up the station. The presenter's voice comes out crackly but I can still make it out.

I try to slow the racing of my pulse by focusing on my breathing. Counting silently in my head as I listen, but my blood fizzes with panic. She wasn't supposed to have been found this soon.

1.

'Police are urging anyone who may have any knowledge about Amelia Taylor's whereabouts back in February to come forward...'

2.

'...The young woman went missing months ago as she was walking home, late at night, from work and has been treated as a missing person ever since...'

3.

'...That was, until two nights ago when her body was found in the Vicory Canal...'

4.

'...Police have confirmed that found evidence points towards her being restrained and held against her will, possibly for months, since she went missing...'

5.6.'...The lead on the case, Detective Jennings, has confirmed that due to the suspicious circumstances surrounding Amelia's Case...'

7.8.'...and the findings of the autopsy, her death is officially being treated as homicide.'

9. 10.

The panic spills over and I pound my fists against the steering wheel until the skin burns. I grip it, my nails piercing the wheel's leather and I can hear my mother's voice spitting its venom in my head. *Stupid boy. You messed it up. You mess everything up. You couldn't protect me or yourself because you're weak and now the world's going to see just how weak you really are.* I scream out into the silence of the truck. Cutting my mother's Taunts short in my head. The sound vibrating in the tin can like interior of the truck, sounding almost inhuman.

I breathe deep until I regain my composure. I decide that I'll worry about this later. My practice on that woman months ago shouldn't deter me from my finale. From enjoying every last sweet sip of it.

I breathe out the frustration, restarting the car and pulling back into the main midday traffic. Silently replying to my mother inside my head, like I always do.

We'll just see about that.

Chapter 29

Ellie

I wake to the feel of tiny hands patting me heavily, complaints of hunger, and demands for pancakes. My throat's rough and dry and as I roll over, the late morning summer sun blinds me from the open curtains. I pinch my eyes shut, waiting for the blobs of color on the backs of my eyelids to subside before I risk opening them again. I squint against the blinding light and am met by Myah's pouting face. 'It's late, Mom.' Matty mumbles from the doorway, rolling his eyes. I glance at him and meet his gaze, shocked at the sudden switch.

He's never called me Mom before. Ever since he uttered his first word, he's called me Mommy. I realise as I look at his soft eyes and dark hair, that he's growing up too fast and I want to freeze this moment in time. Stop the transition that's about to happen from my sweet little mommy's boy to the moody teenager he'll one day become. 'How late?' I croak, pushing myself up onto my elbows and peering over at the alarm clock on my side table.

Did I set it last night? I'm suddenly wide awake. The numbers 08:40 staring me in the face. Jesus Christ, they're right. It really is late and they're going to be late for school. I can already picture the judgemental glares from the teachers. I fling back the bed covers and move faster than I have in the last week.

It's 09:30 by the time I'm parked at the bottom of the school steps. I hurry them in through the main reception, the kids entrance now firmly shut and secured, with repetitive apologies. I try to ignore the judgemental grumbles and frowns from the school receptionists, their faces looking startled at the creased mess of the kids' clothes and unbrushed hair. I only had time to either make them look pretty, or feed them. I chose to risk the school's image rather than the starvation of my offspring. *So, sue me!*

It's only when I'm back in the car, my clothes sticking to me in the heat, that I remember I forgot to ask Myah about the locket. I make a mental note to bring it up at pick up. I take a moment to pull my sweaty hair up into a high ponytail, luxuriating in the brief respite of a draft on the back of my neck, when the loud shrill tone of my phone blares from the car's speakers. I berate myself for forgetting that it's connected to the hands free as adrenaline sharply spikes my fingertips. Anxiety flows freely through me when I see Elaine's name flashing on my phone. A big ringing threat. I know I need to answer. I know I need to get back to work and I think today is as good of a day as it will ever be. At least I've actually slept a decent amount of hours last night. I take a deep breath, rehearsing my apologies in my head, and swipe the call to answer. Elaine's sharp bite of a voice fills the car from the still connected hands free speakers.

'Ellie. Hello!? Are you there!?'

'Hey Elaine. Yeah, I'm here. Listen-' I start to apologise, the anxiety thumping in my ears.

'No, Ellie. *You* listen.' She cuts me off and I swallow the urge to cry, tears prickling in the corners of my eyes. I refuse to let her spite crack me at my already frayed edges. 'You don't turn up to your tutoring sessions, send me some cryptic text message about a family emergency. No explanation. You just ask me to reassign your students for a few days. Now it's been a week and you haven't contacted me. You've been screening my calls. Haven't bothered to respond to any of my messages or voicemails. Haven't told me what the hell you plan on doing.' She takes a tactical deep breath to help her continue her rant. I try to take advantage of it and go to speak but am spoken over, 'So, when exactly were you planning on telling me what's going on? Are you coming back to work? When?' The silence hangs for a few moments whilst I try to keep the tremble out of my voice. Try as I might though, my voice still comes out a feeble squeak.

'It's all sorted now. I can do my sessions this afternoon.' I mumble. There's no point in telling her what happened because women like her just don't care. I bite my tongue instead, reminding myself how much higher than minimum wage my salary is in this job and apologise. 'I'm sorry for being so unreliable. My clients, have they been...' I don't get to finish as she starts speaking over me again.

'The Johnston's have decided to go elsewhere for Anastasia's education. A loss I'm sure we'll both feel considering the connections the Johnston's have.' She pauses for another moment and I swear I can almost hear her hiss at me like a feral cat in the interim. 'I hope whatever apparent week-long emergency you had was worth it. You're on the ropes with the rest of the families' whose sessions you've missed so be sure to grovel next week.

The Harrisons will be expecting you at ten for Bartholomew's session. Oh and lucky for you I've managed to find you a new tutee to replace Anastasia. I've sent the details to your work email. Your first session is scheduled for three. Do *not* be late.' The disconnect tone bleeps as she hangs up on me.

How the hell am I going to manage a three o'clock session and school pick-up? I feel overwhelmed. Like all of the energy from my restful night has evaporated with Elaine's voice. I don't feel at all ready for a new tutee session, never mind the other children scheduled for this morning.

I text Tilly practically begging her to pick the kids up for me. As much as I hate Freya, I have to admit that I feel her absence acutely, like an annoying hair you can't quite grasp when it's tickling your face. I did rely on her for the kids pickups on the days my sessions ran late. The only non-selfish thing she's ever been willing to do because even though we don't get on, she does adore her niece and nephew. Now though, I guess, I'll have to think of an alternative. I check my appearance in my small compact and try to cover some of the dark circles with concealer. I negotiate with a higher power that I don't look as horrific as I think I do.

I can almost hear the higher power laugh in my ear as I pull out and head towards the Harrison's house a half hour drive away. I feel resentment gnaw when I realise that Elaine must have expected me to come back today no matter what since she already has new tutees lined up.

I'm almost at my destination when Tilly's reply pings through the speakers, assuring me that she can pick the kids up. I thank whatever higher power there may be, that I don't have to ask my mother.

My stomach is painfully empty by the time I finish my one o'clock session. I didn't have time to stop off and get anything between Bart's and Harry's sessions and I feel woozy with hunger now. I open up my emails before I pull out of the Smith's large five car drive to find Elaine's email with my new tutee's information. I need to know where they're based before I can contemplate and plan out lunch. I ignore the consistent emails from Elaine over the last week, pulling them over to the deleted folder without opening them. The first lines give me enough information to know that every single one is her asking where I am and when I'm planning on coming back. Each email is more furious than the last. She's even forwarded some of the parents' direct complaints and concerns about my abilities and capacity as a teacher. Betrayal sticks in my throat like a bubble. Some of them, I'm not surprised by but there are a few who I thought I'd made friendly working relationships with, bordering on out of bounds friendships even. Yet, there they are, calling me incapable and unprofessional.

I try to swallow the betrayal bubble, reaching the email with my new tutee's info. I pull it up and scan the information.Laurie Parkett. Fifteen and a solid B student in all subjects except for English where she is sitting waveringly at a low C. Her parents want someone to help her improve in all subjects with a focus on English to try and achieve a straight A report card by the time her GCSE's begin next year. I feel for the girl. Achieving a B grade is an achievement in itself but for these higher-class parents, nothing's ever enough. You could get complete

A's in almost all subjects with some of these parents and they would still gripe and barb over the one C grade you got. Even if that subject happens to be an elective.

I read through the rest of the information about Laurie's very full schedule of school and extracurriculars. Leaving only three hours a week free for tutoring sessions. I decide to work out the logistics of days and hours after we've had an initial consultation and head to the demographic information so I can plan out my route. The blood drains from my head but somehow I can still hear it drumming through my ears. My heart rate pounds so hard I can feel it against my hand when I grip my tightening chest. The edges of my vision begin to blacken and it spreads across my vision, threatening to overtake me. The panic attack takes over quickly and with vengeance and I have to open the car door to get some air. I gulp in the humid early afternoon warmth and I stumble from the car, trying to concentrate on my breathing and clenching my teeth, wishing the attack would let up. I can feel the smoke from raging flames infiltrating the back of my throat and making my eyes sting and water but I know it's not real. I know I'm not back there. In that house. In the fire. But it feels as if I'm there all over again.

Eventually, the panic slowly subsides and I breathe in large gulps of air. My muscles release from the tension and my heart rate slows to almost normal, if still a little elevated. Once I can see normally and breathe again without hiccupping, I get back into the car.

I debate calling Elaine and telling her that she needs to reassign Laurie Parkett. That I am not able to take on this particular tutee but even thinking of it, I can hear her voice. Elaine does not need me. She has plenty of decent tutors in her private company now. I may have been the first one to join when her start up was small and unknown, only a handful of middle class families on the roster. The hours were long and the pay small but now it's grown. It's large and prestigious now with many tutors on the payroll. She won't hesitate to fire me now and considering the liberties I've already taken this week, I have no choice but to suck it up. I put the car in reverse and wonder how the hell I'm going to manage this. I couldn't even look at the address without going into a full blown attack.

How am I going to go back there? Back home? Back to the house I grew up in? Back to the house I nearly died in? Back to the house my father *did* die in?

I guess I'm about to find out. Because Laurie Parkett and her family are living in our old house.

Chapter 30

Detective Dawson

I can't get Amelia's face out of my head. The blue tinge in her lips and pallor of her skin. I can't help but feel like it's my fault. I failed her. I let her down. I should have been looking harder. Now I'm here, walking down the cold corridors of the station's basement where the morgue sits with Amelia's parents trailing behind me.

They're clinging to each other like any sudden movement might actually shatter them to tiny pieces on the worn tiled floor. Mrs Taylor hasn't stopped sobbing since she opened her front door and saw me standing there. I guess it was written all over my stoic face because she crumpled to the floor in a wailing heap before I even had a chance to say it. Mr Taylor rushed to her aid and held her whilst searching my face for answers he didn't want to find.

In ten minutes, we'll share in the misery of seeing the corpse of Amelia Taylor whenever we close our eyes. Luke thought me crazy to want to go and tell the Taylor's myself. He was more than happy to leave the bad news to the homicide department but I couldn't let that happen. I had been speaking with Mrs Taylor regularly for the last few months. Usually, the conversations consisted of her begging me to look harder and me telling her I was doing everything I could but there was nothing new to follow. I wanted the news to come from me. The woman they associated with the friendly face of the department. The woman who was fighting for their little girl.

I guess now they won't associate the hope of finding Amelia with me anymore. All they'll think of when they hear my name is the image of their daughter stone cold in the basement of this building. The victim of a heinous crime this Detective couldn't save her from. I wish I could protect them from this but we need someone to officially identify her. Since she had no personal identification on her when she was plunged into the canal, this is necessary. Mrs Taylor flees from the room when Charlie pulls the white sheet back gently. She was careful to keep the markings on her body hidden as much as possible where the sheet remains. Even so, the professional stitching holding their only child together after the investigative autopsy still stands out garish and black against her white bloodless skin.

Mr Taylor and I stand silently, looking at Amelia as we try to ignore the wails of his wife filling the corridors. He's remained straight backed. Firm and brave faced as he's faced with his dead child but his eyes glisten in the harsh lights. I know that, as soon as his wife falls asleep tonight, he will be silently sobbing into a cushion on the sofa. I have to swallow the lump in my throat, ignoring the prickle of tears in my own eyes. This isn't the time or place.

'Mr Taylor,' I clear my throat, 'can you confirm that this is your daughter, Amelia Taylor?'

'Yes.' It's barely a whisper when he responds. He suddenly looks so old and worn down by life. His grey, wispy hair suddenly looks thinner, his face so furrowed I could see all of his wrinkles and pores in the light. 'I want to see it. I want to see what he did to my baby.'

'Mr Taylor, I would strongly advise against that.' Charlie speaks gently, looking to me for support.

'I agree with doctor Keenley, Mr Taylor. I think it's better if w-'

'Show me.' His voice is a hiss. Firm and demanding and It shocks me. In all of our conversations and meetings over the last six months, he's always struck me as a gentle soul. But I guess no one's a gentle soul when their only child is brutally murdered. 'I want to see what that monster did. What you lot *let* him do because you didn't look hard enough. I want to see all of it.'

Charlie shoots me another warning look, but I nod slowly. 'Show him.'

I suddenly have to fight the pricking behind my eyes even harder because he's right. We should have found her. If we did, she wouldn't have been through half of what's happened to her. Charlie pulls the sheet from the bottom end first, slowly folding it upwards, careful to still give Amelia as much modesty as possible. I involuntarily gasp at the deep purple bruises dotting her legs. I'd seen them already but the discoloration is getting worse and I'd tried so hard not to look too closely before that I didn't quite see the extent. Charlie gives me a sympathetic look and then does the same motion with the sheet from the other end of the table. I gag silently, grateful that Mr Taylor's back is to me so that he doesn't see. The burns are extensive and deep, clearly infected. The bruising over her chest is a deep blackish purple and matches the bruising on her neck from where she had ultimately met her end.

'He bleached her hair?' he asks me, stroking Amelia's now blonde hair gently. 'Why would he do that?'

'We believe that he may have wanted Amelia to look like someone else.' I say gently, trying to decide how much to say. Amelia's once naturally deep black hair has been bleached a light blonde. Her hair is damaged from the harsh chemicals which were used to make it the desired shade, it looks rough and dry, and I cringe imagining how different it must feel to Mr Taylor now than it would have done before she was taken. Or when he used to plait her hair when she was small with her whole life seemingly ahead of her. Mr Taylor's resolve breaks then, and he whimpers. He takes his daughter's hand and cries quietly. Charlie and I wait patiently, careful not to interrupt a man saying goodbye to his baby girl and careful not to break down ourselves.

I regret agreeing to do this myself. When Mr Taylor composes himself, he starts to cover his daughter gently back up. It looks like a father tucking his daughter in for a nap, only this one is eternal, and she won't be waking up and the bed is a cold hard slab. As he pulls the cover back over her feet he stops, peering at the inner side of Amelia's foot silently. I glance at Charlie, but she looks as unsure as me.

'He did this too?' Mr Taylor asks Charlie the question, pointing a shaking finger. 'Why?' Charlie takes a step closer and peers closely at what he was pointing to.

'What is it?' I crane my neck to try and see what they're looking at.

'It's a small tattoo.' Charlie tells me. 'It's fully healed. I thought it was old. Mr Taylor... did Amelia not have this tattoo when she went missing?'

'Amelia hated tattoos.' He says matter of fact. 'Needles petrified her. She would never have gotten a tattoo.' Charlie makes eye contact with me, and we're both thinking the same thing; That whoever took her has branded her with this tattoo.

'It looks like an astrology sign.' Charlie tilts her head looking more closely. 'It's not very well done but it was taken care of. No sign of tissue damage from infection. It was cleaned regularly and cared for properly. From the pigmentation of the ink, it must have been done basically as soon as she was taken. It looks like the symbol of Pisces.' Mr Taylor audibly gasps and starts to slowly back away from the table. Charlie looks at me meaningfully. 'Amelia's date of birth is April twelfth. Her astrology sign is Aries.' She mumbles. 'Not Pisces.'

Chapter 31

Ellie

I don't know what I expected. Windows cracked? The house alight and bursting with flames? Paint peeling against the heat? Clouds of thick black smoke curling up into the air? The dark black ash of the singed panelling and the wide gaping hole where the roof has fallen in?

I guess I expected it to look exactly as it had the last time we went there. After the fact, when my father's body had been pulled out by the firefighters and police officers that had worked beside him during his long-standing career. Their hearts ripped open almost as much as ours as they walked through the rubble to find him. It was a burnt-out, blackened carcass then. There was nothing left. The fire had raged hot and high and wiped out any semblance of our former lives.

As we all stood there, taking in the fires aftermath, I remember thinking it was almost poetic. Like a physical symbol which reflected how we all felt. The house, much like all of us, was never going to be the same again. We were all going to be scarred and damaged, pieces were going to be missing which could never be replaced. The largest piece being my father who would never check the locks before we went to bed or make sure the porch light was on if I worked the late shift at the movie theatre again. I remember laughing; a spluttering, loud sound when the black body bag containing my father was carried out and onto the back of an ambulance. Or at least, the body bag with the only part of my father they could find amongst the rubble and ash: his charred skull and part of his right arm. They only knew it was him because of a metal plate screwed into the tibia bone – a shoot-out injury from a bank robbery case.

My mother had shot me a horrified look when my laugh had rung out in the solemn silence, Freya glaring at me with equal measures of disgust and hatred. But the irony of his body being taken away in an ambulance had struck me as odd and amusing. You never really thought about how stupid that was in movies, when a person's body would be taken away by a vehicle meant to preserve and save a life. It felt unnatural for them to take him quietly back to the hospital to officially declare him dead. Even though the body-bag should be a clear enough indication.

We'd gone back days after to see if anything could be salvaged. We stood on the path in silence, all of us smelling of musty second hand clothes and sofa surfing. We were all still badly bruised and burnt, inside and out. Our lungs were still coughing up black smoke as we all tried to recover. I remember scrubbing myself furiously for days but never quite managing to extinguish the smokey smell of the fire from my pores and my hair.

We walked slowly through the rubble. Our bodies anchored down by grief, my feet felt heavier because of my guilt. My mother moved through the wrecked carcass of the house sobbing quietly. Freya sobbed loudly. I walked through in silence with shame filling every pore. Every crunch of gravel or trip over a brick had me wanting to run and never look back.

We found next to nothing salvageable. It was all burnt beyond recognition. My mother had managed to find the only thing within the whole sad state of the house which wasn't burnt to ash, one half of a singed photograph of the four of us. It was burnt and brown at the edges and I'd been completely burnt out. Leaving my family how it always should have been, just my mother, father and twin. She kept it framed on the mantelpiece from then on. A constant reminder to me that I was as meaningless to my mother as our home was to the fire that ravaged it. Except, I didn't need a photograph to remind me of that.

I guess it makes sense it wouldn't be like that now. Yet, as I stare at the house from my car window, I still can't quite make my brain process what my eyes are telling it. Every time I blink I can see the red hot flames, feel the heat of them on my face and my armpits start to sweat. I have to hold my breath and remind myself there's no smoke now. I blink the images away angrily, not wanting that one night to define my whole life. But who am I kidding? It did define me. It defined us all and it was my fault. It will always be my fault. It feels like poetic justice that I would be forced to come back here and walk through the newly built home where a different family now lives.

The house has been rebuilt in a modern image. All sharp edges and monochrome colours. But, you can see it still has the layout of the original house. The garden has been laid with Astro turf, it's bright and green and hurts my eyes when I look at it. The path is cobbled and leads up to a large black porch with one of those stereotypical porch swings. The house stands monstrously tall compared to the Gardener's and Caldicott's on either side. Their houses look the same as they always did. Quaint and well kept. I stare at each of them in turn, still bitter that the elderly couples on either side of us never heard the screams. Never sensed that something was amiss with the family who lived next door.

The Gardeners had always been nosey. The type of neighbours who peer over your hedges and send 'anonymous' notes through the letterbox about the grass lengths and the late night noises of the televisions. Yet, on the night it really mattered, they didn't hear us; Not the cries, the screams, the shouting. They didn't even smell the gasoline, the smoke. It was only when the sirens wailed to a stop, the three of us crying in a trembling heap on the curb, that the Gardener's and the Caldicott's finally came outside to see what all the fuss was about. I wonder if either of them are still there, still alive. Whether they still use the most horrific night of my family's lives as a conversation starter at the monthly mixer. Discuss why it happened, who is to blame and debate over how my father, the Chief of police, did not see it coming. As if it affected them. As if it was their place to discuss it. I internally berate myself. I need to stop letting that night rule my life. I need to approach this like any other tutee. It's a whole new house, freshly built. There are no ghosts here. Not if I don't let them be.

I take a deep breath and ring the bell. It's an unfamiliar, shrill tone. Nothing like ours used to be. It serves as a further reminder that this is not the home I once knew. It may stand in its place, but there is nothing that remains of my former life. It takes what feels like an age for a petite woman to answer the door.

She's middle aged, the first signs of old age creasing at the corners of her eyes. Her blonde hair is held tightly in a bun atop her head and she's wearing a polo shirt and bright white trousers which make my eyes hurt as much as the fake grass. She's barefoot and looks like she's trying to give the appearance of someone who is having a restful day at home when in reality, it probably took her hours this morning to make herself look so "effortlessly" good. I paste what I hope is a warm, open smile on my face and pray It doesn't look as constipated and strained as it feels.

'Good morning. I'm Ellie, the tutor you hired through Ivy Education.'

'Oh, my goodness!' She laughs and I wonder what the joke is. 'I completely forgot! *So* sorry. I'm Laurie's mom, Grace. Please, come in.' She takes a step back and opens the door and I hold my breath as I pass the threshold. It's brighter here now. There are so many windows, it's a miracle the house stays standing. The walls of the hallway are painted a pale yellow and the carpet lining the large staircase looks like you could sleep on it. I hold my breath as I follow her through the hall. I find myself making a firm effort not to look too closely at anything.

The house has been rebuilt in the original layout. Stairs to the left, living room the first room on the right, the dining room after that with a large alcove joining it to the kitchen at the far end. Even though the layout is a copy – paste of ours, that's where the similarities to my childhood end. The rooms are slightly bigger and are a lot lighter and airy. Pale pastels, whites and creams give the house a homely feel which we never had as children. My mother was always adamant that the house should be glistening and constantly ready for visitors. She used to rattle on about how we needed to make an impression because of how important my father was. Sometimes, I think her obsessive cleaning was just a way to fill her long, boring days of being a lonely housewife. The house is tidy but clearly well-lived in. Discarded jackets and empty cups on the counters, half used candles and dust lining the skirting boards. Tears sting the backs of my eyes and I try to ignore the dull ache in my chest. It's so much more like a home now than it ever was when we lived here that it makes me feel hallow. Lonely.

'The agency said you come highly recommended.' She smiles cheerily, clearly oblivious to my discomfort in her home. She gestures to the breakfast nook in the corner of the kitchen. The table's cluttered with letters and the type of discarded junk that normally accumulates on a kitchen table. She apologises repeatedly as she clears it away, regardless of my continuous reassurances that I really don't mind. 'They said you've managed to get nearly thirty students' grades increased by a minimum of thirty percent. That's impressive!' She beams as she points to the kettle questioningly. I feel myself blush as I accept her offer for tea.

'I suppose on paper that's true.' I try my hardest to make my smile look sincere and not like I'm on the verge of a panic attack. It proves difficult though, since I am. 'But really it's the children. I find most kids don't realise what they're truly capable of. I just help them to recognise it, find easier ways around problems and help them come up with a way which works for them.

I helped a former student improve in English by encouraging his love for writing short, fictional stories about aliens. I focused quite a few of our sessions on that before we started working on his school syllabus. His parents were dubious at first; Didn't see how it was going to help. He's at Harvard now and well on his way to becoming editor of the school paper.' I sip my tea to stop myself from rambling anymore. I realise I've been spewing on and on so much that she's had time to make me a cup of tea and pass it to me without me so much as taking a breath. 'Sorry. I'm rambling' I blush redder.

'No, no. That's amazing.' She beams. 'Well, Laurie is doing extremely well at the moment, her teachers say it's looking promising...' *Here it comes, but...she's just not good enough.* The muscles around my mouth strain from the effort of trying to keep the disdain from my features. '...but she doesn't feel that way, unfortunately. I've tried to explain to her that it doesn't matter. Ivy league or not, she's still my smart cookie. That her worth isn't purely the sum of her academic achievements.' She sighs.

I feel guilt eat away at the disdain. I had just assumed the worst. I was so convinced that Grace was cut from the same cloth as my own mother. I'd just assumed the tutoring was her idea, that she was pushing her daughter to breaking point. 'There's so much pressure these days from academics. These institutions forget that these kids are just that...kids.' I smile empathetically.

'Exactly.' She blows out a breath as if she's been holding all the tension in her lungs. 'She'll be home from netball any moment now. Something else I've tried to talk her out of doing. I've told her so many times she needs to rest too but she loves Netball. In fact, I think it's the only afterschool activity she actually wants to be at.' She laughs affectionately and I feel myself joining in, the tension of being back here I'd felt so strongly two minutes ago suddenly diluted. I almost forget I'm even in a house built on the tainted soil of my childhood. Almost. A couple of hours later, Grace is sees me to the door and says goodbye to me like we're old friends and it almost feels as if we are. Her and Laurie are such lovely people, and their relationship is one I hope I'm currently cultivating with my own children.

We spend the entire time talking about Laurie and her strengths and weaknesses. How she likes school and her friends. Grace even confided in me that Laurie's father isn't around much. She'd looked sad when she told me that they're still married and very much in love but that his job means he works late and oftentimes spends weeks across the country. I turn as she sees me to the door,

'I won't charge you for today's session. Call it a consultation, to see if the fit between Laurie and me seems right. She's a lovely girl, I'm more than happy to become her official tutor if that is what you both wish.'

'Oh, definitely.' She nods so enthusiastically I'm convinced her head is going to snap off her shoulders. 'Stroke of pure luck that that flyer was shoved through the letterbox, a clear violation of my "no flyers or leaflets" door sticker.' She chuckles jokingly but abruptly stops when she sees all the blood drain from my face.

'Sorry.' I swallow, my throat suddenly dry and croaky. 'You said you got a flyer?'

Ivy Education doesn't do flyers. It's one thing Elaine is adamant about. She says flyers are a waste of money, paper and ink which people throw out as soon as it's floated to their doormat. She prefers the undeniable word of mouth with a bit of social media coverage and online forums which have done wonders for the company's image and income.

'Yes.' Grace looks wary of my sudden change in mood. 'It came through the door a few days ago. It had all the information on. Even your name and a couple of others on the back with reviews from previous tutees. I was going to throw it straight out but Laurie saw it and well.. you've seen how adamant she is to get the best grades possible. She practically begged her father.'

'Do you still have it, the flyer? Could I take a look?' My head and stomach are suddenly swimming with the same anxiety I felt when I first read the address on the file.

'I think so.' Grace shrugs and starts rummaging through the hall console table, tutting at all of the fast-food restaurant menus. She's muttering something about clearing this thing out when she finds it and hands it over.It's quite small.

The paper's glossy and saturated with information. It has the Ivy Education logo and slogan along the top in fancy italic writing and lists the average grades and percentages of improvement which we advertise on the site. It has the company's phone number and email address along the bottom but doesn't look like anything Elaine would create. It's plain and lacklustre. Plain white with black writing. The type of flyer Elaine would scoff at. She would say it doesn't even grab the eye, so why bother spending all that money on getting it printed. Might as well just do a Facebook post, it's quicker and easier. That's what she would have said if someone presented her with this flyer and I suddenly feel even more nauseous. 'The reviews are on the back.' Grace nods encouragingly. I flip the leaflet over with shaking hands.

My name is the largest and is bold and centralised. There's a fake quote from a tutee called "Eugene" who I have definitely never tutored before. I scan over the other names and quotes and the corners of my vision blackens. The only other tutors mentioned are brand new, with much smaller success rates than mine and all of their names and figures are much smaller and not as easily readable. It's almost as if they're just there to fill the space and make me look better.

'Bit strange really,' Grace shrugs, clearly not understanding the gravity of the current situation. 'Bernadette up the road, her son is failing science and mathematics to a concerning degree but when I brought up the company and suggested she use the flyers that were put through, she had no idea what I was on about. No other mom's on the road seem to have gotten one either during the PTA meeting last week. It's as if ours was the only house it was posted through. I guess we're just lucky that we got the last copy and here you are, how perfect!' she smiles.

Somebody wanted me here. At this address. In this house. The house which took the place of the one which nearly killed my entire family.

But why? Who?

Chapter 32

Detective Dawson

'If I have to read one more article or forum post which blames a person's actions on the phase of the moon or the fact that something or other is in retrograde this week, I'm going to pluck both my eyeballs out with tweezers, Mollie. *Tweezers.*' Luke groans dramatically. I laugh in spite of my current state of mind.

'Listen,' I hold my hand to my chest in mock hurt, 'the last new moon was awful for me because Saturn was being a complete and utter shit.' We both splutter into bouts of laughter.

I look over at him, both of us still giggling, and feel warmth towards him that wasn't there a few months ago but has gradually been growing over time. Despite the fact that Amelia's case is no longer ours, he's still here. Well past when his shift was due to end. Well past when the dayshift packed up and left and was overtaken by the night shift. I've been buried so deep in the old files, it was like a blink. All of a sudden, I looked up and it wasn't Sonja from day shift vice in front of me, but Terry from nights. It amazes me that Luke humours me like this.

Stays and joins me in my obsessive need for answers. As soon as the case became a murder investigation and we finished handing over our investigation report, it was no longer our prerogative or responsibility to figure out what happened to Amelia Taylor. Yet here he is, helping me. Looking through mountains of files and past homicide reports. Trying to find any tangible mention of horoscopes. Anything that could help. When we can't even claim overtime for the five hours we've been here, hunched over these files. I know I should be letting it go. Should be leaving it to the highly capable and revered homicide Detectives. It's not as if I have any right to be investigating something so outside my purview. My knowledge of homicide investigating is limited to what we were taught during the academy. Yet, I can't let it go. I can't get it out of my head. I have so many questions. My head spins and aches with the gravity of it all.

'Judging by those eyebrows Lorell, I don't think you've ever handled a pair of tweezers before, mate.' I wiggle my eyebrows at him, and we both fall into fits of laughter again and it feels good to ease the tension. To take a moment away from the weight of the situation and remember were allowed to have fun.

'Seriously though, who believes this shit?' He breathes out, shaking his head.

'Whoever murdered our girl it would seem.' I sigh. The image of Amelia's bruised body flickering past my vision.

'Question.' Luke holds his finger up as if he's my student. If he were my student though, he would've waited for me to call on him before he carried on. 'If our perpetrator believed in all this crap, wouldn't there be more signs of it? Ritual style markings, stuff like that. But Amelia Taylor only had that one small tattoo. What if it has nothing to do with astrology or moon phases or whatever?' He holds up a few files for effect. 'All of the crimes I've sifted through so far, have at least *something* which suggests ritualistic crimes. Our girl, nothing but that one tattoo.'

'So, what? You don't think it has anything at all to do with the star sign? But then why bother putting it there at all?' I compulsively pull the lid of my pen off and on, trying to make sense of what else it could mean. My brain circles around something I can't quite put my finger on. Frustration and confusion congeal. Coffee. I need coffee.

'I don't know,' Luke groans. 'I just... it seems strange to me. I just can't put my finger on it. I need glucose.' He makes a b-line for the kitchen.

'Coffee please!' I shout after him.

I'm reading through a report of domestic abuse turned suicide where the victim had been marked with astrology symbols burned all over her waist and hips. She'd said her husband, who had been high on LSD at the time, had explained to her that it was because their love was, quote, "written in the stars." When my phone rings, I frown at the caller ID and shove the cell between my ear and shoulder, still skimming the end notes of the awful criminal file.

'Detective Dawson.' I yawn into the phone, pushing the file away. Not our guy. The case was an isolated domestic incident involving substance abuse; no other charges or similar victims.

'I think there's something seriously wrong going on.' The voice on the other end trembles.

'Miss Dolloway? Is that you?'

'Yes.' Ellie replies. She sounds like she's crying, and I press the phone tighter against my ear. 'Someone's out to get us. They're sending me things. Signs. I think something's seriously wrong. Freya might be in danger.' I try not to sigh audibly.

'Miss Dolloway, we established there is no concern for your sister's wellbeing. She has chosen to leave of her own volition. Has something happened which makes you feel that is incorrect? Have you heard from Freya?'

'No, I haven't heard from her. It's not that but there's been *things* happening. They sent me her locket. There was a Dahlia. Someone made a fake leaflet so that the family living in our old house would hire me. Do you understand? Someone's doing these things *on purpose,* and it only started when Freya went missing.' She can hardly get the words out before she's overlaying them with more. Rambling, desperate. My head spins and I try to take in all the information but none of it makes much sense and I'm sure this is just the result of extreme stress.

'I'm sorry Miss Dolloway but none of this is making much sense.' Luke's come back from the kitchen with no coffee in sight and is trying to understand the conversation mid-way through. 'Who exactly is "they"?' I ask.

'I don't know.' The desperation and despair in her voice has me feeling sorry for her and I know I shouldn't do this, especially since we're now off the clock, but I find myself telling her we'll be there in half an hour.

The silence in the car ride over to her house is stoney. Luke tuts at me and huffs the whole way, wanting to make his displeasure at having to drive half an hour out of the city into the suburbs clear.

'Listen, we were working anyway. We needed a break from all the paper. What's the harm in going out to see what all the fuss is about?' I nudge Luke's arm as I ring Ellie's doorbell and get a grumbled response in return.

She looks dishevelled. As if she's still spiralling. Even though she's heard from Freya. Her hair looks tangled, and her face is red and tear stained. She's tried to cover the dark circles under her eyes from lack of sleep, but she's cried all the concealer off. Her hands are shaking and she's jittery, her eyes scanning the street behind us nervously.

'Did you see anyone?' she whispers. 'I don't know if they're out there.' I glance over my shoulder and try to see what she's looking for, but the street's quiet. The only people around are a couple of joggers and one dog walker, who barely glances in our direction. She's clearly paranoid.

'Shall we go inside?' Luke uses his soft voice. The one which always works. I squash the pang of jealousy again that he has such a way with women. Her eyes take one more sweep of the street before retreating into the house.

We follow her through to the living room and sit quietly on the sofa. She doesn't sit, she paces the floor quickly, stopping every now and then to glance behind the drawn curtains. I'm about to ask her to sit down and breathe when I hear a high-pitched childish laugh from upstairs. I glance at the clock. It's 23:00 PM on a Tuesday. I don't have kids myself but I'm almost ninety nine percent sure it's not some sort of school holiday. She sees me eyeing the stairs questioningly.

'I couldn't get either of them to go to sleep and there's no way they're going to school tomorrow so it doesn't matter that they're up so late, anyway. They can sleep in late if need be.' Her voice is defensive, challenging me to question her parenting skills so she can bark and bite. When I don't comment, she carries on. 'Someone got to her. Got to my Myah. Put that goddamn locket in her backpack. I'm sure of it.'

'Slow down, Miss Dolloway.'

'Please, stop calling me that.' She snaps and then apologises just as quickly for the sharp tone.

'Apologies, Ellie.' Luke walks across the large living room in two long strides and takes Ellie's hands, slowly guiding her towards the sofa on the other side of the room. He sits her down and then takes the seat next to her. 'But please, slow down. We're trying to understand what's happening and why you're so upset.'

'I'm sorry.' Ellie starts crying then. Not loud, ugly crying but quiet and reserved. She wipes the tears as quickly as she can. I get the impression she's not a woman who cries often. Or at least, not a woman comfortable with others knowing she's upset.

'You mentioned someone got to the children,' I encourage her. 'Did one of the teachers tell you about something which may have happened?'

'Nothing like that.' She sniffs. 'But, I know there's someone watching them. They got close enough to Myah to put that goddamn locket in her backpack.'

'What locket?' Luke takes out his pocketbook and flicks to a clean page and I resist the urge to do the same. I don't want her to feel like she's being interrogated.

'Freya's locket. She never took it off. Ever since her childhood sweetheart gave it to her, she's worn it. I haven't seen her without it in almost a decade.'

'You found a locket in Myah's school bag which holds resemblance to this locket?'

'Not a resemblance. It is the locket. The exact same one. It has the same engraving, the same slight nick in the side.' She pulls a small silver heart shaped locket from her jeans pocket and passes it to me to look at. Sure enough, the locket does have a very slight dent in its side. So small, you wouldn't even see it unless you were looking.

'Did the children spend a lot of time with their Aunt?' Luke asks gently but I can hear the edge behind it. He doesn't think we should be here

'Yes. They have a very good relationship.'

'So, it's possible that Freya may have gifted her old locket, a memento which meant a lot to her, to her niece who she was very close with before she planned to leave?'

'Absolutely not.' There it is. She's closed down. After so many years working in the police you learn to see it. The precise moment when you lose a suspect or a witness. The moment you cross the line between the friendly Detective there to help and the enemy there to poke holes in their stories. 'There is no way Freya would have parted with this necklace willingly. It was like... like a limb to her. Even when she moved on, married, she still refused to take that goddamn necklace off.'

'She never removed it to have it cleaned? When she was swimming? When she was sleeping?'

'No. The only time she has ever removed it was her wedding day. One singular day.'

'So if Freya never gifted the locket to Myah, how do you propose it came to be in her possession? You said someone planted it there, why would someone do that, do you think?'

'I. Don't. Know.' Ellie looks at me exasperated. 'Fine. You don't believe me about the locket, that much is obvious but what about the other stuff. I assure you Detective, I am not mad.'

'Right, the other stuff.' Luke blows out a breath of irritation, flicking back a page in his notebook for effect but I think we all know it's blank. 'You mentioned a flower of some sort?'

'That's right.' Ellie nods firmly. 'Someone purposefully gave it to the kids when we went to visit my father's grave. A clear message.'

'Your father's grave? Is it not possible someone had merely brought some flowers for a lost love one and gave one to the children as a kind gesture? People usually leave flowers as signs of remembrance, do they not?' There's a moment thick with silence and Ellie's eyes glisten with fresh tears. She clearly decides not to push the issue, convinced Luke will shoot down any further suggestion she makes because she changes direction abruptly.

'The leaflet then.' Her voice is shrill again. 'Someone purposefully put a leaflet advertising my company. Me specifically, too. Through the door of the house where my father was murdered.' She stands and storms across the room, clearly irritated but still charged with adrenaline and pulls out a crumpled glossy leaflet from her handbag.

I notice she passes it specifically to me, bypassing Luke's out-stretched hand. He covers the frustration well. I read through the leaflet and pass it over to Luke. I pretend not to see the glare Ellie fixes on me. This is his show today, I'm rolling with it. He looks over the leaflet briefly, front and back, and clears his throat.

'Ellie.' He sighs. 'This doesn't really prove anything except that your company has decided to advertise its services to increase clientele.'

'That's just the thing.' She puts both her hands on her hips. In this moment, I can see teenage Ellie; Stroppy and giving her parents attitude. 'We don't advertise with leaflets. Never have. Never will. Elaine, the owner, doesn't believe in wasting the trees for something people will glance at once and then use as a coaster.'

'So, you think someone went to all this trouble to make leaflets and distribute them, just so you might end up working back at the house you grew up in? To what...prove your sister is in danger?' There's a beat and I know Ellie's resolve is starting to crack. I see it sweep across her face, if only for a moment. The doubt.

'Only that particular house had that leaflet posted through their door.'

'But this leaflet has more than just your details on. Is it not possible for the occupants to have asked for, or been assigned to any of these tutors on the leaflet?' Luke's voice has softened.

'I suppose you're right. But my name features the most.'

'A testament to you no doubt.' He smiles.

'But, why only make this one leaflet, only post it there?'

'Maybe they distributed it to multiple streets and only had one left for your old street. How would the person who created this one leaflet for the sole purpose of you returning to that house, even know they would use it? That they would seek out a tutor? Isn't it likely they wouldn't have? I think a person going to all this effort would have to have been extremely lucky for all of this to fall in place so neatly.'

She sits back down next to Luke. Her shoulders slump. I know he's finally gotten through. That she sees this for what it is; A woman missing her sister who left so abruptly and brutally from her life, she has to create specific reasons for why she would no longer want to get in touch with her. It comes out as a whisper when she speaks again and I almost miss it. She doesn't direct the question to either of us and I feel like it's more a question for herself then for us.

'But, who else would know about the Dahlias?'

Chapter 33

No One

It's like a bubble at the back of my throat. Uncomfortable and inconvenient. Serving no purpose other than to infuriate me. Because I am. I'm infuriated. My head feels fuzzy with it. How does she not see it? All of the small inconceivable tremors in the universe which have led me here, to her. These things I've left for her, like a treasure hunt of my broken heart. Which she ripped apart with her bare teeth and chewed on, only to decide it was rancid and spat it back out like it was nothing. Now, she looks as defeated as she once made me feel.

Ha. Serves you right you bitch.

She hasn't seen anything yet. As soon as I saw the Detectives leave, I had to come back here. To her. To the one I can control. I lean over her. Trail my eyes along her body and take it all in. I want to remember every last inch. Every last pore on her skin. This is my masterpiece. My legacy. I half expected her to be numb to the torture by now. To have succumbed to her injuries but she's surprised me. She's beaten the odds and she's still going. She's still fighting. Her eyes gloss over with fear and it reminds me of my mother. Of how her eyes looked so similar. Right before the light went out.

***

Seven years ago

My stomach churns and my mind races through all of the worst possible scenarios. Every time I hear a siren or switch on the news, I find myself holding my breath. Waiting. Always waiting. For someone to have found him. To make the connection between him and my mother. To find their way here and let themselves in. I imagine what it would be like. Whether I could get to the back door quick enough. Whether I would feel right leaving mother if I did. The type of man that would make me. I go to work and I'm convinced people are staring at me. That they know that creeping just below the exterior is someone who could do that to another man. Someone who is perfectly capable of mutilating the body of a dead man. Of slicing him up into small pieces to make him easier to get rid of. Who has had another man's cold and congealed blood paint his hands and matte his hair, without so much as batting an eye. Someone who spent the entire time mutilating someone's body, wishing it was his mother's.

She wept and wailed. Hit me repeatedly on the back with her tiny fists while I took him apart. Like it wasn't her who had fucking killed the man in the first place. Like it wasn't her fault we were in this mess. Every hit had me seeing red. Not just from all of the congealed blood, but because I wanted to smash her skull against the kitchen tile and tell her to shut the fuck up.

When it was done she went silent and she stayed that way. For weeks. Fifty-eight days to be exact. She didn't utter a single word to me. She spoke to the mailman, the neighbour, the fucking bible bashing idiots who came to the door. She spoke to the waste of space's bully of a son when he got home and lied effortlessly through her teeth. Wept as if she was broken hearted when she told him that he'd said he didn't love us anymore and that he left. She even told him that it didn't matter that the shit stain was gone because she loved him like he was her own, unconditionally. The betrayal burned hot and red for weeks, the injustice biting at my skin. She spoke to every single other possible person she could but she didn't speak a single word to me for months. As if in punishment for what happened. Punishing me for her own actions. She would cut her eyes at me and wail openly at unexpected intervals in my face but she would not acknowledge me when I spoke. She refused to eat the meals I made or the food I brought.

She's treated me like a living ghost and I hate her. I hate her. I hate her. That was until this morning, anyway.

This morning, she greeted me with a massive smile and half a cup of lukewarm tea when I got up. She acted as if nothing had happened. She chatted away to me like any other morning back when it was just me and her and I cried. I cried with relief and with sorrow. The tears came thick and fast. Syncing perfectly with the gurgled sobs which spread like waves through my body and out of my throat. I cried like a pathetic little baby and I hated myself for it. My step brother laughed hysterically at me. I hated her more for making me cry. For making me look weak and embarrassing me when it was her fault. It's all her fault. The anger only seemed to feed the tears until I was almost growling at myself in-between the sobs.

That was when she burnt me with the cigarette she was smoking. The laughs rolling from my step brother's mouth increased with amusement when she crushed it hard and deep into the flesh on my forearm and told me to stop crying. I realised then that it was never that deadbeat who tainted my mother and made her a monster but that she'd been this person all along. It was with my cheeks wet and the smell of my own flesh burning filling my nostrils, the hysteria of the two of them filling my ears, that I decided to kill my mother.

Chapter 34

Detective Dawson

Vada wraps herself around my legs and mews, her eyes circling the half empty tin foil pot of duck Chow Mein on the table next to me. I sigh and shoo her away, trying to focus back on the array of paper fanned out across the dining table. She bounces back, rubbing against the chair and my legs, mewing more aggressively. It's a cry which *says: I'm just going to resort to jumping paws first into that tin in a minute and then you won't have a choice but to give me some.* So, like I always do, I cave. I flick a couple of pieces of duck to the floor and carry the rest to the fridge to stretch my legs.

My phone pings and I rush back, hopeful that it will be Charlie with more information about Amelia's case but it's not. It's Nathan. My ex who, even though we broke up six months ago, I keep finding myself falling back into bed with. Regularly. We'd broken up over a casserole when we both agreed that the love just wasn't there anymore. We'd gotten together young and once I made Detective and he started his own financial company, we found that we had both grown up and sadly, apart. Yet, even though the love was clearly gone, the sexual chemistry still bubbled and we'd been using each other for stress relief for months. Lately though, the visits have become less and less and I don't find myself craving his touch much at all these days.I try to pinpoint the moment that changed as I read over his simple "tonight?" text message.

My heart palpitates with nerves as I think about another man who's been to my place. Luke. I realise how long ago it was that he came over for the first time. He stayed with me for hours. A case had overwhelmed me, and I had an all-consuming need to bring the missing person home. I feel disheartened when I realise it was Amelia's.I look over at the work on the dining room table and think that maybe I should take a break. Have some meaningless fun and decompress for a while. Then I remember the look of anxiety filling Ellie's face when we left earlier and suddenly, I can't bring myself to. I text Nathan back with my excuses and put my phone on silent before I go back to the uncomfortable dining chair.

I don't know what I'm looking for exactly. I'm half expecting the answer to just jump up off the page and scream *here I am!* Or something ridiculous like that. I didn't bother telling Luke when I dropped him home that I was planning on looking through the old Chief Dolloway case files to see if I could get any more information on the family. I made a big show of stretching and yawning and kicking him out so I could go home and rest. He didn't look convinced, but I think he was just so desperate to have a shower and nap, he didn't argue. Then I ran by the station and signed out all the old files. I planned to camp out at my desk, but my stomach had growled so loud half the office had turned to look at me. So, instead I decided to pick up Chinese and bring my obsession home with me. I've never been capable of setting healthy work, life boundaries.

I find it unfathomable how little we actually know about the Chief's case. From all of the logs, I can see that the department put in an unbelievable amount of time and resources to try and figure out who it was that had entered the Dolloway's residence that night. Yet, none of it was enough. They never found out who the guy was. What his motives were. There were speculations of course, there always are. Detective notes and theorisations are all stacked in a box about criminals the Chief had put away but were now out. Personal enemies of which there were very little outside the confines of the law. There were links to a number of local break ins leading up to that fateful night, but all avenues were dead ends. So, disappointingly, the Chief's murder remains a mystery. A cold case which is so cold it's almost frozen. I skim over the investigation summary and crime scene photographs again, my eyes stinging from the effort, another sign I need to take a break.

The house burned to rubble and ash so most of our knowledge of what happened that night came from the eyewitness testimonies from Kathrine, Freya and Ellie Dolloway. Mrs Kathrine Dolloway had explained that she was woken in the early hours of Friday morning on the twenty ninth of October almost eight years ago by the sound of her husband, Chief Dolloway, inputting the pin into his bedroom safe and retrieving his gun. She said that he had told her that he heard breaking glass downstairs and someone moving around. He told her to stay put and call the police before he crept out to confront the intruder. Kathrine had started unlocking her phone when a strangled cry came from the direction of her daughter, Freya Dolloway's room. She described how motherly instinct had taken over and she had abandoned her phone, not having dialled the police yet, and ran to her daughter's aid.

At this point, she claims that she was so focused on making sure that her daughter was safe, she didn't notice the smell of gasoline in the air.

What she had found when she ran in was Freya face down on the floor, pinned there by the weight of a man in a balaclava kneeling on her back. He had pulled the cable ties holding her wrists tight as Kathrine had run in and then swung around, pointing the butt of a gun at her. He told her if she made a sound, he'd kill Freya. To protect her daughter's life, Kathrine Dolloway had surrendered to the intruder's will. The intruder had them both tied by the wrists and ankles, sat upright and was kneeling behind them when Chief Dolloway came back upstairs.

He had pressed his gun against the base of Freya's skull and told her mother if she tried to warn him, he would sever her daughter's spinal cord with a bullet. Similarly, he had told Freya that if she tried to move or warn her father, he would kill her first but then her mother and father would follow. They all sat there silently, eyes trained on the back of the bedroom door, listening to the Chief walking back upstairs. He had gone back to his and Kathrine's room first but when he found the bed empty, he had called out and started looking. Kathrine and Freya had both stayed silent, the only sounds were theirs and the intruder's frantic breathing and the sound of her husband searching for her. When the Chief had reached Freya's room in his search and pushed the door open, gently at first to try and avoid waking what he thought would be his sleeping daughter, he had assessed the situation in three seconds.

The light from the hallway spilling through the door was just enough to light up the section of the floor his wife, daughter and the man holding them hostage were knelt. He had raised his gun immediately, announcing himself as police but that didn't matter when the intruder had the upper hand. He had two hostages and a gun; the Chief only had his gun and experience. His experience told him that whilst he may be able to save one of them, take out the man, the gun pressed against his daughter's head would definitely go off before he managed it. So he had surrendered, dropping his gun and kicking it to the man across the floor. Leaving all three of them to the mercy of the mad man who had entered their home.

Kathrine explained that he had then forced them all downstairs, using the threat of his gun to control them. At this point, they could see and smell the gas which seemed to cover every surface and they were so scarred that the spark of the bulet would set alight their home, that they'd remained compliant. Kathrine recalled how he had beaten the Chief unconscious in front of them and every time they made a noise; he would threaten to shoot him dead. Once the Chief was incapacitated, he had reiterated his earlier threats that if they tried anything, they would all die one by one and had then gone back upstairs to get Ellie. The only Dolloway who, at that point, was still sound asleep in her bed and oblivious to the violence downstairs.

Then, the testimonies get vague and strike me as weak from an investigative point of view. That's what I'm finding difficult to wrap my head around. The testimonies up until this point are all detailed, specific. Almost too specific. But as soon as Ellie joined the mix, the testimonies thin out. It's entirely possible that it may just be a trauma response. From the little they did share, the violence seemed to increase from that point on. There was no doubt the intruder was malicious, sadistic, and got off on playing the family members off of one another. Emotionally abusing them and threatening to kill the others whilst being physically violent. So, it wouldn't surprise me if their minds had blocked out the finer details in an effort to keep their sanity intact and some sense of control. But it's the similarity which strikes me.

The testimonies were almost exactly the same. They seemed re-hearsed even. Kathrine, Freya, and Ellie had described the assaults, the threats and the violence in the exact same manner. The same order.

They all described how the Chief had gotten loose, having used a sharp piece of glass from the broken window the intruder had used to gain entry to the house to cut his ties. He had stabbed the intruder in his thigh and had broken his wife free whilst the man was howling on the floor from his wound. His wife was the only one he managed to break free before the intruder had launched himself on him from behind. They had started fighting. They rolled around on the floor and threw each other into furniture. The intruder had shot the Chief in the shoulder but he had kept going, screaming to his wife to get their children and unborn grandchildren out of there. It was as Kathrine was breaking her children free that the second bullet that went flying had sparked the gasoline soaked into the living room carpet and set alight in a huge blaze of orange and red.

The fire had spread thick and fast because of the amount of gas saturated across the house but Kathrine had managed to break her two daughters free, even in the blaze and thick smoke and they all made it outside. The neighbour had reported in her witness statement that she had seen the flames through her bathroom window when she got up to go to the bathroom in the middle of the night. When she'd come outside, she said that the three Dolloway women were sat silently on the grass of their front lawn, watching it blaze. The Chief and the intruder had burnt to ash along with the house.

I don't know what it is yet. What they are all hiding. Only an instinct swilling in my gut – telling me that they are all liars.

Chapter 35

Ellie

I don't know why I'm here, standing in Freya's apartment. After the police left yesterday, I was so on edge I couldn't sit still. I'd put the kids to bed early. Too early. I had to close the curtains and doors to fake night-time. A decision I'm sure rocketed me to the top of the bad mothers list and bought me a fast-track ticket straight to hell. I just couldn't calm my mind and I knew if I spent too much time around the kids they'd notice. They're both clever and I can't let either of them know how scared I am.

Because I am. Scared. I don't feel safe unless I'm in my own home, locked behind my doors and windows. Even then, it feels like someone's watching me. From the shadows outside the house. Every slight shadow makes me feel exposed and vulnerable and if it weren't for my kids I'd be running. Far and fast. Because whoever it is that's out there, they only have bad intentions. I can feel it in my gut. I'm also convinced it's in some way linked to Freya. I find myself loathing her more and more each day. Convinced, somewhere in the back of my mind that if she had looked after herself better, kept herself safe, we somehow wouldn't all be in this mess.

The hate burned hot and fast and was starting to scorch my veins so I needed to get out. To do something. Try to keep my family safe from whoever it is out there. Because I know there's someone out there. No matter what the police say. I ignored my gut once before with disastrous consequences, and to hell if I ever do that again. I didn't know what else to do so I'd begged Tilly to come and look after the kids for a few hours. She'd agreed, the cost being a bottle of the deepest red upon my return and had been kind enough not to mention the fact the kids were in bed at 6PM when she got there. Although she did give me a look which I'm trying not to read into but I'm sure is a similar look to those I'll receive one day in hell. Now, as I stand here, trying to decide where to start in the mess that is my sister's life, I'm starting to think this is actually a complete waste of my time. But I also don't know what else to do. I feel hopeless and agitated. I've never coped with heightened stress very well and the ache that started behind my eyes a few days ago has bloomed into a full-blown migraine which is relentless no matter what I do or take to try and subdue it.

I know the Detectives think I'm overreacting and that my lack of sleep is leading to an explainable paranoia over what they deem to be insignificant and unrelated occurrences. People brushing me off isn't exactly new to me, so I don't know why I feel such abject resentment and irritation towards them for just doing their jobs. I knew as soon as they left, I needed to find something. An unquestionable piece of evidence that all is not as right as they believe it to be. So here I am, standing in Freya's chaotic place, a stack of final notice bills in front of the front door, wondering where to start. I decide to start left to right, in a clockwise search to hopefully find something that can help me, even though I know it's useless. Both me and the Detectives have already searched, and it isn't exactly a large area for three people to cover. The chances of any of us missing some vital piece of information is unlikely but I don't know where else to start. If the police aren't going to take this seriously then I'm going to have to take matters into my own hands and do the dirty work myself so that they have to protect me and my children. My phone sounds in my jeans pocket and I don't even bother to look. I already know who it is. My mother. Since Freya disappeared into thin air, her beratements and accusations have become insurmountable.

My mother's hatred for me isn't exactly a secret and I know deep down that she only humours my presence in her life because of her connection to her grandchildren but I don't think I really knew how deep rooted it lay until Freya wasn't around.

With Freya gone she has no one else to concentrate on. It's like Freya stepped out of the way of the light and now I don't have her shadow for protection against my mother's venom. So, I've decided to ignore my phone whilst I do this. If there's an emergency, Tilly will call, not text and I learnt a long time ago to give her a ringtone specific to her. To warn me before I answer the call on loudspeaker around other people or in the car with the kids.

I block out the persistent rings and notifications from my mother and focus on the task at hand, scouring through my sister's entire life for any sign of what the actual fuck is going on.

🔥

It's dark out and I'm seconds away from pulling my hair out by the time I get round to checking Freya's desk again.

I haven't found anything helpful so far. In fact, the only thing out of place I've noticed is that Freya's wardrobe looks somehow thinner and more empty then the last time I was here. I brush that confusion aside though because it's stupid.

On one hand, I didn't pay enough attention to much of the flat the last time I was here to be sure there's clothes missing now which weren't there before. On the other hand, if Freya really did willingly up and leave, it makes sense that some of her clothes would be missing. That she would have taken them with her. Right? Tilly called a while ago to say that she's going to open up a tab of bottles I owe her if I don't hurry up and relieve her of her babysitting duties soon. So, because I was rushing around to try and get out quickly and convinced there was nothing to be found, I almost missed the photographs in Freya's drawer.

There's a pile of them. Glossy black and white photographs printed on high quality paper. They shine as I pull them out. I try to remember if I saw them here last time, if I'd somehow missed them but I have no recollection. The drawer was definitely full of pens and half filled with junk. No brand-new glossy photographs in sight. I hold my breath, flicking between them and ignoring the fact my heart is going full throttle and I'm not even sure why. I glance over the photos until I reach the fourth photo in the pile and my breath catches in my throat, threatening to choke me. All of the photographs are of Freya; Her face is covered in thick makeup, her eyes and lips showing up dark against her pale complexion in the black and white film. She's wearing an incredibly short sequined dress which catches the flash of the camera.

She looks... trashy. It's the third photograph which makes me pause and clogs my breath in my lungs. In this one she's looking directly into the camera and her eyes are glazed over. She looks like she's looking right through me and she looks absolutely terrified, tears collecting at the corners. Her mouth is slightly a jar and although the image is in black and white, like an old-fashioned movie, the patches in her mouth look like blood. I have to remind myself to stay calm as I carry on looking through the print outs, but they only get worse.

By the last one I'm crying silently, tears making wet greasy spots on the photo's surface. Freya's looking at the camera, tears running down her cheeks. A dark gloved hand is snaked around the front of her throat, gripping the edge of her neck and pulling her face to stay towards the camera. The grip is so tight you can see deep grooves and imprints in her skin under the fingertips. Her head is held in an unnatural position and her eyes scream at me. I remember to breathe but it comes out as a gasp.

My fingers are trembling with the rest of my body as I struggle to find Detective Dawson's number in my phonebook. I grab at the images, her face... my face staring back at me as I wait for the Detective to answer. The anxiety itches at my throat. My fingers tremble so much the photographs jolt out of my hand and land haphazardly all over the floor. I start grabbing them back up when I notice a messy scrawl across the back of the last image. The one where she's being strangled to look at the camera. Detective Dawson answers the phone and asks how she can help but I stay silent. I stutter my apologies at accidentally calling her and hang up because the words written across the back of the image tell me not to. Literally.

Isn't she pretty? Pretty like you. Speak to the police again and she'll be a pretty corpse.

Chapter 36

No One

She needs a break. It's obvious. She took a lot longer to resuscitate this time. I was almost scared I wouldn't be able to pull her back. That all of this would end prematurely. I need to control myself or she might die for good before I'm done.

I learnt my lesson on the last one. The brunette. She was meant to be here for a lot longer but then I got so far ahead of myself that she closed her eyes for the last time. Even after I wasted all of that time bleaching her hair, my nostrils burned from all the fumes, because she didn't look enough like her. She was such a nuisance afterwards. Even more so than when she was here.

I'd thought the squealing, pleading, coughing, choking, and shocking amounts of defecation and human filth was annoying but none of that was as irritating as having to lug her dead weight around and get rid of her. It reminded me of dragging that useless piece of trash's body down to the basement. Me doing all the hard work taking him apart in pieces to fit better into the barrel of acid we used to dissolve his body. My mother was sobbing the whole time like she was dis-traught. Glaring at me every time we put another piece of him into the bubbling liquid, as if it was somehow *my* fault. She'd somehow come to the conclusion that he was dead because of me. It made me sloppy. Thinking of my mother when I got rid of the other woman and I didn't weigh the body down properly.

I pace.

Back and forth.

Back and forth.

The repetition calms the panic screaming through me. I need an outlet.

Chapter 37

Detective Dawson

'So, she just claimed it was a butt dial and hung up?' Luke took another bite of his needlessly loud burrito and chewed it like a dog.

'Exactly.' I scrunch my nose and try to ignore the slobbering sounds, praying the lift will hurry up so I can get as far away from the sound of him eating as possible.

'But you're worried, aren't you? You think there's more to it than that?' He shoves the last piece of burrito into his mouth and scrunches the wrapper up and I silently thank the heavens.

'I don't know what it is.' I sigh, trying to roll the tension out of my shoulders. I didn't get any sleep last night and my limbs are screaming but my brain wouldn't stop turning. Over and over. Flicking between Amelia and Ellie. My gut clenching and twisting, its subtle signal that all isn't right. That I'm missing something, but I don't know what it is. 'Charlie sounded like she was about to burst into tears when she called, I don't think we're about to get good news.' I'm frowning so hard I can feel the tension in my eyebrows. My resolve telling me to ignore the gnawing in my gut for the time being until we have all the facts. Facts I think we might be about to get.

Charlie's call had pulled me from the brink of pure insanity reading through files and files of dead ends last night. After Ellie Dolloway's cryptic phone call I'd gone back to scouring the Dolloway's history, determined to find something, anything. But the frustration was so thick and strong by the time Charlie called that I'd almost squealed with excitement and gratitude. Then I heard her voice. It was strained and thick and I could tell it was taking all of her might to get the words out. Even though she'd only told me that there were things I should know and to come and see her. That's how I know whatever it is she wants me to know is nothing good. Something bad enough to take all the fight out of one of the most seasoned and strongest medical examiners for miles. It still shocks me.

The smell of death which seems to seep from every nook and cranny of the morgue. The chemicals are the strongest, stinging my eyes and nose like they always do but even with all their toxicity, I can always smell it. That undertone of death. I can't count the amount of times I've been in here but as we step off of the elevator, the sensory overload of the smell and the bright fluorescent lights still nauseates me. Charlie's waiting for us when we go into her office. She's already made two cups of coffee and set them down on her desk in front of the two chairs opposite hers. We don't share pleasantries like we would normally. Something in the quiver of her features tells me it wouldn't be the right thing to do.

'Tell us Charlie.' The pause gives me just enough time to notice that she hasn't made herself a drink. Her cup is stained but empty. She must feel as nauseous as me. Both of us are in the same boat but at different ends. She's at the front and can see the incoming storm ready to consume us. I'm at the back, feeling the chill in the air but I can't see clearly how bad the waves are yet.

'I now have all of the results back from Amelia's full autopsy. I already gave you the basic run down of my initial external examination of course but there's been some... developments, which I know you would want to know.' She takes a deep breath and I can almost scream at her to just spit it out. Whatever it is. I can just about hear her over the blood rushing through my ears when she speaks. 'I did the full works. X-rays, body fluid tox screens including blood, eyes, teeth, nails... all of it. Organ examination, brain tissue sampling.'

'Charlie.' I reach across the desk and grip her hand, the trembling in her fingers only adding to my unease. 'We know how an autopsy works. Please. Just tell us whatever It is you found.'

'Right. Sorry.' She breathes out all of her tension, rubbing her shoulder. 'I'll give you a copy of my full report of course just because I know that you'll want to be able to look back on the details. But, in essence, Amelia Taylor was held in captivity and tortured for several months. I can't give an exact timeline of course but all signs point to her being held between the night she disappeared and around ten to twelve days ago when her body was weighed down in the lake.' It's crazy to see the visible change in Charlie's persona.

I can almost pinpoint the exact moment when she leaves her emotions behind, stepping so easily into the shoes of a professional pathologist, completely separate and compartmentalised from the horrific details she's relaying.

'During that time of captivity, Amelia underwent extensive torture. There's organ and tissue damage which is extensive. In all honesty, I'm surprised she lasted as long as she did. She had been tattooed or rather branded and according to all social media presence and the evidence of bleach in her hair follicles, her hair had been bleached blonde repetitively during her captivity. It looks like her appearance was important to whoever held her. They kept on top of the bleaching, there's barely any root growth. Her nails were also manicured and painted. From my investigation it looks like this guy's signature is...' her face creases in anguish, 'resuscitation.'

'I'm sorry, did you just say resuscitation?' Luke speaks for me. I can't find my voice. My mind's spinning. My palms are clammy.

'Yes.' Charlie opens the file in front of her and pushes it under our noses, pointing to pathologist scribbles over the torso of the human diagram on the side of the page. 'There's significant bruising to the torso area. Broken ribs, a punctured lung, there's significant remodelling on parts of the ribs. Some remodelling is thicker. It looks like they have been broken, healed and then broken again several times. The muscles of the heart and bruising around the oesophagus and trachea show a pattern of strangulation to the point of cardiac death and then effective resuscitation.'

The room's spinning, my vision swimming. Luke and Charlie are still talking. Charlie spews pathologist jargon I don't understand and Luke probes for more information, desperate to understand exactly what it is Charlie's telling us but I don't hear a word. Their voices reach my ears muffled and I don't have the energy to concentrate enough to make them clearer. I cut through their chatter, my voice barely a whisper but my insight is enough to stop their chatter abruptly. They both look at me, dismay and agreement clear across their faces.

'He's playing God.' I mutter. 'He's practised this. He knows enough to keep the routine up over months of torture and captivity.'

'Yes.' Charlie sighs and I know she knows what I'm getting at when she says the words I'm not yet strong enough to vocalise, 'he's had practice. Amelia isn't the first and she won't be the last. Fisher and Harding agreed. Whoever he is, he isn't finished.'

Chapter 38

Ellie

I finally realise I've been staring at the photos of Freya for hours when Tilly's ringtone slices through my train of thought. I gather all of the photographs up and shove them deep into my bag. I wonder whether, if I bury them deep enough, they might cease to exist, except I've never been that lucky.

I don't remember the drive home. I may have run multiple red lights or even run a cyclist under my wheels without noticing. Muscle memory kicks in and before I know it, I'm parked up outside my house with no memory of the drive back. I can only hope that one or more tickets don't fall through my letterbox in a few weeks, an accumulation of all of the driving rules I violated during my journey home.

As soon as the door closes behind me, Tilly starts rambling about having a life of her own, but her rant dies in her mouth when she sees my face. As soon as she asks me what's happened, the dam bursts. Ugly racking sobs spilling over. My cheap, thin cardigan is no match for the volume of tears and mucous coming out of me.   She drags me into the living room and shuts the door as a noise barrier between my hysteria and my sleeping kids. She pushes me down onto the sofa and takes a seat next to me and then she waits patiently for me to compose myself.

It feels like a never-ending tidal wave of emotion and I can't seem to stop the tears. If it had just been one continuous feeling, I probably could have handled it without all the theatrics; If it had just been shock, or just been grief, or even just anger then I would've held it together. But, what I didn't understand is why I feel so guilty and helpless. I somehow feel like this is all my fault. As though I have somehow wished this on all of us by believing my life would have been better and more simple without Freya in it. Maybe this is my karma for everything that happened before somehow and I guess, if you boiled it down to its core, that would be right. Tilly sits silently until the sobs have stopped and the hiccups start before she speaks.

'Tell me what's going on, Ells. I haven't seen you like this since we were seventeen.' Neither of us voice the time she's talking about but we both know. For a moment, I worry my voice won't work if I try to speak but once I start, I can't stop.

The words come out rushed and fall over themselves as I explain everything to her. They come out at three times the normal speed as I rush through. Partly because I'm sure that if I breathe a single breath or take a pause, she'll start speaking but I need to get all of it out first. Then I finish, ripping the printed photos out of my bag with a flourish and shove them into her lap. Her silence feels static in the air. Giving it an eerie presence which I swear I can almost physically feel. I've never known Tilly to not have something to say. She's a woman of strong feelings and an even louder voice. When she finally does speak and tells me to, 'go get wine'

I could almost laugh with relief. I scramble to the door, relieved to be able to do *something,* even if it is just to pour large volumes of wine into glasses. My hands are still trembling. Not quite working in coordination with my brain so I waste half of the wine on the kitchen counter as it sloshes. The waste is still running down the sides of the glass, dropping red teardrops into the carpet, as I carry them back through to the sitting room.

Tilly's sat cross legged in the middle of the floor, looking closely through the horrendous photographs. A heave travels up the back of my throat as I glance at the thick, black threat stained into the back of the photograph. I choke the gag back with a large gulp of wine, purposefully diverting my gaze as I pass Tilly her glass.

'Jesus fucking Christ, Ells. What have you gotten yourself into?' She's shaking her head, looking through the photos over and over. 'What the fuck has *Freya* gotten herself into?'

'I don't know what to do, Tilly.' I ignore the quiver in my voice. I can just be myself around Tilly. I've always been able to.

'Tell me you ignored this *psycho* and showed the Detectives these.' She reads the answer in the expression on my face. I can tell because she shakes her head and looks like she's about to throttle me.

'They said they'd kill her if I did that, Tilly.' My voice comes out a pathetic squeak and then my hands are trembling so bad again I have to put my glass down on the floor. 'What was I supposed to do?'

'So, what?' she throws her hands up in the air, 'what exactly are you planning to do Ellie? Because you certainly can't do nothing. Clearly whoever this person is, is holding Freya against her will. Planning to do God knows what to her and you're going to... what, exactly? Just not tell the police?'

'I....I....don't know.' I hold my head in my hands, listening to the sound of the blood rushing through my ears in time with the thumping in my head. The sound of my anxiety and helplessness. We sit in strained silence for ten straight minutes. Both of us no longer want to look at the photographs but neither of us are able to tear our gaze away either.

'Do you know who it might be? Whoever it is, who has her?'

'I wish I did. I'd have gone to the police if I knew. I wasn't even entirely sure until I saw these photos. It was just a horrible feeling. Things have been happening – strange things. For a minute a few days ago, I thought it might have been...' I hesitate. Tilly makes a motion with her hands to tell me to spit it out already. 'I thought it might have been...*him.*'

Recognition ignites in her eyes and she sighs quietly, stroking my hand. When she speaks it's as if she's trying to talk me down from a ledge; slow, gentle, soothing.

'It can't be him, Ells. You know it can't. He's gone.'

I swallow the lump in my throat and nod with a reassured calmness. She's right. I'm overthinking it. Seeing clues and symbolic messages which don't really exist in the coincidences happening around me. She spreads the photos out, looking at them closely, inspecting each one intently. How she manages to look at them so closely without vomiting seems impossible to me. She moves across the floor, so her back is to the sofa next to where I'm sitting. She holds the photos elevated in front of us and I have to gulp wine again to fend off the vomit.

I see it through the corner of my eye first. It's more a feeling before I even look at it properly. The tiny hairs on the back of my neck prickling almost painfully. My unconscious mind is trying to tell me I need to pay attention. So, I look. I have to consciously drag my eyes back to the photo Tilly has held up and is scrutinising. My vision's blurred with the haze of wine and the threat of another migraine, but I still see it. It almost jumps off the glossy page. I stare at it for a few long moments. Trying to get my memory to work inline with my thought process. I swear I've seen it before. I just can't place it. It's the worst photograph. The one where they're clutching Freya's neck, holding her face towards the camera. The hand is on the edge of the photograph, the edges ever so slightly blurred and out of focus but I can still make it out.

A round gold ring. Large and bulky on the index finger. There's grooves in it, mapping out some kind of symbol. They're not obvious, looking almost random with how they're lined on the main face of the ring but they look unbelievably similar.

'What?' Tilly looks between me and the photo and I realise I'm almost glaring at it. 'What do you see?' She scrutinises the photograph; her eyes darting from side to side as she tries to see what I've seen.

'That ring. Does it look familiar to you?' My head throbs louder as I frown. Trying to pull something from the recesses of my brain. Something I know is there, just out of reach. I'm clawing at it, trying to bring it into focus but my eye muscles twitch from the effort. With how deep Tilly's frowning at the ring I can tell she's trying just as hard to make sense of the indents in the ring.

'It looks like... some kind of...' she tilts her head slightly, 'I don't know... like a signet ring?' It hits me then.

I don't want to say like a freight train because that's just so cliché but that's what it feels like when the memory lurches through the haze in my head to the forefront. Like a train hitting me right in the face and suddenly I can't breathe. Because I have seen that ring before. When we were teenagers. Every graduating class were given the option to buy one when they hired their gowns and caps. It was a symbol of the academy's prestige. A real expensive "fuck you" to the cheaper, public schools in the area. Most of the male graduates would buy one.

Scholarship kids would save all year to buy one just so they'd feel more high level and on the same playing field as their fellow classmates who were brought up with only silver spoons in sight.

'Oh my god, Tilly!' I gasp but she still looks confused. 'Whoever took Freya, they went to our high school.'

PART TWO

SEVEN YEARS AGO

Chapter 39

No One

It's faster than I thought it would be. Asphyxiation.

I'd been reading up on murder for weeks. The different ways I could kill her. Which techniques were more efficient or more effective. I Researched for hours the types of toxins I could buy without any red flags to mix into her tea. Slaved over learning the different knots you can tie in a rope; either to crush and constrict blood vessels or to lever the neck to one side, snapping it. I even practiced a few on myself, with fail safes to make sure I didn't kill myself. I'm fed up of the bitch, not suicidal.

That's why it took me so long to finally do this, to finally kill her. Not because of any kind of conscience but because I'm indecisive. I'd been deliberating over it for weeks but then she'd upset me. Spitting her putrid phlegm in my face like I was trash and I snapped.

I lunged at her. Pinned her down. Dug my fingers and nails so deep into her throat that I could feel her heartbeat thumping against my fingertips as I strangled her.

I felt it when her pulse stopped. Now I feel disappointed. I scrutinise the scene for a whole minute. Feeling depleted. I expected it to be better than this. Like the world would be set, somehow, right. That I would be able to breathe again. Except, the air feels the same. Stale and penetrating.

I'd watched her give up, her nails not scratching so hard, her eyes not so petrified. It was almost boring after that. I realise, too late, that It was too quick.

The sound of a piercing scream startles me out of my daze before I realise the sound has come from me. something deep and almost primal taking over.

I want to do it over and over again. Watch her die more than once. See the terror in her eyes for longer than the seconds it took me to strangle the air out of her. I want her to suffer as much as she's made me suffer.

Then, the idea. It blooms beautifully in me, replacing the dread with excitement. I know what I need to do.

I pull her by her fat, swollen ankles onto the floor, my hands pushing so deep down in her chest I can almost feel her ribs straining, ready to snap.

My skin crawls at the thought of having my mouth anywhere near her decaying teeth and tainted saliva but I do it anyway. Breathing the life back in until she gasps, her eyes springing open. Full of confusion at first, then realisation and then pure unadulterated dread.

'Ah, there it is.' The smile feels unnatural on my face. 'You're alive because of me, mother. I brought you back. Maybe next time, I won't'

Chapter 40

Ellie

I sip the watered-down punch, marvelling at all of the dresses swishing and swaying on the dancefloor to the music thumping out of the gymnasium PA system. I'm grateful Mrs Henry is manning the food and drinks table like a new and enthusiastic patrol officer. She's trying her hardest to make sure none of the students can get within two millimetres of the punch bowl with the mini flasks, filled to the brim with the cheapest, liquor from their parents' stash, hidden in their pockets. It means I can drink the punch without worrying about the life growing inside of me. Although, looking around the dancefloor, it's clear that even with Mrs Henry's watchful eye, half the year have managed to sneak drinks in anyway and have been gulping them in the toilets. I wonder how many of them think they look glamorous and agile as they dance around, their view romanticised by a drunken haze as they flail their arms and spin. From the scorn on Mrs Henry's face, I think she knows her efforts have been futile too. Half the hall is already drunk and it's barely 9PM.

I rub my stomach self-consciously; my babies are both very active tonight. I wonder if it's the music. If they're dancing too. The thought of them doing the macarena makes me giggle out loud and I catch myself, blushing at how stupid I must look. Giggling in the corner with my watered down non-alcoholic drink, hugging the wall like I've been doing since we got here.

'I can't remember the last time I saw you smile!' Tilly makes me jump as she shouts loudly against my ear all of sudden. Her approach was masked by the thumping of *girls just wanna have fun* bass.

'It's so loud in here, I can barely hear you.' I find myself giggling again and I almost cry because it feels so good and I can't remember the last time I felt this... ok.

'Did you see Victoria? Talk about a wardrobe disaster.' She does some sort of mocking flouncy dance, jumping midway through and then clutching her own dress to her chest, faking the horrified look on Victoria's face earlier when her dress had completely ripped and fell away, exposing her sweaty breasts to half the class.

'I feel sorry for her. The memory of tonight is going to be permanently seared into everyone's brains. Knowing you, you'll be bringing it up at the reunion in ten years.'

'Like I'd be caught in this shit hole in ten years. No thank you. Come dance!'

Before I can voice my objections, Tilly grabs my arm, forcefully pulling me and my very large twin bump across the dancefloor, through the throng of drunk dancing graduates. I have to apologise to everyone as I fall into them. They all look at me with unfiltered irritation and underlying judgement as they tut and shake their heads, whispering to their friends as we pass, motioning towards my clearly pregnant stomach. I can feel the good mood waning. My attempts to be a normal teenager for one night is as pointless as Mrs Henry's military guarding of the refreshments table. I want to cry by the time we're in the middle of the dancefloor and Tilly's dancing around me with no care in the world, clearly oblivious to the stares from our classmates. Then I hear one of the girls in the swarm around me shout to her friends over the music.

Only, it's during the momentary pause in between songs and her words shout out in the quiet, drawing everyone's attention. Their heads spinning in our direction, 'God. This slut's taking up half the dance floor because she couldn't keep her legs shut!' Heat radiates up my neck and across my face and chest, tears searing at the corners of my eyes. Everyone's turned to look, their eyes piercing through me, humour dancing over them. The girl who shouted it has the decency to look mortified for a few seconds before someone I can't see bursts into laughter and everyone else follows.

The tears are free falling by the time I'm out the main building doors and in the parking lot. The mascara I so pointlessly put on a few hours ago now runs in dirty dark tracks down my cheeks. The cold bites at my exposed arms but I barely notice. I'm stumbling down the steps when I feel the surge of nausea. Humiliation mixed wrongly with the anxiety and cheap punch in my stomach and it's now climbing its way back up my throat. I just about make it to the bush before the vomit escapes my mouth. It comes out as a darkish red tinge from the punch and the sight of it makes me heave and puke again. I'm wiping the back of my hand across my mouth, my head thumping when a hand is suddenly thrust out in front of me. I noticed the ring first. The gold top reflects the outdoor light above. The curves on the top distinctive of the school emblem. It's so ugly I don't get why any of the students in the graduating class have bought them. I take the tissue, mumbling a thank you and when I look back to see who my saviour is I feel ill all over again. Oliver, the school's most notorious bully.

'Don't know why you're looking at me like that,' he scoffs. 'You're the one with puke down your chin.' The heat's back in my cheeks and I quickly wipe at my face with the tissue, mumbling my apologies. 'You're not fooling anyone you know.' He says it with such lack of feeling that it turns the back of my neck cold. 'Claiming it's Bobby's. He's been telling anyone that will listen that it's not his. Been saying you're a complete slag all over the field.'

He might as well have taken the cigarette he's casually puffing on and burnt me. Tears are prickling at my eyes again and I silently beg myself not to start crying again. When the nurse at the clinic had taken the babies measurements and given me their due date, I felt crushed and overwhelmed. Their due date is later than I thought it would be, so now I know for certain that they're not Bobby's. I'd hoped and prayed to anyone who was listening to let them be his, but I guess luck wasn't on my side.

I'd debated not telling him. Wondered if I could bury my head in the sand and convince both him and me that they were his. That it isn't so much of a mess but I couldn't do that to him. I had to be as honest as I possibly could. So I told him. All of it. Every horrible, heart wrenching detail. At least, everything except for who.

I don't know what I'd expected his reaction to be but him effing and blinding and calling me a "God damn lying slut" was definitely not it. I think I always knew he had an edge to him but I just never expected to be on the receiving end. The fact that he's been telling people anything about the situation at all makes my stomach and my heart ache.

'Maybe people should mind their own business.' I stick my chin out, trying to hold firm but I feel my lip tremble and the smirk on his face tells me he saw it too.

'Oliver! There you are! Come on, I thought we were goi-.' Freya falls into the back of him and nearly shoves him right over into me before she catches my eye and rolls her eyes. 'God. You're still here?' She stumbles again and has to grip on to Oliver's arm to keep her balance. I can see her nails digging into his skin from here and the mix of humour and disgust on his face as he watches my sister struggle to keep herself upright sends a shock of anger through me.

'She was just about to tell me who really knocked her up.' Laughter ripples between the both of them and the anger surging through my body is eaten away like acid, humiliation taking hold once again.

'Oh, please!' Freya is so drunk she sprays spit with every syllable. 'She'll just lie. First, she said it was Bobby's and then she made up this story you won't believe. My parents didn't even believe it.' My palms start to itch and I can feel my heart pounding at the base of my skull and I have to push my nails hard into my palms to try and focus, nurturing control over the panic attack I can feel bubbling just below the surface.

'Freya. Please. Don't.'

'Oh really?' Oliver pretends he didn't hear me, cocking his head towards Freya and urging her to go on.

'She said she was *raped*.' Freya hiccups. 'By someone at our school, but she won't tell me who. Lies are ugly on you Ellie, you know that?'

Chapter 41

Freya

My head is fuzzy with alcohol. I can feel the last cup of cheap vodka and flat Cola bubbling and swimming in my empty stomach. It makes me feel faint as the car swerves from lane to lane. Oliver has the music on loud, bass thumping through the car and vibrating in my chest and limbs. It feels good. The loud thumping of the bass and the vocals of the lead singer drowning out the noise in my head. I look at the time on the dash. 01:06 AM. It's nearly time and the thought relaxes me. I say a silent prayer to Scott, letting him know I'll be with him soon.

I see the sign for Bea Rock and smile to myself. It seems fitting that Oliver would be driving me to the secluded woodland with its clearing where all of the college students have their bonfires and keg parties. The car park is an area of dead grass and gravel; where young, drunk, and horny teenagers go to do everything their parents won't let them do in the house. Where Scott and I shared our first kiss.

We park in the empty car park. I'm just aware enough to tell that there's still no bonfire set tonight. I feel simultaneously relieved and irritated because on the one hand it means there's less people to try and stop me. But on the other hand, it means Oliver will be less distracted when I do and I was counting on him being distracted by some blonde in a skirt so short it's more of a belt. I only needed him to drive me here. His job is done but now I have to try and figure out another way to distract him enough that I can make it up the hill to the cliff side.

All of a sudden Oliver's leaning across the car, sticking his tongue, which tastes like cheap cider, into my mouth. I let him kiss me for a few seconds. Wondering if maybe it will help take my mind off Scott for a few minutes if I do let him touch me when his hand starts to creep up my dress. Then I realise that the only thing that's going to take my mind off Scott is if I do what I came here to do. So, I push Oliver off, muttering excuses about being too drunk and stumbling out of the car.

I don't remember the climb up the steep hill by the time I'm finally standing at the top, leaning against the pathetic excuse of a barrier. A strip plank of wood, nailed in place to the beams, shoved roughly into the earth. I giggle at the idea of some public safety rep looking at the steep fifteen foot drop over the edge of the cliff side. Tutting and sucking his gums looking at the jagged, rough rocks sticking out of the cliff face and the cars speeding past on the gangway below at the national speed limit. Then thinking, *Yep. We need to put something to stop people from falling to their death* and then putting a pathetic plank of wood there. Nodding approvingly once it's put in place that his work here is done. The public is saved.

It doesn't take long until the giggles are wracking sobs, tears streaming down my cheeks. Looking up at the heavens and I wonder why this had to happen to us. I've never thought of myself as a bad person but now I wonder, almost obsessively, what I could have done to make the universe want to turn around and throw me a big "fuck you" by killing Scott.

I'm moderately aware of Oliver when he makes it to the top of the hill behind me. His breathing is deep and laboured from the steepness of the climb.

I expect him to start telling me not to. To start spewing rubbish about silver linings and happiness just around the corner. Offer me a cup of tea and a warm bath because according to all the crisis hotlines, the consumption of a leaf grown in fields of Asia is the cure to depression, grief and heartache.

At the idea of that, I snort. The loud laugh rings in my ears and I'm acutely aware of how psychopathic I must look right now. I'm thankful there's no keg full of judgemental, teenage onlookers going on right now.

I clamber over the pathetic wooden plank barrier and stand with my back firmly pressed against it, my arms holding me in place as my feet slip on the loose earth, bits of soil and rock crumbling over the end and falling into the dark below.

I wonder for a split second if Oliver is going to try and stop me. I look over my shoulder and almost jump with fright. It's almost enough to make me plummet over the edge before I'm ready. My heart skips and thrums through my ears when I see he's closer than I thought. Less than an arm's length. But he's not trying to grab for me, to stop me in any way.

He's just standing there. His arms crossed across his body, head cocked ever so slightly to one side as he watched me. He doesn't look alarmed or worried in any way. Just purely dumbfounded and curious and my throat goes dry.

I tear my attention to the steep drop and decide to count to ten and then jump. I've only counted to three when I'm suddenly plummeting through the air. The wind is fast and cold through my hair and bites at my chest and arms. I'm confused for a split second. Unsure why I went so early. Did I slip? A part of my mind argues with the rest. Telling me that I definitely felt a large hand on my back just before I fell. Applying pressure. Almost like a push.

It's about halfway down, the fall seeming to happen almost in slow motion, when I'm staring at the jagged rocks hurtling towards me, that I realise I don't actually want to die. That I want to live. You hear about stories of people who throw themselves off of bridges and survive, that they changed their mind once they'd jumped. That they'd been relieved when they didn't. That it was almost euphoric.

That's how I feel. Euphoric in the realisation that I want to live. Even with the pain. I want to be able to feel it. I start flailing my arms, trying to grip on.

The last thing I see is a ledge in the cliff face which I'm heading straight for, before it all goes black.

Chapter 42

Ellie

I find hospitals bleak. What is it that people call them? God's waiting rooms? Or is that nursing homes? Either way, they sweat death and the odour makes every room reek of grief and despair. Part of me wonders if the maternity wing smells different. If it perspires life and smells of hope and love. I feel acutely anxious that it somehow doesn't. That I'll be bringing my babies into the world shrouded in negativity and that will somehow affect them, infiltrate them and fester in there somehow.

As I look at my sister, bruised and battered and being kept alive by something as flimsy and unreliable as a man made machine, I wonder if we were both doomed from the start. That if we hadn't been born in this hospital that reeks of death, we somehow would not be here right now.

The machines pulse and beep in the quiet of the room. I watch my mother hold her breath each time a machine goes quiet for a second too long in the rhythm, the relief visible in her face and dramatic exhalations when the machine wheezes or beeps again.

My father stands in the corner of the room. His face scrunched in agony as he watches one of his children fight for her life while there's nothing he can do but watch and wait.

Her surgeon had come in about an hour ago when they brought her back to the private room. One that's been shoved at the back of the ward and I'd wondered silently if they use this room purely for the lost causes. The people they don't expect to make it, kept isolated in this back corner of the ward, away from the other patients and family members in the intensive care unit. As if death is contagious and they want to keep the other patients safe from my sister. The surgeon looked melancholy and sympathetic as he tried his best to answer our questions whilst remaining too vague and nondescript to really be telling us anything. Simply responding with, 'We've done all we can. All we can do now is wait and see if she comes round.' So now we wait, suspended in time whilst the rest of the world goes on.

'This is all of your fault.'

I look up, alarmed. My mother's shooting daggers at me so sharp I feel them rip through the tendons around my heart. I'm stunned. Too shocked by the amount of venom in her voice to respond, to defend myself. I look at my father for help but he just sighs heavily and rubs at his face with both his hands, pretending to not see, to not hear.

'You know how fragile she is. You should have stayed with her tonight. Been there. Stopped her.'

'I'm sorry.' My voice is small, insignificant. The apology is empty.

'I wish it were you.' She's crying now. Dry heaving as she talks. 'It should be you in that bed, fighting for your life. All the lies you've told. Vicious, malicious lies about that young lad. I wish it were y ou.' It's at this moment that my father decides to step in. Physically striding across the room and gripping my moms shoulder with a firm grip. Speaking quietly but firmly when he tells her, 'That's enough,

Kathrine.' But it's too late. The words are already out in the universe. The damage is already done.

🔥

It's almost another three whole days before Freya starts choking. Her body starts to thrash and heave. My mother starts screaming and multiple nurses and a doctor rush in and smile. Actually smile and I want to scream at them to stop that. She's dying. Why are they smiling?

Then a small brunette grips my mom's hand and speaks encouragingly, telling us not to panic. That this is good. That Freya's fighting the tube. That she's breathing on her own and she's awake.

The sounds get worse before they get better. They pull at wires, flick switches, press buttons on machines urgently and pull the long tube out from down Freya's throat and then she vomits. Clear bile, coughing and choking, pushing at the nurses who are trying to give her a bowl and move her hair.

I feel relieved that she's finally awake but it strikes me as I watch my parents fuss over her, that I don't feel a rush of joy. I should be screaming with relief that my twin's alive. Running to her and telling her never to do that again or I'll kill her myself. Crying happy tears. Like you see all the actors do in movies. I feel relief but it's more for the fact that now my parents can't blame me for her death. That I won't have their grief constantly hanging over me, blackening any happiness I may ever feel again because my mom wishes it were me that was six feet deep. I wonder whether that makes me the monster my mother believes me to be.

It's after my mother's stopped crying and climbed into the hospital bed next to Freya, like she's a bed-sick toddler, my father having gone downstairs to get them both more coffee to cure the adrenaline which has eaten away to fatigue, that the nurse quietly knocks and comes in. She's all sunshine and roses.

'Apologies Mrs Dolloway, but there's a few kids here asking to see Freya. I wondered if she was strong enough and ready for visitors yet.'

'Who?' Freya's voice is strained and croaky from the tube and the hoarseness of it makes me cringe every time she speaks.

'Harriet, Oliver, Reggie, Bobby and... Connie?' the nurse looks unsure for a moment, trying to remember the names.

My vision swims, anxiety scratching at the inside of my skull. My breathing becomes laboured but they don't seem to notice my discomfort. They're too busy working out who the hell the nurse meant when she said Connie and why 'the nerd from the theatre is here'. Apparently, It's only obvious to me that, by Connie, the nurse had meant Courtney.

The babies stir, making my stomach feel light and squirmy, one of them kicking me hard in the side. Almost as if to tell me to calm down, to control my breathing because they can feel the cortisol levels too but my breathing still comes ragged and unhinged.

'Jesus Christ Ellie, why are you hyperventilating? Anyone would think it was you lying in this hospital bed with your bones broken and stitches stinging.' Freya tuts and rolls her eyes when she sees the state I'm in. My mother looks over and I can tell by the irritation on her face that she doesn't really care that I'm ridden with anxiety and fear, she just wants me to shut up too.

'Go get some air Ellie. You're upsetting your sister.' My mother turns away from me then, fussing over Freya's hair like she's about to be interviewed by a TV crew rather than visited by her friends.

The nurse looks at me sympathetically as I stumble out and asks me if I'd like some water or to sit down at the nurses station for a moment. I want to thank her for her kindness, lie and say that my mother's coldness and my sister's narcissism doesn't bother me, but I can barely catch my breath. I smile small and hope that she can see the gratitude in it but I suspect as I'm rushing to get through the busy ward to the exit that I probably just looked like I was having a meltdown. Which I am.

I concentrate on the few steps in front of me, watching my feet and counting my steps to try and focus my mind on something other than the panic. My vision swims and blurrs, I can hear my own breath in my ears and my chest hurts with the exertion of how fast my heart is beating. One of the babies' is going nuts in my stomach, flipping and kicking furiously. Battling against the panic attack at the same time.

All of a sudden I feel exhausted and weak. The room spins. I grasp the wall for balance and then there's a sea of blue as nurses rush to my aid, all of them gripping me and pulling me to sit on one of the uncomfortable plastic waiting room chairs. One of them is feeling my pulse and saying something to me but I can't hear the words over the blood thumping in my eardrums.

The blue suddenly turns white and I feel myself jump before I realise it's just a paper bag that someone's handed to me. They push the opening against my mouth and I can read the words "breathe slowly" on the nice looking nurse with blonde hair tied so tight on top of her head I wonder if she has a headache.

It feels like hours before the room finally stops spinning and I can breathe again. My limbs feel like lead and my eyes are aching with exhaustion. I just want to curl up in bed. All of the nurses retreated back to actual patients about ten minutes ago but Blonde headache nurse still sat with me on the uncomfortable plastic chairs in the hall.

The water she's given me is ice cold but feels heavenly as I sip it. She checks my pulse rate again, applying pressure to my wrist with two fingers and counting silently as she stares at the small clock on the far wall.

'How are you feeling now?' She asks softly once she's done. Her shoulders and face are visibly relaxing so I'm guessing my heart rate is in normal range again.

'I'm sorry.' I mumble. 'I'm sure you're really busy and I feel fine now. I don't know what happened back there but I feel much better now, you don't have to sit with me anymore.'

'Have you had a panic attack before?'

'No.' I lied.

'Do you want to talk about it? Whatever it was that triggered the attack?' I can tell she knows I'm lying about not having one before but neither of us voice it. Leaving it as an unspoken truth we both know instead.

'My sister's a patient here. I think it's just the stress catching up. We didn't know if she was going to make it before. She's doing much better now though.'

'I can imagine that hasn't been easy whilst dealing with a pregnancy too.' She motions towards my stomach and I wrap my arm around it protectively. 'Do you want me to go and get your parents?'

'No.' I say it too quickly and the concern jumps back into her features. 'I mean, that's ok thank you. I'll tell them myself. I should be getting back to my sister's room now anyway.'

'Ok love.' She still looks apprehensive but I see her quickly glance at the clock again and I know she's already switching her focus to the patients who are actually assigned to her care. 'Take it easy now. I think you should speak to your obstetrician too about the attacks. Just to be safe.'

'Will do.' I lie again but she's already on her feet and retreating back to the ward on the opposite side of the corridor.

I take a deep breath and head back the way I came.

Chapter 43

Freya

My mother's still fussing with my hair when they all walk in. They look so worried and concerned as they all shuffle through and stand by the door. As if they're scared that, if they make any sudden moves, I might pull one of the needles sticking into me out and use it as a makeshift weapon to slit my carotid. They don't realise that in all this mess, the one good thing that came out of it all is that I realised I want to live.

'Well, don't just stand there. Where are the chocolates?'

It's a stupid joke but it seems to work. The tension almost instantly dissipates. Courtney marches over, and grabs me into a tight hug. The needles which are still sticking in me wiggle and press deeper, stinging.

'Careful. Careful.' I gasp but hug her back just as hard. Smelling the fruity strawberry shampoo she's used since we were ten and feeling relief that I'm still here to smell it.

'We got you these.' Harriet is next to cross the threshold, passing me a small bunch of sunflowers. The yellow colour is harsh in the hospital lights and the stems slightly wilted from the journey over.

'Thanks.' I smile but then shove them in my mother's direction, not arsed to make a show of smelling them. She should know I hate flowers.

I look back over across the room and blink in confusion. The nurse had been right, that spotty theatre kid is here. My bones are aching too much for pleasantries so I cut right to the chase,

'Sorry... Ronald is it? Not too sure why you're here it's not like we're fri-'

'Reggie.' He cuts me off. Suddenly, his eyes are doing that thing again. When they seem to look right through me. 'My name is Reggie.' 'Right.' I shift uncomfortably, pinned under his angry glare. 'Sorry... Reggie. Don't take this the wrong way but we're not exactly friends so why are you here?'

'I thought...' he suddenly looks less menacing and more shy. He shuffles from foot to foot, looking everywhere but at me and biting his thumbnail. 'He only said one of the twins... he didn't specify which. Not when he told us.'

'Not when who told you dear?' I push the urge to roll my eyes at my mother's use of the pet name on someone she doesn't even know. Who shouldn't even be here.

'Mr Fuller.' Reggie sighs. 'He's mine and Ellie's manager at the theatre. When he told those of us on shift, he just said he'd heard one of the Dolloway twins was in hospital'

I cringe at the joint mention of us. As if we're one in the same person. A pair who come together. We're not. I'm nothing like my nerdy, friendless, boring, and attention seeking sister. I'm better.

'He thought it was Ellie,' I clarify for my mother. 'That's it right? You came because you thought it was Ellie who was hurt and in hospital. That's why you came, because your friends?'

'Errrm... yeah. That's right.' He nods but he doesn't look sure.

Then it strikes me. This poor bastard has a thing for my sister and she doesn't know it. I repress the laugh surging up my throat. The poor kid's got a thing for my sister who got knocked up by some other bloke. Must sting.

'Well it's not.' It's the first time Oliver's spoken since they all came in and I feel my stomach drop.

I glance over and meet his eye because even though he's speaking to Reggie, he's looking straight at me. Unblinking. I get a sudden memory of the feel of a firm hand on my back just before I fell and I consciously remove it from my mind. It's stupid. He wouldn't have done that.

He told me last week during the midway point of the game, when we'd both found ourselves sneaking out behind the bins for cigarettes, that he'd had a thing for me since he joined the school last year. That he'd always kept his distance because he knew I was with Scott and that I was, quote "a too good for him rich girl," but then Scott had died and now I'm just as broken as him. We bonded over our shared trauma, mine a dead first love and his a dead mom. He wouldn't hurt me. Would he?

Chapter 44

Ellie

It's the following Saturday when we finally get to take Freya home. It feels like any other Saturday once she's in the house. After a brief fight between our father, Freya's wheelchair and the slight lip in the floor by the front door, all seems almost normal.

My mom still won't look at me and is trying to pretend that me and my pregnant stomach don't exist. My father is trying to keep the peace without actually doing anything of real substance to solve the family rift at all.

As soon as Freya had haphazardly manoeuvred from her chair to the sofa, her casted leg and bandaged arm almost lost from sight as she sunk down into the soft cushions and demanded a drink like a bedridden grandma, my father had disappeared off into his study. The door shut firmly and the sound of the lock clicking echoed through the hall to the living room. Not that my mother had noticed his quick getaway. She was too busy rushing like a slave to get Freya everything she was demanding. A drink. The remote. The lights dimmed. Wait no, now it was too dark and gloomy, the lights turned back up.

I retreated as soon as I could safely slip away, feeling every bit my father's daughter as I closed my bedroom door softly and breathed a sigh of relief. If I had had a lock on my door, I would've locked it like him too.

I throw myself down onto the bed and stare at the patterns in the old popcorn ceiling. I feel bone tired and stale from day after day spent in the hospital and back-to-back late and morning shift I've just worked. I should have refused really, given how far along I am now and how stressful the week had been with Freya in hospital. But, I needed the cash and the Halloween event is my favourite one of the year. It's always a big affair when the horror movies screen and we all dress up. It was hectic and tiring but it was fun. At least, most of it was. When I wasn't walking on eggshells with Bobby, that is.

I know I should shower and eat something relatively soon to make sure I get to sleep at a half decent hour but I can't seem to drag myself off the bed. The duvet is so comfortable, so inviting and soft that I just want to melt into it. I yawn, trying to rub the tiredness from my eyes, staring at the pattern in the ceiling which looks kind of like a surfer on a wave. I'm wondering if the plasterer put it there specifically and why my parents still haven't scraped the old fashioned texture off and replastered when I fall asleep.

🔥

The smell hits me first. Raw and clogging. Something acidic but sweet. It permeates the air, thick and almost stifling. It takes me a few seconds to realise what it is. Gasoline. I blink in the darkness trying to figure out where it's coming from despite the onslaught to my senses that I didn't expect. It takes me a few moments to realise I must have fallen asleep, the only light in the room comes from the streetlamp outside the house, cutting through the netting over the window and casting a gloomy white light across the floor.

I sit up. My stomach growling with hunger and my lips dry. I cough against the stench of the gas. I swing my legs over the edge of the bed and stand.

My feet sink into the sodden carpet, the sound squelching like muddy grass in winter. The smell of gasoline is suddenly stronger and I realise the carpet is damp with it.

Confusion and panic creep in. I'm suddenly reminded of the note left on the doorstep. Warning me that none of us are safe.

Something across the room catches the light from the window, drawing my eye to it and I squint in the darkness trying to figure out what I'm looking at.

I freeze. Paralyzed. I want to scream and run for the door but my feet won't move. It's as if I can't control my body, my eyes travelling up from the butt of the gun which is glinting in the darkness, aimed directly at me. It's the eyes I see first. Piercing and shining bright blue in the light.

My grandma used to always say you could tell a lot about someone and their heart from their eyes. These eyes shine with malice and ill intent and I clutch my stomach. As if the extra flesh and bone in my arms will protect them but I know it won't.

I glance briefly at the door, judging the distance to it. Wondering if I can make it. Weighing up the pros and cons of trying. It was only the briefest glance, the briefest consideration but the intruder sees it.

They take three steps forward, walking into the patch of light.

I scrutinise them. Realising they look male, broad and tall. He's standing with repressed agitation, stepping almost compulsively from one foot to the other. Like an excited child waiting in line for a fairground ride.

'Move.' The voice is authoritative but somehow sounds immature. He motions towards the door with his gun and in the movement I see the safety is flicked off. Any other average person probably wouldn't notice that through the fear and the room's darkness but I have a police Chief for a father.

I wonder where my father is. Where my mother is. Where Freya is. Why no one's noticed the overpowering smell of gas. I wonder how he got in. I realise that they might all be dead. Killed in their sleep. If I hadn't woken up, would I also be dead? How long has he been standing in the shadows, watching me sleep? I shiver with the question, adrenaline making my skin prickle as I try to figure out what to do.

'For fuck sake. *Move.*' His voice cracks slightly. The demand is not sounding quite as gruff as it did earlier. He sounds young. Almost familiar. I get a slight prickle of recognition and I try to place it as I do what he says, walking slowly across the room. My feet are squelching on the wet carpet.

I gulp back tears because I'm sure I know what his plan is. To kill us all and then burn the evidence, our house and bodies down in flames. Like those families on TV. All those family members who had their homes broken into and burned down with them still alive inside. Staring at the end of his gun, my feet wet with gas, I realise that we're the next hit. We walk through the dark house until we reach the living room. There isn't much light in here either, the curtains are drawn and the only light is from the standing lamp in the corner. The one that my mother uses to read.

My hands start to tremble when I see my family. All of them lined up in the living room on the floor, one of my father's t-shirts ripped apart and tied round their heads, gagging them and stifling my mom and Freya's cries. They all have their hands tied behind them with some sort of thick rope and I uselessly wonder where the hell he managed to find that in the house. The tears start when I realise he must have brought the rope with him. My mother and father's legs are also tied behind them as they kneel on the floor. Freya is seated down, her legs stretched out in front of her but also tied, the pressure nearly ripping at her cast. Her left arm is at a weird angle from where it's been forcibly tied, still bandaged, behind her back to her other arm. My mother and Freya are huddled together, whimpering behind their gags, both sobbing and looking at the man in the balaclava in terror. He shoves me hard by the shoulder to the floor and I twist just in time for my hip to take the brunt of it instead of my stomach. I suddenly feel very alone once he's tied me too. Almost jealous, that my mother and Freya are cowering together, excluding me like always. Always the black sheep of my family. I realise how ridiculous my thoughts sound and swallow the resentment, focusing on the intruder who is pacing back and forth.

I look at my father and notice the anger in his stare. He isn't sobbing, isn't gasping or pleading. Isn't even trembling. He's stone cold. I can almost feel the ideas turning over in his mind as he scans the room subtly whilst the intruder is distracted. Trying to find something to use to get us out of this. Suddenly, I feel almost relieved. Like I know we're going to get out of this. That's when the torture starts.

Chapter 45

Freya

It's been hours and he's enjoyed every second of it. I stopped crying an hour ago, it seemed to only excite him, and I refuse to give him what he wants. He's done unspeakable things to us. Over and over again. Each in turn, whilst the rest of us are forced to sit and watch. I tried to close my eyes at first, but he'd fished out superglue from under the kitchen sink and threatened to stick my eyes open with it if I didn't watch him cut my mother in twenty places. Slow and deep, making her scream in pain, my father shout from behind his gag and Ellie whimper in the corner.

He's finished with Ellie again now. Her right eye is swollen and bleeding. She's been stripped down to her underwear and I can see the dark patch on her pants where she's pissed herself. I close my eyes, forgetting the threat of the superglue for a moment, needing to give myself a second before he starts with me again.

That, apparently, is when the intruder takes off his balaclava.

Ellie's scream is piercing. It's as if it vibrates off the walls and I open my eyes to glare at her in annoyance. Why the fuck would she scream? Doesn't she realise she's just going to aggravate this mad man?

I look from her to the intruder, to check he isn't about to shoot my mother or father or worse, me, because my twin's a fucking idiot.

I hadn't realised he'd taken his mask off. The spots dotting his chin, nose and forehead shine greasy and red, even in the dim light. His hair is thick and dark. Greased down across his forehead with sweat from where the balaclava had flattened it.

It takes me a few seconds to place him in the dim light, I squint and concentrate hard. The files of everyone I've ever met flitting through my brain like flipping through a cookbook to spot a particular recipe. I gasp when I finally figure out why he looks so familiar. I'd seen him just days earlier. We all had.

The spotty nerd from the theatre. The one that works with Ellie.

My memory fights through the fog of fear, trying to bring the realisation to the forefront. I frown, willing it to clear so I can remember his name. The realisation starts dripping from the memory fog of clouds in my head like the slow, subtle shower of raindrops at the first sign of a storm. Until the memory shoots into my brain full force, now torrential rain in my head.   Reggie.

According to the clock on the mantel, it's been a full twenty minutes that Reggie has sat in silence. He stared at us the entire time. He's hardly blinked, and it's made the way he's slowly glowered at each of us in turn, even more sinister.

He had a stupid smirk on his face the entire time, which only seemed to deepen with humour each time one of us yelped or my father looked at the objects around the room which could work as weapons.

Then, all of a sudden, Reggie stands and uses a small but deadly looking pocket knife from his boot to cut the ties on our ankles and orders us all to stand up and move. The gun keeps us compliant like silly little sheep. He chuckles under his breath the entire time he herds us. We follow, my leg throbbing as I struggle to limp on it, pain searing my muscle with each hop, into the dining room. He demands we all sit down at the dining table. Something which we haven't done in almost a year; ever since my stupid sister had got herself pregnant and decided crying rape would dampen my parents' shame and distrust of her. It didn't. That's why we haven't sat at this table in months.

Reggie sits himself in my father's chair, at the head of the table, his dirty and scruffy old trainers resting up on the table top. He leans back casually like he's at a friend's backyard table rather than holding a family hostage at gun point in the middle of the fucking night.

We all sit like dolls in a child's dolls house, our hands all rested on top of the table as instructed, straight backs and heavy breathing. The air smells metallic, the gas he's covered the house in starting to seep into the dining table and dry.

He points his gun at each of us in turn. Letting the butt rest directly pointed at us for a few seconds each. My dad may be the police Chief but I've never felt comfortable around guns. They're deadly and unpredictable and in the hands of someone who is clearly insane, it's a recipe for disaster.

'Let's chat.' Reggie's voice sounds too high pitched. Too merry for the situation at hand and it puts me on edge.

He should be uneasy, panicked, unsure. Twitching the curtains, checking that nobody noticed the commotion, in case police sirens suddenly cut through the air. On their way to arrest him for breaking and entering, damaging property and holding us hostage. Yet, he seems completely at ease. His limbs and shoulders relaxed, his eyes watery with excitement. He's enjoying this. This isn't going to end well.

He rips the duct tape from my mom's lips first. She gasps, the skin around her lips red, raw and sore.

'Take whatever you want.' She sounds terrified and I want to go to her.

He ignores her, pulling tape from my dad's face next. He knows better than to offer him money. He's been a cop for years. He knows that's not what he's here for. He can tell. He knows if he wanted money, he wouldn't have bothered waking us. He would have just stripped the house clean whilst we slept. Instead, he took his mask off and showed us his face. He's tormenting us like this. His intentions are much more ominous than a simple house theft.

Then it's my turn. The tape brutally pulled from my face, the skin around and on my lips stinging like carpet burn. I screw my eyes shut against it, licking my lips to try and subdue the prickly feeling, the sticky residue tasting rubbery and tangy. He rips the tape from Ellie's face last and rubs his thumb down her cheek against the red hot skin where the tape was roughly pulled. She recoils from it. He might as well have slapped her. I'm wondering why when she surprises me and speaks.

'Reggie,' her face still holds that same look of pain, still making me wonder why. 'What do you want? Just tell us and we'll do it. Just let us go please.'

He laughs loudly. The laugh is fake and somehow makes him sound even more mental than he looks.

'I told you what I wanted Ellie.' He sits in the empty chair next to her, pulling it up close and then resting his chin on his hands, elbows on the table. He looks like he's just having a casual chat with a friend. It makes my stomach flip to think that, if it weren't for the gun still hanging from one hand, the scene would look almost normal to someone walking past the window. 'But you ignored me. You rejected me. I thought we had something. A connection. Like you were the only person who saw me. Really saw me.'

'I do see you Reggie.' I cringe because even I can tell by the way she says it that she's lying and I know it's not going to end well if she keeps trying to placate him when her poker face is so shit.

'No. No. No. No. NO!' the chair hits the wall so fast my brain barely has time to process it before he's on his feet.

We all notice too late that he's headed for my mother before he's dragged her to her feet. He's holding her crying against him, his forearm pressed hard against her throat. She's wailing and scratching at his arms, shouting to my dad to help her.

Then my dad's on his feet, about to lunge for Reggie when the gun's pointed square at him and I want to run. Scream and run, hide and not come back out until I'm sure he's gone. Reggie screams at my dad to 'sit back down!' and I hold my breath, praying in unison that my dad doesn't sit down, that he takes him down but also simultaneously praying that he does so that my mom doesn't get shot instead. I only realise I've been holding my breath when my dad chooses the latter and sits back down, his face full of fury and his hands clenched so hard his knuckles are pale with exertion, and I let the breath out in one long blow.

'See Ellie. If that were true...' Reggie starts rambling, still pinning my mom in place with his arm, '...you wouldn't have kept this from me. You wouldn't have been avoiding me. Ignoring my calls. You wouldn't be lying to everyone about what happened.'

'I didn't lie, Reggie.' Ellie's basically whispering now and I want to scream at her to shut up and just agree with whatever the hell he's talking about.

'What is he talking about, Ellie?' My mother gasps.

'Yeah, Ellie. What am I talking about hmm? Shall I tell her or you?'

'Reggie, please just stop this.'

'I guess we're going with me then.' He sighs, leaning in closely, mouth pressed against my mom's ear, making her squirm and fight against his grip. 'You see, Mrs Dolloway. Ellie and I are in love. Not one of them stupid teenage crushes, but real love. Or at least, I thought we were...'

'Reggie, you've got this all wrong.' Ellie sobs.

'...only, I guess I was wrong because, after we spent our first night together...' I cringe because the idea of my sister sleeping with someone, even in the midst of all this fear, makes me cringe.

'...she changed her mind. Decided I'm too poor and not good enough for her. She thinks it was a mistake. Only, instead of just breaking up with me, she's started going around calling me a rapist.'

'It was!' Ellie's hiccupping and I don't know what to do. I look to my dad for guidance but he's already slowly edging his chair closer. The tension in the air is so thick. The argument between them has us all so distracted, none of us have noticed that my dad is now almost right next to Reggie and my mom.

'NO IT WASN'T!' He bellows. 'It was not that. You love me. I know you do! But you got scared when you realised I got you pregnant and you panicked!'

The world stands still and I feel winded. My brain's trying to process exactly what is happening. What he just said. I don't have enough time to think about it before my father has lunged at him. Tackled him to the floor. My mother flies off in a different direction.

None of us noticed the flames until my mother's already crawled to me and untied the knots in the ropes keeping my hands together.

Chapter 46

Ellie

The flames are licking up the curtains by the time my mother and Freya have untied the knots in my rope. It looks like Reggie tied mine a lot tighter than theirs. I don't even have time to analyse and worry about that right now. She's screaming at my father to let him go. That we need to get out. The air is thick and my throat feels like it's swelling. I keep coughing to try and clear the smoke from my lungs but the gas has accelerated the flames. The fire spreads fast and furious. I watch my father fighting with Reggie on the floor, trying to pull the gun free and subdue him, my mother screaming at my father to get out, watching Freya trying to pull my mother out of the smoke, begging her to move.

Another cough crawls up my throat and my eyes sting. I decide I need to protect the lives of the only two people in this room that can't look after themselves. My children. I make a split-second decision.

I run. Through the house. Outside to the front garden. Coughing and spluttering, breathing in large gulps of fresh, clean, oxygen rich air. My body is trembling and my legs feel strangely cold and are stinging. It's only then I realise I've urinated all over myself and being out in the open street like this, I feel suddenly self conscious and embarrassed. Which is absolutely ridiculous, considering my house is on fire right behind me.

I feel a hand grip my shoulder from behind and I panic, shock zaps through my body and I'm on the verge of fight or flight again before I realise it's Freya. She's panting, gripping our mother's hand so tight I'm convinced that neither of them can feel their fingers. I look behind them, expecting to see my father sputtering and coughing along with us but he's not there.

I look at Freya, a million questions running through my mind. Panic seizing at all of my joints.

Then she shakes her head. A silent gesture which says a thousand words and I know it's over. My father's gone. In that very moment, it feels as if my heart breaks but I also feel relieved and for that, I hate myself. Because I feel wretched that my father is gone but I'm also relieved because Reggie Walters burned along with him.

I hate police stations. Almost as much as I hate hospitals. So, it seems only fitting we would wind up here so shortly after Freya's hospital stay.

The air always smells almost damp with coffee and pastries and sweaty old men. I've always hated police stations because they were so bleak and boring and seemed to be where all of the worst of humanity congregated. I spent so much time in the break room in this very station whilst I was growing up that I know, the chip in the skirting is from where I accidentally crashed my toy car into the paintwork on one of the weekends my father had been called in whilst my mother was out of town. That the seal on the fridge is so old that anything you put in there only lasts a day but that the station doesn't have enough money to replace it. That the Styrofoam cup of water I'm holding in my hands, which feels fuzzy as I rub my finger against it, costs roughly seventy nine pence. That the tissues my mother is pulling from the box in the middle of the table are so cheap, that she has to use three just to wipe her tears without it crumbling into pieces.

The three of us sit in silence. Waiting for someone to come and take our official statements. About how the Chief of police, my father, burnt to ash in the fire that consumed our home. My mother had hissed quietly at us, urgency in her voice, when the first wave of emergency services had arrived, to tell us not to tell them the truth. That the truth would only bring our family shame, cloud the heroic way my father died to protect us. She'd looked at me pointedly, glancing down at my stomach as she spoke. She said it didn't matter that we knew who it was, we had to pretend that we don't. Claim that it was one of the perpetrators from the string of break ins coming to take my father down as the lead investigator. That he never took his mask off but my father had taken him down. I'm too raw and exhausted to argue. My father is dead...and it's because of me.

My stomach rumbles loudly and Freya shoots me a look of disgust which says *how could you possibly be hungry at a time like this?* and I want to scream at her that I'm goddamn pregnant with twins, that's how. But, instead, I get up and head over to the fridge, hoping someone on the night shift has brought a yoghurt.

'What unearth is that!?' My mother's voice is shrill and cuts through the silence so suddenly, I feel dizzy.

'What?' I ask, turning to look at her. She's staring at me. Well, not exactly at me per say, but at my feet. I frown, unsure what the hell she's going on about until I follow her eyeline and realise.

'Seriously, Mother?' I laugh even though it's really not funny. 'That's what you're concerned about right now? That I got a stupid little tattoo on my ankle?'

PART THREE

PRESENT DAY

Chapter 47

Detective Dawson

Jasper looked at me like I was losing the plot in the early hours of this morning. I'd asked him to pull everything he possibly could on the Dolloway family and their immediate circles, including any links between them and Amelia Taylor. He'd been in the midst of making himself a coffee, still looking half asleep because of the early hour, with sleep crumbling in the corners of his eyes. In all honesty, I couldn't really blame him for thinking me mad. I must have looked like an insane woman; hair erratic and the dark circles under my eyes making me look half dead or like I hadn't slept in days. Which I haven't. It's eating at me that there's something I'm missing. It bites down and chews in those twilight hours when I pretend to sleep.

The notion that, if I can just find the missing piece, it will all make sense. It bites down with sharp teeth and shreds sleep from me with each layer of flesh it gnaws through. I don't know why but my instinct is telling me that figuring out what the Dolloway's are purposefully omitting about the night of the fire, will lead me to Amelia's killer.

I'm entirely aware that I could be completely off the mark. Especially since we haven't actually found any proof that they're linked.

Yet, something about the fact that Amelia's killer is clearly twisted enough to have practised his techniques, gives me a sinking feeling that is near impossible to ignore. I've never believed in coincidences and the fact that the Dolloway twins are blonde and both Pieces are not lost on me. Jasper isn't looking at me like I've lost the plot anymore though, now that he's found something. Now, he looks as wired as me. He pulls up all sorts of digital code which I can't make the faintest sense of. He rambles on about IP addresses and digital footprints for a good ten minutes before I lose my patience.

'Jasper.' I snap. 'I need you to tell me in plain English and I need you to do it now.'

'Right.' Disappointment ripples through his features before he pulls himself together. 'You remember that website Freya was a part of, XXX Nasties?'

'The cam girl site. Yeah, I remember it.'

'Looks like our girl Freya wasn't the only local girl using the site to make some extra money. Amelia Taylor also has a profile. Although, she wasn't as security conscious as Freya and didn't bother to use a screen name. She just signed right up with her legal name and details.' My brain fights itself, trying to slot this new piece of information into the picture I have of Amelia Taylor.

The loving and thoughtful daughter and mother that her parents spoke so lovingly of. The supportive and selfless friend her friends and colleagues raved about with such adoration and admiration, with this version of her as I look over XXX Nasties page. Trying to fuse the reserved girl her colleagues described her as with the woman dancing half naked in front of the camera, sucking her fingers and responding to the requests of perverts. With a smile. My brain feels numb from the effort. I can't believe how we never found out about such explicit online behaviour in the original investigation.

'How did this not turn up when she first went missing?'

'Her dates of activity were between 2017 and 2020.'

'The year she got pregnant.'

'Exactly. Looks like she decided the use of the site wouldn't fit into motherhood. She last posted in the winter of twenty nineteen and then completely stopped using the site altogether. It didn't show up in our original digital searches because we weren't looking that far back.'

'We always assumed whoever took her would have entered her life recently.' I'm clenching my teeth so hard that my jaw starts to ache.

'You think this vic's death and your missing person's case are somehow connected?' Jasper raises an eyebrow at me and I can read the curiosity in the way his fingers twitch on his keyboard.

'I don't know. Maybe.' There isn't much I can really tell him. It's not like I can go *well until this little snippet of information, there hasn't been any evidence to suggest a connection but now I'm starting to think I might not be so bat shit crazy after all.*

So all I do say is that I need to know if Freya and Amelia have ever had the same clients or the same members of the site interact with them before. I want to scream when he says that's going to take a bit longer and that I may as well go get some sleep in the meantime. I stop myself from ranting and raving about how we don't have time. That, if I'm right, Freya Dolloway isn't as safe as we first thought and that we need to find her right now. Because at the moment, I don't have any hard evidence that I'm right. So, instead I head to the espresso machine in the station lobby.

My bones ache and my feet sting and cramp as I walk, the next twelve hours of my shift stretching out in front of me. Reminding me why I should have gone home and to sleep properly yesterday but now, instead I get to be grumpy and twitchy from caffeinated liquid for the rest of the night. It's as I step off the lift that I hear it; Shouts and expletives from an angry civilian, arguing with Morgan on the front desk.

My internal struggle debates whether to turn right back around and just use the cheap, half stale powder that the government is trying to pass off as coffee instead. The screaming seems to kick up a notch, as if that's even possible, and the Detective in me who doesn't want to leave Morgan to fend off the screamer alone, wins. As I turn the corner it shocks me to see that it's Tilly Parker screaming at Morgan. Her hands, heavy with rings, waving about, her massive frizzy red hair looking somehow much more fiery today. Her face is red from all the screaming. All of a sudden, my craving for caffeine is forgotten.

'Ms Parker.' I cut in loudly, giving Tilly no choice but to stop screaming and twist round to face me, 'What seems to be the problem here?' I make eye contact with Morgan for a split second, nodding to let her know she can back off and find refuge in the back office. She visibly relaxes, her shoulders slumping and she whispers a silent 'Thanks, Molly.' before slipping out the back.

'Freya. Freya's the problem!' Tilly throws her hands in the air and I watch her inhale deeply as if to rev up her voice box. Ready for another onslaught. I open the closest door and motion for her to go inside before she can start. She's looking at me with a confused and questioning expression when I follow her in and close the door. Looking around the room, I realise why. 'You're kidding me, right?' She laughs without humour as she motions to the five by six space around us which is piled high with boxes and shelves of office supplies. I hadn't realised that I'd pushed us into the reception supply closet.

'We can go and try and find an empty office in this extremely busy station, if you'd prefer.' I fold my arms, trying my best at looking the part of a firm and strict Detective. It feels unnatural somehow. A role normally reserved for Luke. I clear my throat and try harder, 'Which, from the level you were shouting back there, I imagine you don't want to waste time doing. So, I'll ask again, what seems to be the problem? I watch the internal conflict dance across her face as she debates whether or not to argue with me. I see the moment she decides it's not worth it, looking up to the ceiling and sighing purposefully loud.

'Ellie doesn't want me to do this. She's going to kill me when she finds out I'm here but someone needs to do something. I don't know what to do. I'm not used to not knowing how to help her.' It unnerves me that her eyes are shiny. She doesn't strike me as the type of woman who often cries.

'She doesn't want you to do what?'

'She's being threatened. Freya didn't leave on her own; She was taken by somebody and whoever that person is, they don't want Ellie to go to the police. They said they'd kill Freya and Ellie thinks they've been following her. Leaving her signs and messages.' I feel all the blood rush to my feet. This is what I've been so afraid of. If I'm right, The Dolloway's are far from safe. I'm about to ask Tilly if she'll make an official statement but her next words chill me to the core.

'She thinks she's next.'

The hushed conversation with Tilly plays over and over in my head all day. I pick my phone up and put it back down every five minutes. Trying to decide how best to proceed. I should tell the Chief. I should ask for the Dolloway case to be re-opened. Grovel that I was wrong and I think we need to start looking again. But Tilly's pleas ring loud in my ears. That I can't make it obvious. Not to go near Ellie in case whoever this lunatic is, means it and they'll hurt Freya if I do.

'So, you've seen these photos?' Luke asks, pacing back and forth across the kitchen which is much too small for it.

I'd ushered, more like shoved, him in here once Tilly had told me all she knew and left. I came back up to the office, pushing Luke mid-stride into the kitchen as soon as I'd found him, ignoring his protestations at being manhandled.

I'd relayed my entire conversation with Tilly back to him and laid out all my suspicions that have been plaguing every waking hour I've had in the last three days. Suspicions now only more solidified in my mind to be true now that Tilly has told me Ellie is being threatened.

I think the home invasion which led to Chief Dolloway's death, wasn't an accident. That, whoever it was, had a motive we don't know about but, I think the Dolloway twins and their mother do.

That Amelia Taylor's death is somehow related to it all but that I don't exactly know how or why yet but that Amelia was also using the XXX Nasties site too which is too much of a coincidence to not be relevant.

That Freya Dolloway is in fact actually missing, taken by somebody and being held captive somewhere but I don't know why. Only a gut feeling that it somehow links to her father's death.

Then I explained Tilly's sudden appearance at the station and how she'd disclosed that Ellie was being contacted, and possibly targeted, by said kidnapper.

That's when he started pacing. The carpet worn down at least a few millimetres in the last hour that we've been talking it all through.

'So, We're thinking it's Oliver James, right? The ex-husband. It's always the ex-husband.'

'I'm not so sure.' I frown. 'If it were Oliver, why would he bother contacting Ellie at all? He has Freya now. Contacting and threatening her twin only puts him in a more vulnerable position. Why bother with the risk?' I slump back in my chair, exhausted. It feels like all I do is run around in circles with this case. I still don't know what the hell is going on.

Tilly had been reluctant to tell me at first. Her loyalty to her friendship with Ellie stood steadfast and strong but she'd eventually told me about the photographs and the alumni ring they both recognised. She told me it looked familiar and that, after much deliberation, she and Ellie believe it to be Freya's ex-husband's.

'That ring though,' Luke throws his hands up in the air in frustration and I can't blame him. 'She said it was Oliver's, right?'

'Right, but she also said half the graduating glass had one. Plus, it's not exactly an exclusive or overly complicated pattern. I reckon, we put that picture of the ring into the search engine and we get back hundreds of hits of similar patterns and symbols. Plus, he's lawyered up to the nines. No way his lawyer takes kindly to us calling him in for an enquiry on a case which, for all intents and purposes, is now closed.'

'You're right.' Luke huffs and falls down into one of the uncomfortable kitchen chairs in defeat. We sit quietly for a few minutes. 'You know what we have to do don't you?'

'Yes.' I scratch at my throat, trying to knead at the bubble of regret there. I know that Tilly specifically asked me not to and that I, under duress, had agreed not to speak to Ellie but I'm about to break her trust in coming to me. We have no other choice if we're going to find Freya. 'We need to speak to Ellie Dolloway again.'

Chapter 48

Ellie

I think I'll remember that exact moment I realised that my sister would be the death of me. It was any other normal Monday evening except I'd put the kids to bed early again. At least, it wasn't still light out this time. Although, whether that was because it was 8PM or, because Autumn has taken over summer almost in an instant this week, I'm unsure. The realisation that Freya would most likely be the reason I meet my end one day, came later.

I was a wine glass deep into oblivion already. I've never thought myself much of a drinker until all of this started. Only now, I realise that alcohol seems to calm the disarray and uncertainty. It helps slot my thoughts back into place when I start to feel discombobulated or disembodied. Something which I've been feeling more this week than I have in years.

I feel exhausted and yet, I can't seem to sleep. The thoughts go round and round in my head. Each one fighting for first place on a never ending race track in my mind. My muscles spasm at the slightest dark thought or faintest noise. I've been trying my hardest not to let the cracks show in front of the kids. I've always tried my best to be the kind of mother that mine never was. To protect them from the darkness and mind melding anxiety which seeped into my soul all those years ago and nested.

No matter how hard I try to smooth the cracks, the kids still seem to notice. Both of them are so attuned to my mood, you'd think the cord which gave them life through me was still firmly fastened between us. Matty has been clinging to me all week. My beautiful little empath knows that I'm on the verge of losing my freaking mind. I'm relieved he doesn't ask me what's wrong anymore though. He knows he won't get a straight answer.

But, even though they both seem quiet around me now, I can tell it's affecting them both. They squabble more. All of a sudden, both of them seem to run on a short fuse with each other and the world. The school had called me in to take Matty home early this morning after he'd pulled a classmate's hair so hard it bled when the tangle of hairs were ripped from the scalp.

I make camomile tea to take to bed to try and calm the nerves. I'd tried to speak to Matty about what happened at school today during dinner and the way he'd looked at me made my blood run cold. I'd always panicked about what the children might inherit from their father. For the first six months of my pregnancy I was convinced that evil was inherent and would latch on to my children like a parasitic disease. Of course, when they were here and in my arms, I laughed at myself for even thinking such a dark and heinous thought. They were perfect. Yet, for the first time in all their years of life, Matty had looked at me with that dark shadow over his face; eyes fierce with venom and anger, and I saw him there. His father. The evil embedded when he was conceived, now shining on the surface.

It was that moment. Looking at that drop of evil in my only son's eyes, I realised Freya would be the death of us. Of me. After all of this, her disappearing was going to be the reason that my life is never the same again. The person I was before all of this, the person my son was before all of this, is almost dead and gone.

The harsh ringtone of my phone echoes loudly off the tiles. I don't physically jump when it does, because there isn't enough energy in me left to jump today, but the shock of the sound causes an unearthly whine under my breath.

I glance at the clock when I see who's calling me. It's nearly 10PM now. So, why on earth is Grace Parkett calling me this late at night?

I've only had three sessions with Laurie so far, two at their house and a third in a local cafe when I couldn't bear to be in that house anymore. I haven't heard from them in almost a week now. I had assumed that Grace went elsewhere when I'd turned up looking like half warmed up death to our last session because I hadn't slept more than three hours in the previous forty-eight.

I watch it ring dubiously and hold my breath when it cuts out. I wait to see if a voicemail notification appears. When it doesn't, I smile with relief, my shoulders loosening, and pour boiling water onto my teabag. I'll call her back in the morning, I decide.

🔥

By the early hours of the morning, after watching late night television reruns, I've almost completely forgotten about the strange call. I don't really pay attention to what's actually showing. The background noise is more of a comfort to my tired eyes than anything else. I keep drifting.

My eyes are heavy and sleep is beginning to take over again. Except, my eyes shoot open with panic every time I'm about to drift off. My dreams are full of ominous threats and shadows in the dark.

The sight of heavy fingers grasping my sister's throat. Then, all of a sudden I can feel them. Nails digging. Pressure pushes on my windpipe as I struggle for breath. My sister's throat no longer hers but mine. Every time I startle back awake, I debate popping an entire tube of pills just to finally get some sleep.

My head's lolling again as I sit on the sofa in the dark, the garish bright colors of the television screen bouncing off the walls and across the ceiling. A throw pulled up tight under my chin against the slight chill of the late hour, when my phone starts ringing again. The sudden sound jolts me awake. The ringtone jarring my tired head. I glance around the room, unsure of where the noise is coming from. Vibration against my thigh pulls me back into the here and now and I pull the loudly ringing phone from under my leg.

It's Grace Parkett. Again. I glance at the clock on the mantel and anxiety swells when I see that it's almost 2AM. I figure it must be an emergency for her to be calling me so late, and more than once. I wonder as I answer the call, what sort of emergency it could possibly be that she would call her daughter's tutor.

But, the voice that answers Grace Parkett's phone, isn't Grace Parkett at all. Their voice comes through low, deep and gruff. Partially muffled as if by some sort of cloth and I'm suddenly wide awake. Gripping the edge of the sofa, my nails fighting with the fabric so hard, I'm sure I can hear it tearing.

'Oh, she finally answers!' The voice chuckles. The laugh is cruel rather than humourful, 'Hey, Ellie. Did you miss me?'

My throat constricts and I can't speak. Can hardly breathe. No, no, no, no, no. It can't be. My logic fights with my instinct in a silent battle. Even though it shouldn't be, can't possibly be, it's him.

'Oh, for fuck's sake. Why are women so dramatic!?' He's referring to the fact I'm currently hyperventilating over the phone, loud enough for him to hear it.

'How?...what?...you're dead.' My voice comes out strangled and stuttered.

'On the contrary.' His voice is way too light and breezy for the current situation and it scratches my ears with irritation. 'I'm alive and well. Here, waiting for you. Freya's here too, also alive and well but not for long. Guess you better get here quick. Don't even think of calling that pretty Detective or her partner either. I'll know if you do and Freya won't thank you for it. I promise you.' '

'What? Get to where?' I stammer, panic for my sister overriding my fear.

'Use that big pretty brain of yours, Ellie. You know where I am. Think about it. Not for too long though, who knows how long Freya has left.'

The line cuts dead. I'm sweating so much my armpits and forehead are damp. I feel a weird concoction of both rampantly terrified and yet, almost calm. Maybe it's because now I know for sure who I'm up against. I only hope that, this time, I'm strong enough to finish it.

It takes me a surprisingly short amount of time to figure out where they are. The call having come from Grace Parkett's landline being the major clue. Back at the old house.

I toy momentarily with the idea of calling Tilly to come and watch the kids. My thumb hovers over the call button for thirty seconds before I decide against it. I put my phone back in my pocket. She'll want to come with me or worse, call the police, and I can't put anyone else I love in danger. I can't carry that guilt too. It'll break me.

So, instead, I shove my old scruffy converse on and run across the lawn to Janet next door. I feel bad whilst I'm hammering on the front door. The poor woman is definitely over sixty and I'm waking her up in the middle of the night to watch my sleeping twins with no explanation. Just an apology and a plea of desperation.

She looks sleep ridden, confused and somewhat suspicious as she looks me up and down. I wonder how ridiculous I must look from her point of view. Standing here, in my scruffy trainers absorbing all of the rain water and my too large raincoat on. My hood up against the pouring rain. I must look absolutely frigging insane and I feel it.

'Alright, love.' She nods, still looking unsure but agreeing. 'Whatever you need.'

'Thank you!' I want to throw my arms around her but don't want to soak her through too. 'They're both asleep in bed. There shouldn't be any trouble.' I turn on my heels and run to my car. Rain water splashes and soaks the back of my legs. 'I won't be long!' I look back and shout.

As I turn the key in the ignition, I hope with every inch of my being, that I'm not lying to her.

Chapter 49

No One

Four Hours Earlier

It's nearly time. So close, I can taste it in the air. It couldn't have come soon enough. She's so battered and bruised that she didn't even put up a fight when I dragged her out of her room and took her to the bathroom.

She was stiff with tension but placid and didn't put up a fight when I stripped her bare and helped her into the tub. The water was almost scolding, and it brought me joy to see her flinch against its intensity when I pushed her head backwards into the water. She tried to hide her terror when I pushed her head below the surface. I knew she was thinking of all those times I'd done this exact same thing in the old metal sink in the basement. Of all the fun we've had.

She needn't have been afraid though. This wasn't like the other times. This is what I've been waiting for.

She smells divine now. Like Lily and Jasmine. The aroma filled the room like a warm blanket of my mother's old shampoos and scents. If it weren't such a big night tonight, I would've taken her back downstairs and ravaged her.

Instead, I control myself. Because, despite what she and her prissy, holier-than-thou family might believe, I'm not a total savage. I have boundaries. I have control.

That's why I have to do this. To end all of this here and now, tonight. To show them all who I really am. That they never got the better of me.

I help her out and take her to the room across the hall. A room I normally actively avoid. She gawks at me in horror. She's not stupid. She grew up in a law enforcement family after all. She knows that the fact I've stopped wearing the mask is because were nearing the finale. She searches my features, trying to work out where she's seen me before. Self-absorbed bitch, she'll figure it out.

The must and damp smell of my mother's old furniture and belongings hang in the air. I take a moment to relish in the memory of snuffing the life from her. Over and over and over again. I pulled one of my mother's dresses from the wardrobe. A pretty pale yellow summer dress. It hangs from her tiny frame and for a split second, I imagine her as having my mother's body.

All folds and sweat before alcoholism ate the fat from her bones. Dermatitis inflamed between her fat from the lack of hygiene. I gag. Shake the memory from the forefront of my mind. It looks much better on her than it did on my mother anyway. I wonder, for a brief moment, if it would look better on Ellie. I decide that it would.

I paint her face. Not too dramatically because I don't want her to look like a slut tonight. It's not her who's the slut, it's her sister. She looks amazing by the time I give her the tea.

She gulps it down, not even hesitating, her mouth dry and chapped, screaming out for the hydration. She drinks it greedily and scoffs the bread roll I give her like a ravenous animal. Her gluttony makes me want to vomit. Memories of my mother ramming food into her mouth, the flesh of her second chin bobbing up and down. Crumbs falling from her hands and mouth, sauce soaking into and staining her clothes.

I guess it makes sense that she would be ravenous. Unlike my mother used to, she's been eating a miniscule amount whilst she's been here with me. When I remember to feed her, that is. She's much skinnier now. Her cheeks look sunken, and her collarbones jut out.

Oh well. She's still alive for tonight and that's all that matters. It's all she's here for. Her sister's the one I'm really interested in terrorising, after all. She's just a means to an end.

The Rohypnol in the tea works fast. I guess it makes sense. With the weight loss, she's much skinnier now, so it would take a lower dose to make her docile. I panic momentarily as I'm putting her in the back of the truck. I might have given her too much. Have I? I decide it doesn't matter either way. She isn't what this is all about. She's meaningless. Worthless even. A means to a more gratifying end.

The windows are dark when I get there. The house sleeps along with its inhabitants. I've been watching them closely, every few days for the past few months. I almost know their entire routine by heart.

For instance, I know that her husband works long hours in the centre of town for at least six days a week. I even called his office to ask for a consultation with him this evening to ensure he'd stay behind late. Only to find out, to my surprise, that he's on a business trip in Germany for the entirety of this week and the next.

This is why I watch them. Why I do my homework first. Because it means that I know when the wife comes down and opens the door warily after my consistent loud knocking wakes her up, that she is almost defenceless. I know that, when I force my way in and pin her to the wall and tell her not to scream, that there's no one about to run down the stairs and tackle me.

I also know that when she says her husband is just upstairs and will wake up at any moment, that she's full of fucking shit.

Chapter 50

Detective Dawson

Given the time of night, I'm caught off guard when an elderly, plump woman with hair shockingly white answers Ellie Dolloway's front door.

We'd debated whether or not to wait until the morning but had decided it might not be worth the risk. If the person who held, tortured and murdered Amelia Taylor and the person who is currently holding Freya Dolloway are one in the same, time is of the essence. The rain's so heavy it's dripping off the hood of my waterproof parka and keeps landing irritatingly on my nose. The sudden change in weather makes me shiver. Yesterday, it was one of the hottest summer's we've ever had. Tonight, it feels like the sun knew what was to come and vacated the premises. Luke looks like a wet dog and I know for a fact it's only a matter of time before he shakes his head like one too.

I hop from one foot to the other slightly, feeling the dirty rainwater splash up the back of my trousers. The plump woman frowns at us in turn and pulls the door closed ever so slightly, pushing it against her squishy side. An ironic move really and definitely an afterthought, considering she's already opened the door without the security chain on. I decide we don't have time for me to give her the old cop lecture about personal and home security at this very moment. Another time perhaps. If I don't see her family crying on the news before then. They'll cry and hold her picture, telling the reporter about how she's always been too trusting. That she opened the door to the wrong person one night. They'll sob and tell us how they always had to remind her to put the security chain on.

'Can I help you?' She asks expectantly.

'Good evening Ma'am, We're looking for Miss Dolloway. Is she home, please?' Luke asks. All smiles and puppy dog eyes. As usual, the woman goes a decidedly deeper shade of pink and tucks her white hair behind her ear.

'Oh, no need to be so formal dear. Call me Pauline.'

'Pauline, can we speak with Miss Dolloway?' I grit my teeth. My patience wearing thin given the situation and an underlying ebb of jealousy that I don't want to admit is there. 'Please?' I add as an afterthought. Pauline tuts and looks at me with great disdain. Clearly put out by the fact I've ruined her flirting.

'She isn't home.' She snaps. All pleasantries out the window. 'Can I take a message Miss...'

'Detective Dawson.' I pull my badge out of my sopping wet pocket and flash it at her. 'And Detective Lorell.' I motion to Luke.

Tthat makes her perk up. I can see the curiosity peaking in the raise of her eyebrows. I imagine she'll be gossiping with the other women down the bingo hall this weekend.

'Oh!' She holds her hand to her chest theatrically. 'What in the heavens has happened?'

I ignore her question. 'Do you know when she'll be back?' I smile tightly.

I wipe moisture from my forehead. Whether it's from the perspiration of anxiety or the rain, I'm unsure. All I am sure about is that Ellie doesn't strike me as the type of woman to leave her kids in the middle of the night for anything not emergent.

'No idea, dear. She didn't even tell me where she was going. Came round all desperate, in the middle of the night. Woke me up by half banging down my door and asked me to look after those poor children upstairs. Didn't even wait for me to get in the bleeding house before she'd zoomed off in that car of hers.' Pauline tuts loudly, shaking her head.

I can see her now, telling her bingo pals all dramatically about what an awful mother Ellie is. She'll shake her head and discuss the absurdity of her leaving her children like that. It gnaws at me though. Alarm bells chime in my head and I don't know why, but I feel like we're missing something. So, I ask Pauline if we can come inside to take a look around.

'I don't know about that.' She frowns, pulling the door tighter to herself again. I wonder if she thinks I'm going to barge her headfirst or something. 'I don't really have permission to allow you to-'

'Pauline.' Luke cuts in and steps forward, smiling at her in that way that makes all women - unfortunately, myself included - weak at the knees. 'We're a bit worried about Ellie and I can tell you're the type of woman who, I have no doubt, looks out for the young girl next door as if she were your own.' *bullshit.* 'So, please. We just want to make sure nothing is amiss and then we'll be on our way.'

She chews her lip, mulling it over. She looks Luke over a little too closely for my liking but then she submits. Stepping back and motioning us inside. I don't know exactly what it is that I'm looking for but I'm hoping I'll somehow know when I see it.

Chapter 51

Freya

I'm so cold my fingers ache. This dress he's put me in is not meant to be worn in the torrential rain. The fabric starch scratches my bruised and broken skin. It feels like drying yourself with a towel when you have awful sunburn. I keep coming in and out of consciousness. My head and eyelids are heavy. I feel nauseous and light headed.

I've been tied to this chair since I woke up. I have no idea where we are and I feel too foggy to put the pieces together. All I can make out when I look around the room is the outlines of furniture and the woman and young girl tied up in the corner of the room.

They look terrified and I want to tell them to run. Get out! Before it's too late. To tell them that he's a maniac and likes to play God. I want to scream but just as I'm trying to gain the energy, my head lolls again and the room goes black.

He grabs my face hard. His nails, dirty and long, stab my cheeks as he roughly shakes my head, pulling my face from one side to the other. I feel like I'm about to vomit and I want to gag but I don't have any energy. The image of him shouting something at me swims in front of my eyes. His voice is muffled and sounds like it's underwater.

I try to push his hands off but my arms are pressed between the wooden chair and the rough rope that he's wrapped around me. It fuses me in place, unable to move. I believe that even if I could move my arms, I wouldn't be able to get my brain and arms to work in coordination. My limbs feel slack and limp and won't move.

I try to scream. To tell him whatever it was that he gave me mixed in with the tea and bread, he gave me too much of it. It's killing me and I want to tell him that he needs to call an ambulance before it takes its toll and kills me.

Then I realise, the thought chipping away at my resolve, that if that does happen, if I do die, he'll just bring me back and do it all again.

I can feel I'm about to lose consciousness again and I fight with every inch of my being not to. I wanted to die when I was a teenager and lost the love of my life. But, being held captive by this maniac, I realise now that I'd do just about anything to live.

He gives up trying to hold my face up. He lets go of my chin and my head rolls heavy on my neck and shoulders. He moves away from me and heads towards the woman and girl in the corner. Their pleads ring out distorted in my ears.

I try to tell them to be passive. To not fight. That it's so much worse when you try to fight him. I open my mouth but my tongue won't move. The words won't form. The drugs dulled my muscle responses.

Then it goes black.

Chapter 52

Ellie

The house is dark. Still. Lifeless. Anxiety twinges in my fingers and tightens my grip on the steering wheel. The rain's coming down so heavily now, I don't know if I'd be able to see anything even if I wanted to. I also know he's not dumb enough to stand near the windows. I know that if I want to save my sister, then I have to go in there. Face all of this. Part of me even feels like I deserve whatever's about to happen.

There's still that little glimmer and whisper of hope telling me that we'll get out of this alive. Like we did last time. Except, lightning doesn't strike the same place twice. Right?

I watch the dash clock creep on for twenty minutes. I want to go across and into the house but my legs are like lead in the seat. My knuckles are white and aching with the excursion of gripping the wheel so tight for so long when my phone pings loudly in the quiet. Dragging me from my state of catatonia.

I glance down, subconsciously knowing who it is before I even read the message which lights up the screen.

Are you going to sit out there forever? Tick, Tock, Ellie. Tick. Tock.

I swallow the bile churning up my throat and turn the car off. I know now that he can see me. That he's watching me from inside the house. It terrifies me that he can see me, but I can't see him. Now the car isn't humming anymore, the sound of the rain and thunder suddenly become so much louder and more ominous than before. I drag myself out of the car, thinking of my sister, of Grace and of Laurie. They don't deserve to die because I was too terrified to get out of the car.

I stand at the bottom of the less than a decade old porch steps. Watching the rain splash and spill down them, the wood stain not budging. I find myself thinking about how old and worn the steps used to be. When we lived here. They were weathered and scratched, chunks missing in some places. My stomach tightens but I have to ignore it. The Parkett's haven't even lived here long enough to ruin the stain on the porch steps. They've been here such a miniscule amount of time and yet, because of me, they might not live long enough to scuff the paintwork on their steps. No one will ever know why it happened to them.

I pull my cell haphazardly out of my pocket, fighting with the screen as rain soaks it, the drops hard enough to select random letters in-between my typed words. I stab at it in frustration. Finally managing to get the text message typed out. I send it off into the ether. Then I take a deep breath and force my legs to move.

I drag myself up the too-perfect steps to the front door. Telling myself that I'll make sure we all walk out of this.

That I'll make sure he doesn't.

Chapter 53

Detective Dawson

My veins feel fizzy with caffeine but I still tell Pauline I'll take a coffee. If only to get her out of the room for ten minutes. As soon as she's rounded the corner in the hall, I'm pulling open drawers and cupboards in the television and side unit. Looking for... *something*.

I can tell from the way that Luke doesn't automatically start searching with me, making huffing sounds and grumbling behind me, that he doesn't approve.

'Shut up.' I whisper, 'if Amelia's abductor also has Freya, we're running out of time.'

'Fine.' He grumbles, leaning casually against the door frame to keep watch for Pauline. When he hears the kettle ping, he goes into the kitchen to distract her, asking about biscuits. I breathe with relief and start looking more slowly. Paying closer attention.

One of the drawers in the living room cabinet catches and I have to pull it roughly to get it open. It's full of junk. Loose cables and spare batteries but it also has the black and white photographs Tilly told me about. She wasn't lying when she said that they're sinister. Goose pimples line my arms as I flick through them. I take pictures of them with my phone - the irony not lost on me - and send them over to Jasper. I ask him to see if he can find anything that might tell us where the images were taken.

I keep looking methodically through the cabinet. Pauline laughs loudly in the other room, the flirtatious falseness of the sound grates against my eardrums. I block it out. Now is not the time for needless jealousy. I have much bigger concerns than my love life right now.

I don't know why I'm drawn to the high school yearbook. Maybe it's because the childhood for the twins is so elusive. Maybe it's because Ellie and Tilly seem too apprehensive to talk about it. Or, that the Chief's death happened at the precipice of their childhood and yet, we know barely anything about it. Perhaps it's simply because, being the daughter of a cold and distant Detective myself, I want to know if their childhood was as lonely as mine was.

Whatever it is that causes the silent pull, I find myself opening it and flipping through the pages. I'm relieved to hear a clatter and splat of fallen water, the fake apologies of Luke for being so clumsy, re-assuring flirty giggles from Pauline telling him not to worry and she'll make him a fresh one. The whirr of the kettle. I bite back the unneeded sigh rising in my throat at Pauline's obvious attraction to Luke. She's allowed to find him attractive. I have no right to be irritated by her flirting. I remind myself again that I have bigger concerns.

I flip through the yearbook. The pages tell a similar story to my own high school experience. The clear divides and cliques. The teenage angst. The popular kids cover nearly every page, the centre of the high school universe.

I find Freya and Ellie's pictures side by side. Until this moment, I hadn't realised quite how different they looked to one another. They

are definitely identical in their features but the way they hold themselves is contrasting.

Freya sits tall, head slightly cocked, smiling so wide that you can see
her molars. She has make-up on and her hair is curled at the ends. The
shade of her lipstick matches her top almost perfectly.

Ellie instead looks defeated. Shoulders slumped and her hair falling
over half her face. She isn't quite looking at the camera and her smile
is almost non-existent, more forced than natural. She looks sad and
my heart goes out to her. I've never seen Ellie look anything except
haunted and I hope that's just because the only situation I've seen her
in is one of high stress and pressure, not because she feels hollow.

The doorbell is loud and shrill, pulling me out of my empathetic
spiral. I glance at the clock and cringe inwardly that whoever has
decided to call round at... almost three AM... on a Friday has probably
just woken the sleeping children upstairs. Luke nods at me as he walks
past, heading for the door, letting me know that he'll handle it. I carry
on flipping through the year book.

Freya's featured a few times in different sections. She smiles at me
from group shots of the netball team and has a few honorary mentions in the fundraisers. There's a picture of her and a very handsome
looking chap entwined and smiling at the camera in the prom royalty
nominations section. They're very clearly childhood sweethearts. I feel
an edge of feminine rage at the patriarchy of it all. Then, a page later,
there's a memorial page to the young handsome chap that Freya was
wrapped around lovingly. I guess he died before he even managed to
make it to prom, he'd never know if he was truly prom royalty after
all. I flip quickly through the last pages, eager to get through it, when
something slips out of the back and flutters to the floor.

When I pick it up I'm surprised to see that it's seems to be an old
print of the school newspaper. Just the one copy. I wonder why Ellie

would keep it tucked away in here at all. Then I notice the picture in the bottom corner of the front page.

The photo's of Chief Dolloway. The same one they used at his funeral service and in all of the local papers when he died. He's dressed in his Chief's uniform, smiling widely into the camera as if he doesn't see horrific things on the job daily. The text to the left of the photograph is a small obituary and dedication of that month's paper to him. I'm guessing that's why she kept it. I imagine she didn't have many photos of her father left after the fire.

I sigh sadly and flick through the rest of the short newsletter. I catch sight of Ellie in one of the featured articles. I read through it.

It's a two-page feature spread detailing the end of year *FAREWELL MOVIE MARATHON*. An event running Friday to Sunday over the Halloween weekend. I scan the article. Looks like it was a yearly occurrence. Where all of the teenagers in the area would meet at the movies for the midnight screening of that year's feature film. Ellie and Freya's graduating year was, ironically, John Carpenter's original 1978 Halloween.

The image included in the article is of all the students who worked at the movie theatre and who were all working that particular showing during said weekend.

They're all wearing Halloween costumes and only half of them look happy about it. You can tell the kids who had worked hard on their outfits and took a real liking to Halloween. There's a very convincing werewolf, a needlessly slutty nurse covered in blood and a Hauntingly white ghost. One young lad had clearly just wrapped himself in cheap toilet paper from home. So cheap in fact, it was ripping and fraying and almost translucent. Another kid hadn't even bothered to dress up at all.

I spot Ellie right away. She was wearing a bright orange and white striped t-shirt under a faded old hooded jacket. Her belly was swollen and large under the fabric which was stretching to the point of almost ripping. Juno. Clever.

'Dawson.' Luke walks back into the room with his cup, Tilly Parker close at his heels.

What on earth is Tilly doing here at nearly three in the morning?

'Detective.' Her red hair is damp and sticking to the side of her face. The curls are even tighter ringlets then they normally are.

'Ms Parker... Tilly. Sorry.' I remember her demand to not be addressed so formally and correct myself. 'What are you doing here?'

She looks like she ran the entire way. She's drenched through and her hands are trembling. She blows little clouds of breath warm vapour into the room when she breathes out.

'Ellie texted me.' She pants. Clearly out of breath. 'Is she here? Why are you here? What happened?'

My palms are tingling again, telling me to pay attention. That there's something not quite right.

'Ellie isn't here.' I frown. 'According to Pauline from next door, she took off a couple of hours ago without explanation. Asked her to look after the children.'

She shakes her head as if to shake away the thoughts, frowning as she tries to make sense of the information. There's rain water dripping off her nose every couple of seconds like mine was earlier and I can't seem to stop looking at it.

'Would you like a towel, Tilly?' Luke says it as a question but he's already heading for the kitchen before she can answer. Not that she seems to have noticed his question anyway.

She's still frowning with concentration. If I could see her thoughts laid out in front of me, I'm sure they'd be racing around the floor, charging for first place. Luke re-appears and hands her a tea towel, his cup having been abandoned somewhere back in the kitchen.

'Pauline?' I ask him quietly, not wanting to disturb wherever Tilly's train of thought is taking her. We might need its destination.

'The doorbell woke the kids.' Luke answers me, also mumbling. 'She's gone to try and put them back down. The boy's clever. I think he can tell there's something going on.'

I nod. Hoping she keeps the kids out of ear shot for a while.

'Tilly, you said Ellie had texted you?' I draw my attention back to her.

She's sitting silent. She's clutching the tea towel in a clenched fist but not bothering to use it to dry her face. The rainwater still falls from her nose religiously.

Drip, drip. Drip, drip.

She seems oblivious to it. Her eyes seem to stare at something non-existent in the middle of the room. My question draws her out and she blinks up at me. I carry on watching the rain water fall from her nose until she answers.

Drip, drip. Drip, drip.

'Right, yeah. It's why I ran over. I was working the night shift tonight. I'm a nurse.' She pulls her phone from her pocket as she speaks.

I work every muscle in my face to keep the surprise from my features. Her abruptness and take-no-shit personality doesn't give me a good natured, compassionate nurse vibe. Although, that doesn't necessarily mean anything. I've missed things before. Missed enough that a kind-hearted mother was tortured for months on end until she died.

'When I saw the text, I asked someone to cover for me and came straight over. Here... look.'

She unlocks her phone and then hands it to me. All of a sudden, she seems to notice the tea towel in her other hand and dries her face. I take a look at the message with no *drip, drip* to distract me. The text message from Ellie had come in an hour ago and I can see why she ran all the way here in the middle of the night when she saw it. **He has Freya at the house. I had to come alone. Keep the kids safe and make sure they know I love them.**

I pass the phone to Luke.

Dear god. She's gone to meet this maniac.

If my suspicions are right, and the man who took Amelia now has Freya, she has no idea what she's walking into. What he likes to do. Against my better judgement, I pull my own cell from my pocket and pull up a picture of Amelia. Not one of the autopsy photographs that I have access to, because I can only imagine what effect that would have on a civilian. Although, I imagine Tilly has seen her fair share of the dead in her line of work. I just don't want to add Amelia's battered body to the images already stored in her head. I can barely look at them myself and I've seen some things on this job. I pull up a photo of her and her daughter.

Both of them are snuggled close on her parents' sofa. The light from the television colouring their faces blue. They're wearing matching Christmas pyjamas that you see people wearing in those cringe-worthy family photo Christmas cards. Except, they don't look cringe-worthy. They look adorable. Both of them beaming at the camera, a bowl of popcorn just about balanced between their knees.

I hand Tilly the phone. A lump of sadness in the back of my throat.

'Do you recognise the woman in this photo?' For a split second, I'm sure she's going to barely look at it but she surprises me. She holds the picture up in front of her and scrutinises it for a good twenty seconds. I watch her eyes move around the photo, contemplating. I'm about to let hope in. Let in that excited hum of possibility that she's about to link all of these missing pieces together. But, then she hands it back to me shaking her head and I feel the hope dim.

'No.' she shakes her head and then, seeing the disappointment on my face, adds, 'Sorry.'

I'm halfway to putting the cell back into my pocket when I decide to try one last thing. This time, I pull up one of the autopsy photographs.

I pinch my fingers and pull at the screen; zooming as close as possible. Trying to include the least amount of discolouration of the skin. The ugly purple and black bruises. Her body is so battered and bruised, that it proves difficult and there's still some dark patches at the closest I can zoom in before it starts to pixelate.

'What about this?' I hand the phone back to her.

She winces slightly but other than that, she doesn't react or comment on the state of Amelia's body. She studies this photograph for significantly less time before she hands it back to me. Except, this time, she's nodding.

'That's the exact same as the tattoo that Ellie has on her ankle.' She says decisively.

Time seemingly slows. I knew it but I was wrong. Or still in denial and unsure. I draw back, trying to think of the right thing to say, my mouth opening and closing without any sound. My stomach swims and my chest feels tight.

My legs prickle with the sudden urge to move. To do something. To stop this psycho from doing what he did to Amelia to someone else. I pace instead. Trying to stomp the nervous energy out with each step.

I don't know what to do. It's not as if I have any real proof that who took Amelia is who has taken Freya. That Freya has been taken at all for that matter. We ruled her disappearance as a run of the mill runaway from financial difficulty and hardship. We gave this psycho a free pass to do what he likes to her. If I take this to the Chief now with just a nagging feeling and a few cryptic messages, a matching tattoo of a star sign shared between millions of people, he'll laugh in my face.

Tilly looks at me questioningly, concern etching her features and pulling her brow down into a deep frown. She's trying to measure up my reaction with the severity of what I've shown her and the way she looks at Luke questioningly, suggests she can't quite make it out.

I glance at Luke. He doesn't look as agitated as me. He's managed to compose himself but I can tell by the intensity of his gaze, he knows what I'm thinking. I carry on pacing. Trying to think. Trying to decide what to do next.

I accidentally knock the yearbook on to the floor with my shin as I pace and the overstimulation of the whole situation makes me want to scream at the inanimate object. Instead, I compose myself and kneel to pick it up. As I lift it back onto the coffee table, the newspaper clipping sways to the floor. Ellie looks up at me from the photograph, her eyes seeming to stare right at me. Blaming me for what's about to happen.

Chapter 54

Detective Dawson

'Oh my god!' Tilly gasps, her hand holding her chest, staring wide eyed down at the photo.

I can't quite read the expression on her face. I'm about to ask her what the matter is. Try to coax the story of their childhood out of her myself. Except, she doesn't like me much, I can tell. It will be a chore to get her to open up to me and we don't have time.

I shoot Luke a subtle look. *You're up flirty, Mcflirterson!* I think. Then I want to laugh at how pathetic I am for thinking that. It's not like it should bother me, how good he is with women. Sometimes it can even help. Like now. I need a get a grip.

Luke rolls his eyes subtly at the look on my face but, sitting next to Tilly on the sofa, uses his best *I'm here to help, you can talk to me* voice.

'What is it?' he asks softly, peeking at the newspaper clipping. I'm wondering if he notices Ellie as quickly as I did.

'This was taken that night.' She's crying now, sniffing as mucous threatens to dribble down her lips. 'When it happened. When they nearly all died.'

'The twenty ninth of October?' I can't help but butt in and ask.

'Exactly.' Tilly looks at me with a scowl but I can't help myself. I have to know what the hell happened to this family. 'We'd all graduated that year. Most of us had started university the month before but pretty much everyone had come back for the Halloween break. It was big, back then. Halloween, I mean.'

'Ellie still worked at the theatre?'

'Yes. I had gone to med school but I was hating it. I was already debating coming back. After what happened with the fire, well, it was the final straw in me deciding to stay. Then I started nursing instead. Less work, less years.'

'So, Ellie didn't go off to school in the fall like everyone else?' I start growing impatient. What she did after school isn't really of interest to me. We're all here because the Dolloway sisters are in danger.

I get the impression that Tilly usually manages to make things which are decidedly nothing to do with her, all about her in some way or another.

'No, of course not.' She looks at me like I'm thick as shit. 'She was heavily pregnant by then, as you can see. She'd decided to hold off on further education since she was having twins.'

'Her parents were ok with that?' Luke looks unconvinced.

'They were complete arseholes to be completely honest. Well, Mrs Dolloway at least was.' Tilly sighs, shaking her head at the memory. 'She made it no secret to Ellie or anyone else that she thinks what happened to Ellie was a stain on the family. She openly demanded Ellie get an abortion for as long as she safely could during the pregnancy.

She told Ellie she was throwing away her life. Used to tell her she was such a disappointment and that she wished she was more like Freya.'

My heart goes out to Ellie. I can't even imagine being a teenager, expecting twins and having your own mother try to bully you out of it. I guess it makes sense she looks so depleted in all of the photos back then. As I'm ruminating on the cruelty some mother's appear to possess towards their own flesh and blood, I realise the abnormal way Tilly described the consummation. Luke notices too.

'What do you mean by, "what happened to Ellie" Tilly?' he asks.

The colour drains from her face and in that moment, the likeness to a oily, white, and wet fish springs to mind. She clearly didn't mean to give anything away just then and I watch her calculate the risk of divulging more.

'Tilly. If you know something that might help us. Help Ellie and Freya. Then, you need to tell us. We think something might be very wrong here.' Luke uses his most soothing tone and it seems to shake loose her reservations.

'Ellie doesn't like people to know. She worries it will affect people's views of the kids.' She chews her bottom lip, the fight between her wanting to help her friend and trying to keep her friend's secret waging war.

'It's ok.' Luke urges, taking her hand.

I want to lash out like a cat and scratch her hand until she lets go.

'She was assaulted.' Tilly's voice breaks and she folds inward, sobbing loudly. 'The twins. Their father... he raped her. He was insane.'

Her voice has risen five octaves and is on the brink of hysteria. I glance at the door, hoping for dear life that the kids upstairs are already asleep again.

'I see.' Luke is frowning so deep it lines his forehead with creases. The silent rage at the men who would harm women radiating, hot and dense. 'Ellie didn't report it?'

'No.' She shakes her head vigorously. 'Her stupid fucking mother told her not to. Said it would taint the family name. That she needed to just admit the mistake she'd made.'

'She didn't believe her.' It's a statement, not a question but Tilly answers anyway.

'No, she never. She was convinced Ellie had cheated on her boyfriend at the time and was trying to cover up her mistakes by crying wolf. Didn't help that her boyfriend was also going around telling everyone that she was a cheat and the dates didn't line up. *Little prick.*' She scowls under her breath.

'What about her father?' I find it hard to believe the Chief of police wouldn't want to go on a rampage until he found exactly who had done that to his child and made him pay.

'Mrs Dolloway is a very manipulative and difficult woman and Mr Dolloway was deeply in love with her.' Tilly shrugs sadly but there's a sliver of venom in her voice now. 'Ellie told me her father had said he believed her and that if she wanted, that he'd take her down to the station to give a statement. At that point though, Mrs Dolloway had spread her poison and Ellie just wanted to pretend it never happened. Until the fire anyway. After that, she didn't see any point anyway. It's over.' 'Luke and I share a look.

'Over after the fire?' I try to dampen the enthusiasm in my voice but the scowl she gives me tells me she hears it.

'Yes. I told you, He was a fucking psycho. Was convinced she want-ed it. That she was *in love* with him. Just because she was nice.' Her face twists like she's just eaten a sour sweet.

'That's why he'd gone there that night. Held them all at gunpoint. Demanded that she admit to her parents they were in love. Wanted her to run away with him and their children. He soaked the place in gas for fuck's sake. Next thing you know, Mr Dolloway is tackling him and the place is on fire. At least, that's what Ellie told me.'

I feel dizzy with information and I have to slow my breathing so that I don't feed the adrenaline with too much oxygen. In...out. In...out.

'Who, Tilly?' I kneel on the floor in front of her.

Like I'm a goddamn Beggar. A druggy, thirsty for a hit and begging her to give me the shoot up. I don't think she hears me. She carries on rambling. The facts are coming out thick and fast. Tears are streaming down her face.

'Except, he didn't die in that fire with Mr Dolloway, did he!?' she cries. Her voice shrill and ringing against the walls of my eardrums. 'Because he's fucking back! He's fucking back and he's got her! Got Freya! He's trying to get Ellie's attention and it's worked because where the fuck is she!? She's gone to meet him! Alone! He's going to fucking kill her! Oh my god!' She claps her hand to her mouth with a gasp. 'That's been his plan all along, hasn't it? It's never been about Freya. It's been about Ellie. He needed to draw her out. She was the end game all along.'

Luke grabs her shoulders then, and shakes her a little. Twisting her round to face him. Flirty McFlirtison dead and gone.

'Who, Tilly?' He sounds as desperate as me. 'Who has them?'

She points a shaky finger down to the newspaper clipping on the floor. The photo of the Halloween fest at the movie theatre.

At the boy who's cheaply dressed as a mummy. Near transparent toilet paper ripping over his face.

Chapter 55

Ellie

I'm petrified and yet, the first thing I think is *wow, he got tall.*

Reggie Walters is broad now. More muscular than he was when we were kids. His eyes are still the same steely cold blue, though. Or at least, the one that's left is. The other looks like a prosthetic. The iris seemingly missing around the pupil. Both of them pitch black.

There's veiny, thick burn scars covering the whole left side of his face. An angry roadmap of how viscous the fire was all those years ago. His eye socket looks almost squished, the eyelid seemingly gone. When he blinks, that one black eye just keeps staring at me. He doesn't have hair anymore. His scalp is bald now and also scarred on the one side. I want to vomit. My heart hammers in my chest.

The door flew open as soon as my hand closed around the handle, wrenching it out of my grasp. He greets me like an old friend; smiling wide, arms outstretched.

'Ellie!' He looks manic. 'You made it!'

We stand in an awkward impasse for a moment. *He can't seriously expect me to hug him?*

I notice the gun gripped in his right hand and my back starts to sweat. I tear my eyes away again to look at him but it's too late. He saw it.

'Oh, this?' he drops his arms and waves the gun carelessly, loosely gripped, in front of my face. I bite the inside of my cheek so I don't scream. 'You don't need to worry about this little thing. Not if you do what I say. So, come on in, Ells. You're late.'

As soon as I follow him into the dining room, my eyes start darting around wildly for something to use as a weapon. I want to run back out. All I can think is, *run, run, run, run!* Except I can't, because Freya's in here somewhere.

'Stay put.' Reggie demands. I stop in my tracks and try to see in the darkness of the room.

Grace and Laurie Parkett are huddled together on the floor in one corner, tied together. They look absolutely petrified. Laurie's hands grip Grace's in the space between their backs so tight that her knuckles are white. Their eyes plead with me to help them but I need to bide my time. If I move too soon, he'll kill us. He's done it before.

I look around frantically for Freya, panic rising in my throat when I don't see her straight away. Then, I spot her silhouette. She's on the far end of the room, deeper in the darkness. She's slumped in the chair she's tied to. A tatty old fashioned summer dress hanging loosely from her slight frame. Her head lolls to one side, her face obscured by her hair. She's so skinny now that I can see her pronounced collar bones and kneecaps, protruding out of almost translucent skin in the dim light.

'Freya!' I run across the room, ignoring Reggie's demands that I don't move.

I just need to get to her. To make sure she's ok. To tell her that I'm here and that I'm going to get us out of this.

It's only when I've made it across the room, my knees sinking into the carpet, hands cupping her bony shoulders - that I notice her eyes.

'For fuck's sake, Ellie!' Reggie huffs, pulling me roughly back across the floor by my hair. So hard that strands of hair ping painfully out of the follicles. I barely even notice.

I'm still staring at Freya, panic coursing through me. My brain is not quite comprehending what's happening. I feel frozen. My body feels heavy. Tension pulsates through my temples.

'I TOLD YOU TO STAY FUCKING PUT!' Reggie booms. He's right in my face now, angry red welts of scars obscuring my sight of Freya.

He pulls back, taking deep breaths. Rapidly at first but gradually slower, his eyes squeezed shut. His mouth moves, silently sounding out words I can't make out, until he seemingly regains his composure. When he speaks to me again, it's almost gentle.

'Listen.' He sighs, kneeling back down in front of me and pushing my hair out of my face. 'I didn't mean for it to happen but you took too long. Don't you see, I did all of this for you. For us. It's the only way I could get you here. She was just taking your place until I was ready. To make you pay. She's gone, my love, and it's all your fault.'

I push myself past the haze in my head, balling my fists tight. I should never have come here. It was futile.

Freya's already dead.

Chapter 56

Detective Dawson

I leave Luke comforting Tilly and slip out, breathing a sigh of relief when I step out of the thick tension of the room. As if the air isn't so stifling out here in the hall.

I walk down the hall, yearbook and newspaper clipping in hand, into the kitchen to call Jasper. Anger ripples through me. How did we not see this? How did we not find this connection? Reggie Walters. Abducting women and torturing them. All practice for this and we missed it.

Now, Ellie's walked straight to him. I realise with dread that Amelia's branded body, her bleached hair, it was to make her look more like the twins. He's been planning this all along. I can't get the image of Amelia's body out of my head. It's permanently ingrained on the backs of my eyelids. Except, now, I see Ellie. Dead. Battered. Bruised. Tortured. All because we didn't look closer. All because I couldn't stop her. We have to save her.

I flick through the book until I reach the yearbook photo of Reginald Walters and hit my speed dial.

He looks like the type of kid that used to fade into shadow. Scrawny, small. Covered in childhood acne, fringe greased to his head, giving him an unwashed air that school bullies must have revelled in using. He had braces back then. Unfortunate for him to have them so late in the school year. They look like crooked scaffolding, pinned against yellow-stained teeth. They catch the light from the camera flash in an unflattering way that only makes them more noticeable.

I'd feel sorry for him if he wasn't a goddamn rapist and murderer.

'Dawson?' Jasper answers on the third ring, his voice raspy with sleep. 'What goddamn time is it?'

'Never mind that.' I talk fast. 'Are you at the office?'

'What? No.' Rustling of bed sheets on the other line. A woman's voice asking him who the hell's calling at four AM. 'Hold on Dawson. Let me go into the study.'

I tap away the seconds it takes him to get to the study with my left foot. Aware that for every tap, the Dolloway twins creep closer to danger. Closer to being strangled to death and resuscitated. To only be strangled to death again. To both being ingrained on the backs of my eyelids alongside Amelia.

'Alright, Alright.' Jasper yawns. 'I'm here. Computer's on. What do you need?'

'Reginald Walters.' I spit.

There's the loud click clacking of keyboard keys for a few seconds, followed by long stretches of silence which makes me want to rip my hair out.

'Reginald Walters. Only child of Frank and Angie Walters. His dad went out to get some milk and wound up in Austria with a woman called Gabriella Calmack when the kid wasn't even two, looks like.

Completely cut his wife and son off. Filed for divorce a year later. Reginald's mother remarried some redneck con man after that. He came with a son of his own. Looks like they moved in when the kids were teenagers and... how weird.'

'What? What's weird?'

'Looks like there's no trace of the stepfather... Victor Stevens... whatsoever, a few years later. Just completely seems to drop off the face of the planet. His wife cleared out his bank account and then there's no record of him making any more dodgy car deals or so much as buying a pot to piss in.'

'Interesting.' I don't know how it's relevant yet, but I will file it away for later, in case I need it. 'And Reginald? Any convictions?'

'A few minor charges of theft when he was about sixteen, seventeen. Most of it's redacted because he was a minor but looks like the general gist is that he hospitalised one of his peers. Witness statements said the kid bullied him.'

So, no other charges of sexual assault or rape.

'Where's he living now?'

'No idea, boss. looks like...' More violent tapping of the keyboard. 'Yep. There's no record of him after high school. He just dropped off the face of the planet somehow. Nothing taken out in his name. No leases, no accounts, not so much as a speeding ticket.'

'What about his mother?' I rub my face in exasperation. Just as we've figured out who the hell we're looking for, it looks like there's nowhere to look.

'There's still an address in her name. A bungalow.' There's a ping in my ear. 'I've just forwarded you the address but don't get your hopes up.'

'Why?'

'According to the state, the house's mortgage is completely paid off, has been for over a decade but it's been abandoned for years. They've only not torn it down because it's a listed building. Something to do with the land and historical significance but it doesn't look like anyone's living there.'

'For God's sake!' I kick one of the dining room chairs in frustration and immediately regret it, pain radiating through my toes.

'You alright, boss?' Jasper pauses his violent typing.

'Just wish the good guys would get a break for a change, Jasp.' I sigh, reigning the anger back in. 'Let's send a unit out to the mother's address. Check it out. Just to be sure.'

'Course, boss.' Jasper moves away from the phone for a few seconds to request a vehicle be sent out on the radio, reeling off the address on his screen.

'What about the brother?' I anxiously gnaw at the skin on my lip. I feel like we're getting nowhere. 'What happened to him?'

'Now, he's a completely different story.' My interest is peaked, ears prickling like Vada's does four rooms away when I take ham out of the fridge. 'He went on to college after school. Looks like, whilst he was brought up rough, he made an effort to get himself out. He's made quite a name for himself actually. Which he changed, by the way. As soon as he hit eighteen, legally changed his name to something unrelated to the rest of the family. Hold on, let me find the record.'

I start tapping my foot impatiently again, listening to the insistent typing. I ignore the twinge in my toes.

'Right. Here it is... oh... oh... now that's interesting.'

'What is?'

'He knew the Dolloway's. He stayed in touch with them after school. More than in touch actually... he married one of them.' My foot stops tapping and I can feel my armpits dampen.

'I'm sorry, what?' I choke. 'What's his name, Jasper?'

'It's James, boss. Oliver James.'

Everything he says afterwards sounds like it's underwater, obscured by the blood rushing through my head.

The only sound over the line for a few long moments is the subtle static buzz of the telephone line and my shallow rapid breathing. My thoughts race through my head like Olympic athletes fitting for gold.

'Dawson?' Jasper cuts through the static. 'You ok?' I drag myself out of the shock and back into the present.

'Can we send out another unit to Mr James' place of residence also.' I start picking the skin down the side of my thumbnail anxiously. 'Tell them to proceed with caution. He's got a stick up his ass. He'll probably call his lawyer. We need to know if he's in contact with his step brother. If he knows where he is. Let me know.' '

'Sure, boss. No problem.' Jasper dials the operator again.

'Thanks, Jasper. Keep digging into Reginald. See if we can find out where he is. I have to go.'

I cut the line on the sound of twenty worried questions coming through because I don't have time.

We need to find the twins and we need to find them now. This isn't a random act of violence. This was planned. Staged. Months of methodical planning. Years even. I race back into the living room, trying to control my facial expression, but from the way Luke and Tilly both stare at me, I assume I don't do too well to disguise it.

'Tilly, I need to know everything you do about Oliver James.'

I'm preparing myself for a debate. For a battle of wills between me, the woman who wants to save these women's lives, and Tilly, who seemingly has decided to hate my guts. I think something in my face tells her I'm not messing around. That this is important because, to my surprise, she doesn't fight me. She jumps straight in.

It takes half an hour before she's told us everything. Half of which we didn't really need to know and was more idle gossip which did nothing but hinder us with delay rather than help but we finally have a clearer picture of the past.

It seems that, when Freya Dolloway had started dating Oliver - then Stevens - now James, it was a couple of months before Reggie had attacked Ellie. Oliver was a notorious school bully, his most prolific victim being his younger step brother.

After Reggie had broken in and killed their father, it would seem that Freya had broken things off with Oliver for almost a year. But then, she was lonely and grieving and she hated Ellie enough to date the brother of the man who had attacked her and killed their father.

Their mother - being their mother apparently - had supported Freya's decision because she just wanted her, apparently favourite daughter, to be happy.

Ellie and Oliver had limited their contact over the years and had barely seen nor spoke to each other unless absolutely necessary. Then, Freya and Oliver's relationship turned sour and they had divorced badly.

The rest we already knew from earlier interviews and the investigation.

My phone buzzes in my pocket and I feel a fist tighten around my gut when I see its Japer. I go to excuse myself but it's futile because he texts me the bad news as soon as the call ends.

No luck. He was co-operative. No sign of the women whatsoever. Police are questioning him now about his brother but not looking promising, says he hasn't spoken to him in years. Are you sure about this? Forester seems pissed.

I want to cry with frustration because we're back at square one and we just wasted half an hour discussing a bloke who, by all accounts, appears innocent and has no clue where Reginald is.

'We need to start looking at this from different angles.' Tilly and Luke look as exasperated as I feel. I glance at the clock on the mantel for the hundredth time since we got here. 04:30 AM.

Anxiety chews at me. I can't help the feeling that we are dangerously running out of time.

Chapter 57

Ellie

She's dead. Actually dead. I feel like I should have somehow known. You hear all those stories about twin telekinesis. An invisible thread which subconsciously ties you together; which no one can see and only you two can feel. Legends of one twin having his arm cut off on one half of the world whilst the other is admitted to hospital screaming his arm, seemingly untouched, is being torn from its socket.

Except, that's only a myth and the real world doesn't work like that. I had no idea that Freya was dead and I don't feel shredded in two because she's hurt.

I just feel shocked and... angry. At Reggie for hurting her. At Freya for letting him hurt her. At myself for coming here like a goddamn idiot completely alone and without backup. At the idea that my mother is going to blame me for this too, she's going to wish me dead instead. I guess there's still time. She could still get that wish.

I laugh. Actually start laughing. Like some kind of unstable psychopath. Like Reggie. Laurie and Grace both staring at me with wide eyes and a little disgust and I can't blame them but I can't seem to stop. The laughs are coming out thick and fast and deep.

I laugh because I always knew that Freya would be the death of me and here I am. Running to her rescue only to find I'm too late. Running right into my own demise.

'Share the joke, Darling.' Reggie kneels down in front of me on the floor, that gun still hanging ominously from one hand. The glint of it in the low light brings me back to the moment. The laugh dies instantly in my throat and I feel terrified again. My heart is hammering in my chest, my armpits damp.

'Please. Stop this, Reggie.'

'DON'T CALL ME THAT!' He roars in my face and I can smell the pungent stench of alcohol on his breath. He hits me on the temple with the butt of the gun and the room spins. Pain splinters through my face. Blood tastes metallic in my mouth. 'That's not my name anymore. That's the name that she gave me! My rancid mother. It's the name of A PATHETIC WIMP.' Drops of his spit land on my face as he screams, and I flinch.

Then he goes quiet again. Closing his eyes. Mumbling under his breath. Only, this time, he's close enough for me to hear him.

'1...2...3...4...' He counts.

I realise in that exact moment, him kneeling only centimetres away, that this is the only chance I'm going to get. I think of my children. Their bouncing curls and cheeky smiles. The sound of their laughter and the feel of their little hands. The smell of their scalp when they were new.

I count down from three in my head and lunge. Right at him. One hand reaching straight for the gun. I scream as I do it, as if that's going to give me anymore physical strength but I'm too slow. The scream only signalling to him what I'm about to do and he twists. Out of my way. Instead of my hand landing on the gun, we wind up in a heap on the floor.

He smells putrid. Like stale body odour and the sickly-sweet hue of gas mixed with alcoholic tang.

The room's so dark, the early dawn light coming from the window, the only source of light. Highlighting us tangled together, fighting, in the middle of the floor.

His elbow connects with my chin, shoving my teeth into my lip and the blood dribbles warmly down my chin. I jab my fingers out in the darkness, shoving my thumbnail right into his eyeball. The one that's left.

He gasps and groans loudly, trying to push me off but I just keep pushing until I feel a pop and a relief of pressure. Blood runs, warm and thick, down my thumb and into my palm.

He pushes me off and my head connects with the wall. My vision is suddenly uneven and whirling. He staggers back, shouting and holding his eye to try and thawt the blood flow.

I push myself across the floor with my legs to get away from him, looking around quickly for a clear path out.

I'm calculating the likelihood of getting Grace and Laurie free, when my foot knocks something solid on the floor. Whatever I hit, skids across the floor towards them huddled in the corner.

I almost ignore it, pushing myself up, looking around for something I can use as a weapon but then, Grace shouts across the room. Her cries are muffled by the gag but she's staring wide eyed at me and keeps looking at the object my foot made contact with.

I squint in the low light and through blurry vision. I realise it's the gun. He's dropped it.

I glance frantically back to him. He's composing himself, muttering under his breath again. Counting. I know I only have seconds before he recovers and comes for me.

I dive for the gun, feeling such relief when my hand connects with the cold metal that I want to laugh again.

'YOU STUPID COW!' He's managed to stand up now.

His shadow's large and broad, looming in the dim light. The blood is still pouring out from his eye, or what's left of it. The tissue is as disfigured and mangled as the skin on the left side of his body. He isn't trying to stop the bleeding anymore. He's completely poised, listening intently for any sound of me.

I know this is it. Now or never.

I lift the gun and point it at him, hoping the muscle memory of shooting paper targets at the range with my father will serve me well enough to finally put an end to this.

I do it just like he taught me. Pulling the safety clip back and squeezing gently on the trigger. Breathing slow and even, slight pressure on the trigger on the exhale.

Inhale.

Exhale.

Pull. There's a loud click. The mechanism in the gun tries to catch the bullet and send it flying, but nothing happens. There's no pull back. No gun powder. No metal.

I try again. Again. Again. But nothing happens.

Panic swirls in the pit of my stomach. I'm acutely aware of Grace and Laurie whimpering behind me. Of my own breathing. Of Reggie's low, guttural laugh.

'It's not loaded. You silly bitch.'

Just like that. The tables are turned again. Favour on his side. Me, undefended against this goddamn maniac. He tilts his head slightly. A menacing smile on his lips, blood staining them red, filling the cracks in-between them. Nothing happens for a few moments. Then he cups his ear slightly and I realise, too late, that he's listening to my gasping breaths. With loss of vision, he uses them to tell him roughly where I am in the room.

He runs.

Head first at me and the wind knocks out of my lungs as he pummels me to the floor.

His knees pin me. His weight pressing down on my chest. He wraps his fingers around my throat. The pressure making my pathetic attempts at taking a breath burn in my lungs. In my throat.

I scratch and claw. Trying to break myself free but he only smiles and squeezes harder. My face burns as much as my skin under his fingers.

Fire courses through my chest. The weight on my chest is dull and claustrophobic.

The corners of my vision start to blur and then go black. The vessels in my eyes pressurising against the force. My field of vision gets smaller and smaller and the panic only makes it worse.

I kick and thrash but he's too strong and I'm getting tired.

My field of vision is now just a small circle of his face.

His rotten, burned face glaring down at me, half covered in blood but yet, still smiling.

I think of my children. Pray to a God that I don't believe in that I'll get out of here alive. Again. Like I did before.

I find myself wondering whether my mother will realise that, in this twisted turn of fate, she got her wish after all.

Chapter 58

Detective Dawson

Tilly fell asleep about twenty minutes ago. Her snoring is slow and steady and almost a lullaby to my tired brain. I have to get up and look out the window, at the early morning dog walkers who are all padded up against the rain which is still going from last night, walking their dogs. Seemingly no care in the world. Just to keep myself awake.

'How are you doing?' Luke comes in with two cups of coffee, looking as close to sleep as me.

'What if we're too late, Luke?' I sigh, taking the cup.

'Don't catastrophize.' Luke slurps his coffee loudly and I grind my teeth against the urge to tell him to just wait until it cools down. 'We don't know anything. Not yet. Give Jasper time. He'll find us something.'

I sit back down next to him, Tilly suddenly rolling over and letting out a loud fart, breaking the tension. We both look at her and then each other and burst out in quiet laughter. I have to hold my hand tight against my mouth to not laugh so loud that I wake her.

'Jesus Christ.' I shake my head.

'Who knew such a tiny woman could moonlight as a tractor.' Luke chuckles.

I slap him playfully on the arm and burst out laughing again. When we finally calm down, I collapse back against the sofa, suddenly exhausted.

'You should laugh more.' Luke sighs. 'You're pretty when you laugh. You don't do it enough.'

My cheeks burn and I try to hide my smile by drinking tea but I don't think it works very well.

'When this is all over. When we find them. Would you...' Luke frowns and I suddenly panic.

I'm too exhausted and nerve bitten for this conversation right now. 'Luke...' I sigh.

'Ok, Ok. Time and place, I know.' He huffs, waving away my reservations before I have time to voice them. 'But this case isn't going to last forever and when it's over, we'll have this conversation. Whether you want to or not because I'm sick of us pretending there isn't something here.'

Jasper saves me from the awkward tip toeing by calling. The ringtone echoes loudly through the room, abruptly waking Tilly who sits to attention as if she was never asleep.

'Jasper.' Luke frowns at the relief in my voice and my chest stabs with guilt. 'Please tell us you got something.'

'I feel dirty from the depths I had to go into the cyber world but, yes.' Jasper laughs at his own joke. 'You want the good or bad news?'

'Both.'

'Good news, I found the connection between Amelia Taylor and Freya Dolloway. Turns out you were right, it was that XXX Nasties site. Turns out they had a few of the same... clients. Only one of them stands out though. He was particularly... specific, about what he liked and he was particularly aggressive when they didn't respond.'

'Specific how?'

'He liked to watch women being choked. To play dead. To pretend he's saved them. Resuscitated them.'

Every alarm bell in my head goes off all at once.

'Who?'

'He used the username "Slitter98683" with both Freya and Amelia. Although, I would appreciate it if we kept the discovery of the username between us. It wasn't exactly above board, how deep I had to go into the site's coding to find it. Also, if we could keep the next bit of information under wraps too...I found an email address.'

'Time is of the essence, Jasper. Come on.'

'Right. Ok, Ok. The email address he used was SylasW2910.'

'As in... twenty ninth of October?' I feel suddenly nauseous that he's sadistic enough to Taunt Freya like that.

'That's what I'm thinking.'

'But, Sylas? What does that mean?'

'Funny you should mention that. That's where I was going next. When I did some background digging on the Walters, I found a distant relative, a great, great grandpa if you will, whose name was Sylas. Turns out it was Reginald's middle name. Reginald Sylas Walters.'

'That's why we couldn't find anything in his name.' I mumble it more to myself but Jasper decides to answer me anyway.

'Bingo, Boss! Turns out, Reginald re-invented himself after the fire. My guess, he was treated at the local hospital as a john doe. There's a record of one matching his description stumbling into the ER with significant burns over the whole left side of his body. Said he worked in a garage and got into an accident with gas and a cigarette. He slipped out when he was well enough before they could take his details, or insurance, but the records say he called himself Sylas.'

'Tell me you ran his name.'

'What do you take me for? Of course I did. Search pinged up a load of Sylas Walter's in the surrounding areas but there's one in particular who stood out. He's set up a ghost account, fake company name and information but there was a bank account set up which took regular deposits each month. My guess? He worked an under the table, cash in hand gig and saved.'

'What does any of this give us?' I huff in frustration. 'Tell me this links to an address.'

'It does indeed.' Jasper sounds absolutely ecstatic with himself but I want to scream that he can pat himself on the back later. I'm about to but he finally gives me something. 'He funnelled a shit tonne into this account over the years, then he brought one singular property.'

'Where, Jasper?'

I grab my coat off the back of the sofa, Luke realising my intentions also gets ready to go. Tilly starts moving too but I hold my hand up firmly in front of her and silently shake my head. We stare each other down for a few moments before she surrenders. Throwing her hands in the air and falling back onto the sofa like a stroppy teenager.

Five, Six, Two, Xavier Drive.'

'Isn't that...'

'The Dolloway's old street address? The one that burnt down? Yes. Yes it is.'

We bomb through traffic at eighty miles an hour down the highway, sirens blaring through the early morning breeze. Between the speed and the light, 6AM early morning traffic on the roads, we get to the Dolloway's old house in less than twenty minutes.

I don't have time to parallel park. I curb the car, the tires scratching against the rough pavement.

I'm subconsciously aware of Luke hissing at me under his breath to slow down. To wait. That back up will be here in five. To stop. Except, I can't stop.

I'm this close. All that stands between me and this psychopath and the lives of two young women is one wooden front door. I'll be damned if I let the five minutes I wait for back up to arrive, be the five minutes that count. The minutes which stand between the Dolloway twins and life.

So I ignore his warnings to air on the side of caution, crouching low and moving fast, up the front porch. My weapon is un-holstered and held level in front of me.

It's a moment before I shout, 'Police! Sylas Walters, put your hands in the air! We're coming in!' That I become aware of Luke close at my heel. Poised. Ready.

It takes Luke two swift and hard kicks to break in the door and then we're in. Moving methodically room to room, Luke at my heel every step. Weapons ready, braced for impact.

We clear the dining room and kitchen first. I feel sick knowing this psycho could be anywhere in this house, waiting for us. I push the anxiety down, deciding that we'll deal with flames if it comes to it. As long as we get these women out alive.

Then we get to the living room and I want to heave. Three women and a small child are scattered around the room, seemingly unconscious.

I run to Freya first. She's tied to a dining chair at one end of the room. Her body is so thin, it's almost skeletal. She smells like lavender shampoo mixed with damp and it makes me gag. I shake her lightly, calling her name.

'Freya! Freya, wake up!' I shake her. 'It's time to wake up! You're safe now.'

I press two fingers to her carotid, praying silently over and over to let me feel a pulse but there isn't one. Her skin's cold and pale. Rigour mortis has already set in.

I bite my fist against the tears burning in the corners of my eyes. I failed her. I didn't make it in time and now she's dead. Just like Amelia. This son of a bitch killed both my missing women. They died not even knowing my name. Not knowing that their faces and names have kept me up all night for weeks. That now they'll haunt me forever.

I pull myself together, trying hard to focus on the task at hand. At the other two women and girl we can still save. I glance over at Luke who is crouched over Ellie's body.

Hope stirs in my palms but then he looks at me with sad eyes, his fingers pressed to her neck. I want to lock myself in a room and never come out. He shakes his head gently and I feel useless. How did it come to this? How did both Ellie and Freya Dolloway wind up dead?

I can't bring myself to check the other woman and child in the room. The innocent bystanders to this whole sordid tale. Just an innocent family who rented the wrong house. The house owned by a maniac. Luke reads my apprehension in the quiver of my lip.

He does it for me. Goes over and checks each of them in turn and then that sad face, that silent shake of the head again.

'So young.' I whisper. Staring at the young girl lying dead in her mother's arms across the room. 'He killed them all, you think?'

'Yes.' Luke sighs. 'From the bruising on their throats, They were all strangled to death.'

'He's gone. Isn't he?' I want to collapse on the floor but I can't seem to make my body move from its spot next to Freya.

'The back door was open.' Luke nods. 'We'll set up a perimeter, a door to door.'

'They're cold.'

'They are.'

'They've been dead for hours.' I shake my head.

'I reckon so, yes, but we'll let the ME decide for sure.'

Muffled sirens sound in the distance, growing nearer. The men and women tasked with saving these women, coming to help. Help which is three hours too late.

Chapter 59

Sylas

I hadn't planned to kill Ellie. I didn't think I even had it in me to do it. Then she hurt me. Like my mother did. Like Victor did. Like Oliver used to. As if I'm nothing. Less than a man. Less than worthy.

So, I snapped. Just like I did all of them years ago when my mother needed to be taught a lesson.

I realised Ellie never truly loved me. She only used me. Used me to give her children and then threw me away like used up trash.

I took her life away like she meant nothing. Because she doesn't. Not really. Those children. The boy and the girl, they don't need her. Mother's only ruin their children. They're too selfish, too self absorbed. They lie and they hit you. They don't protect you when they should.

I'll be everything they ever needed and more. When they're ready. When they're old enough to come looking for me. For their father.

I'll be here. Then I'll tell them exactly the type of bitch their mother was.

Chapter 60

Oliver

I knew that Reggie was up to something. He'd been living in my basement for the last six months since he reappeared in my life, half his face mashed up and a twisted assumption that I owed him. Just because the break ins when were younger had been my idea. He seems to have forgotten about how he'd gone completely off script and started burning shit down. Once I'd realised what he'd been doing right under my nose, I'd beat him senseless and told him we were done with the break ins. It was too risky with the Chief of police on our tails.

Especially since I'd started sleeping with his daughter. Freya hadn't been what I expected. Back then, I thought she was weak and pathetic. Wallowing in self-pity when her guy had died, vulnerable and useful. She was so damaged; I'd thought it would be fun to play with her. She'd even gotten up on a cliff ledge in front of me and I couldn't wait to watch her splatter. I even helped her when she faltered, and she'd second guessed herself. I'd given her a shove to help her take the next step, a leap if you will. But she'd surprised me, she was resilient and had come back swinging. She didn't even seem to notice I'd pushed her off that ledge.

Then Reggie had gone and burnt the Dolloway's house down, with the chief in there, and disappeared completely. Freya had latched onto me then, and I couldn't find a way out. To try and keep the heat off of me, I pretended to be in love with her, even gone as far as to marry her. She was a nightmare, but the sex was good and of course, it seemed to have worked.

I should've slammed the door in Reggie's mashed up face when he'd reappeared, but I haven't learnt my lesson clearly, so I invited him in. Now he's gone and killed them fucking twins and the police are knocking down my door again.

I think I've done enough to throw the scent off of me again. All I can hope for now is that Reggie isn't stupid enough to come back. But I've been wrong before.

EPILOGUE

Chapter 61

Detective Dawson

One Year Later

The coffee shop is so congested with the morning rush that it takes me two whole minutes to spot Tilly's fiery red hair in the back corner. I push my way haphazardly through the herd of people, ignoring the tuts and huffs and side eyes as I force my way through.

Tilly looks like she's actually slept this week. Her hair isn't so flat and the circles under her eyes are not so dark. The last year has been rough on her. Losing Ellie was like losing a sister for her. Now, I think, I identify with her more than I thought I ever could. We'll both always be Haunted by the Dolloway twins. Except, she's brighter today. She's even smiling which I don't think I've ever seen her do.

She's hunched over a colourful drawing of what looks like some weird deformed alien. Then, I get closer and notice the tail and the collar and realise it's supposed to be a dog.

'Cool dog.' I point and smile. Myah Dolloway beams at me, all gap toothed.

Matthew Dolloway glances up from his own drawing which looks significantly darker and more moody. I smile and wave but he just sighs and goes back to his drawing. My heart aches for him. I can only hope Tilly has kept good on her word which she made to Ellie when she agreed to be godmother, that she will always look after and protect him.

It had come as a shock, to say the least, when Kathrine Dolloway had point blank refused to take her grandchildren in as their legal guardian.

'My precious baby girl is dead. I want no part of them.' She'd hissed.

It had taken me a few seconds of confusion before I realised she wasn't referring to Ellie as her precious baby girl but to Freya, and to Ellie merely as the reason she was dead.

I had felt inexplicable rage and hurt for the twins but couldn't force her to take them. After a battle with social services, that only left Tilly. As their god mother. I'd expected her to say no. Thought she had too much of a free spirit for that but she had humbled me when she hadn't even hesitated. The twins have been officially under her guardianship for four months now and all appears to be going well. I think Ellie would be happy with how it turned out.

'Kids, go get yourselves an ice cream.' Tilly gives both of them change and hurries them off to join the line.

I take the seat Matthew has vacated and we watch them for a few moments before getting into it.

'Any news?' Tilly asked hopefully.

'Oliver finally gave us some addresses to try.' I sigh. 'But as of yet, we haven't found him. He also admitted to telling Sylas where to find the spare key in the brickwork to get in. Although, he admits it was during a conversation about robbing her. She had some of his cash stowed away under the floorboards. He didn't realise what Sylas was planning to do, it would seem.'

Tilly's shoulders slump. 'He can't get away with this.'

'I'll make sure he doesn't.' I say it with conviction but the more time that passes, the more doubtful I become that we'll ever find Sylas Walters.

My phone buzzes and I check it quickly. Smiling despite myself when I see that it's Luke.

Don't forget to pick up the peppers for dinner tonight babe xx 'Oh, someone's getting some.' Tilly teases, laughing at my blush. 'It's that big Detective chap, right? Your partner?'

'It's... new.' I smile.

I didn't expect the trauma of finding the Dolloway twins and the Parkett's like that to bring me and Luke closer together but it did. I was trying my hardest not to let my obsession with Sylas Walters cloud everything good in my life so I'd agreed to let Luke cook for me tonight. A date night he'd said. So I will remember the peppers and I will enjoy my evening with my boyfriend and I won't think a single thought about Sylas Walter. Or at least, I'll try not to. At least, for tonight.

'Have you found anything more from the house?' Tilly asks, pulling the conversation back into the dark.

'No. Nothing more.'

When the team had finally made it out to a house owned by Sylas Walters' mother, we'd realised that he'd been holding his victims there. The utilities were off with no electricity but there was hair, nails, blood, human faeces and urine in one of the rooms. From the peeling, mouldy wallpaper it looked to be his mother's old room. He'd bricked up the window, blocking the light and the way out. Tortured his victims in the basement. There were clumps of hair found in the basement sink's drain. I say my goodbyes with Tilly and am standing up when I notice the picture Matthew had been so closely drawing. My stomach drops and I feel the breath catch in my throat.

The drawing is of a person. Seemingly, a man. Tall and broad. There's angry red lines and gashes drawn all over his face. Deep red blocks over the eyes. When the kids come back to the table, I point to the picture. My heart is hammering.

'Who's that?' I ask Matthew. 'Oh.' He frowns. 'That's the man that I saw at the park last week. He said he's my daddy.'

My blood pressure spikes. The blood rushes to my feet. My head swims.

I guess I won't be getting my romantic night of peaceful thoughts after all.

Author Note

If you have made it this far, I would just like to thank you from the bottom of my heart. Even if it wasn't your cup of tea! As an indie author who self publishes, every reader is important to me and any sort of recognition, whether it be a review on social media platforms, selling websites or even just a recommendation to a friend, helps me immensely. So, if you enjoyed any part of this novel, I'd really appreciate it if you'd put in a good word for me with your reader friends or post a review online. If you'd like to hear about any of my works in progress, upcoming releases, or sales / promotions, please do sign up to my monthly author newsletter.   KJ.

Thank You

There are a few people I'd love to thank for their help, skills and encouragement which helped me to not only write this book, but feel able to share it.

My amazing husband, Alex. Who has always been my biggest supporter and has always encouraged me to pursue my dreams. He's never been much of a reader and yet, still read the entirety of my book in a week. Without his love and support, and his patience with my constant idea dumps, ramblings, anxieties and self-doubt, this book wouldn't have ever gotten finished.

One of my closest friends Lacie, who has read multiple versions and drafts of this book and has not complained once when I've asked her to start re-reading it all over again! I couldn't ask for a better friend to share this accomplishment with, nor a better person to be able to call one of my confidants, supporters and friends.

Lelanie, who proofread and corrected my many a spelling, grammatical and formatting mistake without passing judgement or comment on how many apostrophes I missed along the way.

All of my BETA readers, who gave their much-needed thoughts and judgements on this novel in its early stages.

Lastly, I'd like to thank my cover designer, Nabin - who took my vision and made it a reality for the cover of my first ever novel.

I appreciate you all - thank you.

Trigger Warnings

As mentioned in the author note, there are a number of possible triggers associated with All The Lies We Told, please see these below.

Once again, please be mindful that these may lend themselves to important elements of the story or possible twists in the plot lines.

This novel mentions and discusses sensitive subjects including:

Reference to Rape / Sexual Assault

Loss from death and feelings of grief

Mention of abortion

Mention of depression and suicidal ideation or attempts

Descriptions of gross bodily harm and injury / scarring

Murder / death.

Please read with caution.

Printed in Dunstable, United Kingdom